Goodbye, Theodore

Candy D. Mitchell

Published by Candy D. Mitchell, 2020.

Goodbye, Theodore
Book 1
by Candy D. Mitchell
Published by Candy D. Mitchell
peculiarfairytales.com
©2020 Candy D. Mitchell
ISBN 978-0-578-74990-7

Cover by: MiblArt
Edited by: Lozzi Counsell

To Nick, for all the adventures, late night nachos, and being the most loving weirdo I could ask for.

To my grandpa who always encouraged me to be myself and do what I love.

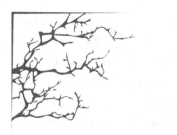

1

The Night emerged from its slumber, only to find the entire sleepy town of Harthsburg not ready to dance in the twilight. As The Night grasped onto every surface, it felt alone. No one was left in his wake to bid him farewell. Instead, the streets lay empty, reeking of terror. All the doors were locked tight. And I mean all the doors—windows, closet doors, garage doors, screen doors, bedroom doors, and, of course, front doors. The Night had never felt so alone in the town of Harthsburg before. He cast his blanket out and kept on going, leaving a black trail behind him. He would have to hope that the next town would allow him to stay, at least for one night. What The Night did not know was that there was an even greater darkness that had entered the sleepy town during his slumber. Oh, yes, a darkness darker than even The Night.

By the morning, the town of Harthsburg would forever be changed. Very few people noticed at first, but one of the few that did was Theodore Lexington. He woke with a startle. As he turned to his clock, it struck past six, and a cold shiver ran through his bones. It was unlikely that the weather could revert to such chilly lengths as it was that morning.

Shivering from the chill in the air, Theodore reluctantly leapt from his bed and stepped into a pair of slacks. He pulled a light gray undershirt over his well-defined chest and grabbed one of the many button-up shirts that he wore for work. This morning, he settled on a champagne color. He never could truly get used to wearing the confining type shirts, but as he put it on he didn't even bat an eye while he buttoned each button since it would keep him warm. He yanked on a pair of paisley socks, before heading down the short hall into the kitchen. Theodore once again went along with his normal routine and began to make himself the worthiest of all breakfasts: an omelet. Or at least, Theodore believed it was as such.

He began most mornings this way, by cracking eggs almost ceremoniously on the edge of his favorite bowl, whisking them with milk, cheese and spinach, flipping and plating the omelet with a flick of his wrist, and, of course, serving it to himself along with his morning tea at the kitchen table, promptly at 6:30. It was a familiar morning to him, for the most part.

However, he noticed the lack of birds chirping outside, the absence of people chatting in the streets, and the surprising gusts of wind that were unheard of in the middle of June. His thoughts lingered on the quiet world outside his windows, almost giving him a pinch of nostalgia that floated out of his mind too quickly to remember where it had came from. Until his nose caught a whiff of his breakfast.

His mind went back to thinking about his date from the previous night. A small but prominent grin appeared, just before he stabbed his fork into his eggs. His grin stayed the whole way through breakfast, and he hoped that he had caused mutual feelings to appear for her; however, he had no way of knowing. But he hoped he would find out later if she too couldn't stop grinning.

Once he had finished, he gently placed his plate into the sink, almost hoping that the clinking sound would make the silence more bearable, at least for a moment. It wasn't enough though, and he couldn't help but debate if he should turn on the television to fill the silence to drown out the sound of the unseasonably blustery wind. Theodore stared at the television set that hid most days in his wardrobe with distaste. He was reluctant to turn it on and had only purchased it to seem normal. Instead he walked over to the radio.

As he turned the knob to his favorite station, silence filled the room. No sound erupted from the speakers. Not even static. He turned the knob just slightly to listen to the next station, but again, pure silence. Now, Theodore was a logical man, so he accounted the lack of sound could only mean one thing: His radio had to be broken because his lights were on, and he had just used his electric stove with no issues. He wondered if it might just be the outlet that was having issues, so he stomped over to the next nearest outlet and plugged it in there instead..

Again, he turned the knob. Nothing. But just as he went to unplug it, he realized that the red light was on, indicating that it did in fact have power. Placing his hand on his chestnut brown hair, he scratched his head while contemplating how this could be. Instead of over thinking what could be happening, he unplugged his radio and walked back over to the table to finish his tea that had more or less gone cold.

When the clock struck seven, Theodore decided, like most mornings, it was time to head to work. He stepped out the door and jingled his keys around to find the correct one to lock the door behind him. A little keychain that said 'Harthsburg National Forest' with a depiction of a waterfall encompassed by a tree line jingled slightly against the door as he locked it. He jammed the keys back into his pocket and turned on his heel down to the sidewalk. The cold breeze continued to weave in and out of his brown hair. It whooshed it up into a semi-mohawk.

Theodore was a simple man and had decided a long time ago that a car would not be needed in such a small town. For the most part, this was a smart decision because his job was a short ten-minute walk and the vital means of living in the center of town were just another ten-minute walk from his work. But today, Theodore found himself, for the first time, regretting his decision to not be a car owner. The cold breeze was more than he anticipated for this time of the year, and he daydreamed about having a little heater blowing on his arms and face. Sadly, he would have to walk to work cold, and not just cold, but alone.

The closer he got to his place of work, the lonelier he felt. By now, he would have already said a grand hello to his neighbor Margeaux Saxon and waved to Edgar Pickins as Edgar grabbed a quick breakfast at the mini-mart. Normally, Edgar, who was known around town as the "nicest guy", would get one of those sugar infested pastries that came wrapped from a factory out of state. The first ingredient, more than likely, was high fructose corn syrup. Had he glanced at the ingredient list, he might have put it down and grabbed something else. No, Edgar was a husky man who could care less about what he shoved down his gullet, and in all honesty no one else cared either. Theodore, however, was the type of man to check his ingredients and had a strict exercise regimen that he was quite proud of. His only vice was the occasional drink. The type that you did in social settings mainly.

Theodore paused by the mini-mart doors, expecting to run into Edgar as he exited the shop. To his surprise, Theodore didn't see anyone inside the mini-mart, let alone him. Not one single person barged out. An eerie feeling crept over him as he took a step onto the one piece of concrete that had a large crack that spread about ten inches long and four inches wide. Despite the unsightliness the gash caused the concrete, Theodore adored it because it had started to sprout little orange flowers, all bunched together. The kind of flowers one would imagine existed in a fairy garden of a little kid's backyard. He couldn't help but pause and admire the flowers today. The quietness made him quite unsteady, but seeing the flowers gave him some reassurance that there was at least some normality.

Theodore lingered for a minute longer than usual at the beautiful flowers, and when he looked up, he let out a sigh of relief at the sight of his co-worker, Darlene Hicks, several yards away. Theodore was about to raise his hand to wave to her when a shadow that looked as if it belonged to the awning above her ever so quickly wrapped itself around her and—poof— she was gone. At that point, Theodore's reassurance had now hit him over the head with a frying pan of alertness.

He thought quietly out loud to himself, "No one in the streets except me now, there's this ridiculously cold weather that's never occurred in this month before, radio silence, and now fucking Darlene just vanished!"

He searched frantically for any sign of her in the sky. If his eyes weren't attached to his muscles, they might have popped out from all the searching he was doing. He looked up and to the sides. He even looked behind him and below him. She was nowhere to be found. His body shuddered with disbelief. Theodore froze in panic and looked down at the only thing that seemed normal in the world around him—the little orange flowers swaying wildly in the wind. But a shadow was growing larger and larger over the patch. And just like that, black. Goodbye, Theodore.

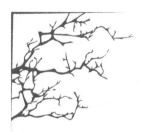

2

A small shriek was heard by none other than Audrey Wilkins, and to be honest, she had no idea if the shriek had come from her or one of her friends that she'd just witnessed disappearing into a cloudy abyss. Yes, she saw the whole thing as Theodore was taken. She poked her now sweating head out from the side of the mini-mart and checked the coast was clear, before running frantically.

Audrey ran past all the old brick buildings that lined the streets with the occasional thick green vines growing up the sides of them, until she made it to her office building, which happened to be the same building that Theodore worked at. A large brown and white sign was above her with the lights flickering that read: *Paper & Things LLC*. Audrey had all the textbook symptoms of a panic attack—heart pounding, body trembling, shortness of breath, and, of course, her sudden thoughts of impending doom.

The seconds ticking past felt like hours, as she banged on the glass relentlessly, staring over her shoulder in horror, terrified that the nothingness that claimed Theodore would envelop her at any moment. She continued to sweat, despite the bone-chilling gusts of wind billowing around her, proving that symptoms of panic can do remarkable things.

Gerald, who was the office manager, looked out the window when he heard the banging on the glass, and ran down the stairs to retrieve Audrey from the outside world that he was now referring to as the "unknown" in his mind. At first, Audrey didn't see Gerald's face as she thrashed about, until finally, Gerald yelled, "STOP!"

Audrey opened her eyes so wide they were the size of jawbreakers.

Quickly, she stepped back, and he opened the glass doors. "Gerald, you're here. I... I thought the whole town was gone," she said with her hoarse voice.

His eyes gazed past her and darted from side to side before whispering, "Get in!"

Before she could say another word, he grabbed her hand and pulled her inside. Once Gerald had shut the doors promptly behind her, Audrey felt a sense of safety like that a blanket gives you when you are scared at night, but in reality is just a placebo. The building reeked of damp. Not the smell of rain, but the stink a load of laundry would have if it was left forgotten in the washing machine for a few days.

"What is that smell?" Audrey wrinkled her nose and looked around at the receptionist's desk that stood to the right of them. The chairs for potential clients were empty, magazines untouched, and the fake flowers that sat between every few chairs looked darker than Audrey remembered, like they too were feeling glum.

Gerald looked at her for a moment, and then glanced quickly over one of his shoulders, then the other, wide eyes darting around. Audrey found herself wondering if it was panic or paranoia that made him seem so uneasy. When he looked back at Audrey, he absently fixed his tie and said soft-ly, "Something bad has happened."

Audrey stared at Gerald blankly. "Something bad has happened" wasn't something you expected to hear in a town this small; this quiet. The words filled her with a terror that chilled her more than the icy wind wailing on the other side of the glass doors had.

Gerald took a deep breath. "I'm not sure what has hap-pened, but most of our friends and neighbors seem to have vanished. I've only seen a few people, and no one so far has had a clue what is going on. Have you seen anything?" His words were rushed; breathless. He stared at Audrey with bulging eyes and a clenched jaw.

Audrey was struggling with the nightmare she had just witnessed, and couldn't find the words to to tell him the truth. So all she said, while she fumbled with her thumbs, was, "No, but the town is empty and I heard... I heard some-one scream."

She wasn't proud of the lie, but it was the only response she could give right now. Gerald, of course, did not know that her pants were on fire, but did assume that her frantic behavior meant that there was more to her story. But instead of pressing her, he just nodded his head.

"Is it just us here?" Audrey gazed at Gerald, hoping for the best possible answer that all her co-workers were still alive.

"Only other co-workers. Janet, John, Winnifred, Claire, Alex, Henry, Wyatt and Eliza are upstairs. I hope others are out there. Maybe hiding out at their jobs too or in their homes?" he replied in a hopeful tone.

While Gerald continued to speak, Audrey looked past him and fixed her eyes on the view outside the window. She strode to the back of the room and stopped directly in front of the large office window. The sky had turned. The milky blue sky was churning like water in a washer into a wrathful pinkish red that glared down upon the town. A color you would only see with a setting sun. It was hardly the time for the sun to take refuge at this time of day. In fact, the sky seemed almost frothing with rage, pressing down on the roofs of buildings in town with its blood red swirls and now forming, dark clouds that promised a raging storm.

Gerald trailed off, slowly turning to look at what Audrey was gaping at. Audrey blinked hard and gave herself a shake, as if to shake off a bad dream and rubbed her hand over her mouth. As her thoughts drifted to the image of Theodore launching into the sky, she quickly switched her thoughts to that of anything else to keep her from erupting into sobs. Work, family, friends. She had spent a wonderful date with him the previous night, and the shock of what had happened to him was too much.

Gerald seemed frozen for a moment, before whipping his head back to look at Audrey. He stuttered a moment, as if he couldn't figure out what to say, and placed his hand on Audrey's shoulder, giving her a light shake. "What does this mean?" he asked frantically.

Audrey turned to look at Gerald's grim, white as bone face, which wasn't something she expected to see from someone like him. His terrified look only added fuel to the fire.

She continued to stare, hearing him but not at the same time. She couldn't make his words make sense in her head.

She tried to take a breath to steady herself, but her body wouldn't cooperate. She gasped in a mouthful of air but felt as if she couldn't force the air into her lungs. Her heart rate quickened as she shoved Gerald off her, struggling to breathe, trying to form a single coherent thought. But her heart hammered in her chest and she started to wonder if she was having a heart attack. Her chest ached, she couldn't breathe, and her vision began to gray. She distantly heard Gerald calling her name and felt his hand on the back of her shoulder, tentative, as she wobbled over to a chair and collapsed into it. The sky raged outside of the glass windows, now a dark bloody red filled with churning black clouds. Audrey squeezed her eyes shut, wheezing rapidly, suddenly feeling as if she may vomit.

Gerald continued rubbing Audrey's shoulder. "Take a deep breath and exhale slowly. I'll do it with you," he said as he took a deep breath in through his nose and slowly released it out of his mouth. Audrey watched him and mirrored his breaths. He stared over her shoulder at the violently swirling clouds, barely able to see the red sky behind them now. Gerald kept murmuring to her, reminding her to breathe, as she worked through the panic attack. Being many years her elder, and having served in the army, he had seen his share of panic attacks and hysteria. Audrey's hysteria helped to ground him, almost as if reminding him that he, a natural born leader, couldn't afford to lose himself to fear when so many needed him to stay calm.

Audrey's breathing was beginning to calm, and she began to hiccup as she recovered from hyperventilating. She wiped her eyes, accidentally plucking off a single eyelash that stuck to her index finger. Instead of making a wish, she wiped it on her pants and gazed up at Gerald. He patted his hand on her shoulder, his face remaining calm and kind.

When he spoke, firm and authoritative, his voice somehow carried the same kindness that his eyes had. "Alright, we are going to join the rest upstairs now and discuss with them what to do." He put his hand under her arm to help her to her feet.

Audrey nodded, knowing that she was stronger than this. She let out a final sigh and climbed to her feet. She smoothed her dark green houndstooth blouse and followed him up the stairs, heading to the third floor. Audrey had always disliked going beyond the first floor of the office building if the elevator wasn't working. It wasn't due to laziness, it was because the stairs creaked with the slightest pressure on each and every step, and they were stained with dirt and grease from the feet that had used them over the years. No amount of and types of cleaning solution the janitors used could remove the slightly slick, slightly sticky layer of filth from the ancient stairs.

Every creak beneath Audrey and Gerald's feet as they climbed the wooden stairs to the third floor was ominous, each noise making her breath catch and her pulse race. She was never usually scared of the dimly lit stairwell, with its flickering fluorescent lights, however, under the circumstances, there was a lot to be afraid of. She stepped onto the third floor landing and was startled by someone rushing forward from the dark hallway.

Relief replaced fear when Audrey's co-worker and best friend Eliza came into view. Eliza grabbed Audrey and hugged her as hard as one would hug their only child after losing them in a grocery store.

"Hi, Eliza! Are you okay?" Audrey stumbled on her words, a bit winded from the descent up three flights of stairs, her tongue sluggish and heart still pounding from her recent panic attack.

"Oh, Audrey," Eliza practically shouted as she continued to embrace Audrey with a tight hug, clearly as hysterical and terrified as Audrey still felt. "I... I thought something had happened to you," she said as she slowly let go of her. They walked down the hall, passing by empty office rooms, before making it to the room that they were most familiar with. Gerald followed behind them quietly.

"I'm okay, but it doesn't seem like maybe many other people were as lucky as us. I hope there are more people out there that are safe somewhere else." Audrey spoke softly, shaking her head as she talked.

On a normal day, the room would have been overwhelmed with the noise of sales calls to businesses who needed stickers, new business cards, or any other marketing materials that they could provide. They would be able to hear the many printers down the hall executing customers' orders, and Audrey could imagine just where Theodore would have been. His flirtatious smile always made its way to her, even when he was on a phone call. But again, today was not a normal day and the open room filled with what would probably end up being a bunch of dusty desks and chairs felt empty as Audrey saw how few people were left.

Gerald looked around the room, taking in the troubled faces of his co-workers. People he barely knew, except in the generic co-worker way that most people could relate to. Although he was always friendly to them, he remained their boss first, and only knew things like what they would eat for lunch and any mannerisms that they pertained, but other than that, he just managed the office.

He straightened his shoulders as he walked to the front of the room slowly, thinking back to when he had led men into war just shy of his twenty-fifth birthday. Gerald was preparing himself mentally, knowing he needed to lead again, knowing that if he did, he could potentially fuck everyone over by making one wrong choice. He could potentially cost them their lives as they went up against... what? He had no idea what they were up against. He blinked hard, scrubbing his face with his hands. He had no clue what was happening out there. He took a breath, removed his hands from his face and took in his co-workers again.

Thin, serious Eliza, wearing high heels and a tight pencil skirt, stood at the front of the small crowd, clutching Audrey's arm. He could see her long, fake fingernails digging in. Everyone stared at him expectantly. He released the breath he hadn't realized he'd been holding, and resolve took over. Gerald leaned his butt back onto the nearest desk, resting his hands on the desk either side of him. As he struggled for words, his brows furrowed. Everything seemed either too frivolous or too horrifying.

"I doubt anyone else will be joining us now. Whoever is left beyond these walls has hopefully found shelter, just as we have..." Gerald paused, swallowing hard as the heaviness of what he just said sunk into him. He cleared his throat and continued, "Now, I know we're all scared, but let's dis-

cuss what information we all have; pool our knowledge. I
you all to realize that with the strange shit going on outside,
we need to stick together and survive whatever this may be.
Wyatt, can you tell the others what you saw?" Gerald spoke
somberly.

Wyatt was the latest employee of *Paper & Things LLC.*
He was a thin, wiry man with sparse, coppery facial hair that
begged to be shaved off. Thick eyebrows furrowed above his
hazel eyes—they were the most striking feature about him,
although today they were red-rimmed, bloodshot and accen-
tuated by shadowing beneath them that made him look as
if he hadn't slept for a week. Gerald stood next to Wyatt
and nudged against his elbow, accidentally startling him. He
turned his sharp, hazel eyes to Gerald now, looking as if he
would rather the earth swallow him up than recount the horrors he had seen. He cleared his throat.

His eyes darted from face to face, taking in each person
now staring at him as he walked the few short steps to face
the few co-workers that were left. Realizing he had been
holding his breath, he raked a ragged breath into his lungs
and scrubbed his face with his hands, dragging his fingers
down his cheeks in a manner that made him look as if he
were peeling his sallow face off. Wyatt's eyes fixed on Eliza,
unblinking and wild, uncertain if these people were ready to
hear what horrors awaited them.

Gerald noticed his eyes latched on Eliza, but before
Eliza, who was whispering to Audrey, noticed, he coughed
to get his attention. When Wyatt noticed, Gerald gave him a
slow nod and said softly, "Please, Wyatt. Tell them what you
told me."

Wyatt licked his lips, wringing his hands in front of himself, and began to speak,

"I... I was walking. Walking to work. Here." Wyatt shook his head. There was no easy way to say it. The words felt all wrong, like they were getting caught in his throat. "Archie—I'm not sure if any of you knew him; Archie Daniels?"

A few people around the room nodded, others just stared at him expectantly.

"Archie was... taken. I saw him... shoot. Up into the sky. I know that sounds insane; impossible. But it happened. He was... taken, by something dark. Something evil, perhaps. It wrapped around him and yanked him into the sky. I couldn't tell what it was, it all happened so very quickly, so fast. I ran and I hid. What if that dark thing had taken me instead? What was it? Where did it come from?" Wyatt's voice began to rise, his eyes mad and wide with fear. Gerald gave him a reassuring nod, and that small action seemed to bring Wyatt back to the present. Before anyone could respond to what he had witnessed, he wiped the sweat from his brow, and backed into the crowd.

Audrey started to feel almost ashamed of herself for not telling Gerald the truth. Wyatt looked like a bomb had exploded in his face, and yet Audrey stood there in horror, but not in utter shock. Although she was still hesitant to speak up, she decided she had to say something now that she knew she wouldn't sound crazy.

Wyatt didn't say anything else, so Audrey nervously walked over to where he was stood. "Gerald, I have something to share as well. Would that be alright?" He nodded his head and drifted himself towards his deskmate, Alex, who was now sandwiched between Eliza and him. Gerald rose his hand to his lips as she stood up front. His confusion would hopefully not result in distrust in her later.

"Everyone, I said before that I didn't see anything, but I lied. I just didn't think anyone would believe me. However, after Wyatt's bravery, I felt like I should speak up too. I saw Theodore taken the same way Wyatt saw Archie." When she landed on the name "Theodore," her eyes became misty.

Wyatt threw up his index finger and pointed it at her, and then everyone else in the room.

His red-rimmed eyes spoke of madness and spittle flew from his lips as he shouted, "See, I'm not crazy. Audrey saw it too!" His eyes frantically searched Alex and Eliza's faces. He squeezed their arms, imploring them to believe him with his bulging eyes. He looked insane, as if the stress of the situation was too much, and those surrounding him backed away slowly.

Audrey went over to him and placed his hands at his sides. Her eyes stared deep into his as she said kindly, "It's okay. I believe you." Although Wyatt was still noticeably upset, her affirmation relaxed his body, and Audrey placed him back next to Eliza, who almost looked like she was glaring at him.

Gerald approached the front again and gazed around the room for anyone else who might have wanted to come forward too. No one did. "Thank you, Audrey and Wyatt, for letting the group know the tragedies you both witnessed. After hearing from you two, I hoped that now we might have have a better understanding of what is happening to Harthsburg by listening to what you've both seen; however, I am left with more questions than before. Can anyone shed light on what is happening?"

Henry, who normally was a quiet man, probably because he sat alone in an office crunching numbers all day as the only accountant for the business, decided after gazing at everyone standing to suggest that some sort of religious awakening was taking place. Audrey, who wasn't very superstitious, thought in her head how absurd he was sounding and drowned out the rest of his speech. "Honestly, who could listen to that shit?" she thought to herself. If you've been wondering if some sort of apocalyptic God situation was taking over, you would be more wrong than when Y2K made all programmers and computer users fear once it became 2000, computers would stop working.

Henry finished on the sentence, "Our sins have finally caught up to us, and now this is when we pay!"

The rest of the group just kind of looked at him, perplexed by his radical comments.

"If that's all, Henry, we'll discuss other options." Gerald sighed. Henry closed his mouth and stumbled to the back, making sure no eye contact was made with his fellow co-workers. Gerald paced for a second, rummaging through his thoughts inside his balding head. It was easy to see that no one in that room had any plans, suggestions, or clues as to what they were going to do next. It became quite apparent that Gerald didn't either, as he opened his mouth and then shut it.

Audrey could sense his frustration and chimed in, "Why don't we relax for a bit, and then maybe when our heads are

a little clearer, we can think of the next step." The head nod-
ding was unanimous.

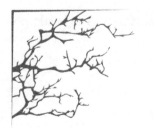

3

Cold. Cold. Cold.

The sound of water pounding against a hard surface came and went. It was too dark to make out exactly where he was, but he could see a sliver of light that beamed down to water. He knew it was water due to the mirroring effect that even the small bit of light provided. Shadows danced upon the water, but whose they were he didn't know. After screaming for what felt like an eternity, his lungs felt sore, like he was getting the flu.

He kept his mouth open in the hopes of catching at least one drop. Five water droplets fell into his mouth as he counted. It was almost like counting sheep, but in this case, he wanted a distraction to stay sane, rather than to help him sleep.

The hoarseness of his breath was just the start of the pain he felt. It had taken a couple of hours, or maybe even days, for his body to snap back to reality, which meant the pain now flowed out of every nerve. He didn't need a doctor to tell him that the wetness on his shoulders was his own blood. The blood had gushed out like a small river for what felt like a few hours when he was first taken to this place.

One thing he was sure of, their sharp claws weren't the deadliest part about them. Although others were taken with him, he never heard them. He knew at least one person had to be there with him—Darlene. He started to think that perhaps she was already dead and that he was the only one left, or she, and the others if there were any, had kept silent after hearing his screams.

No one had restrained him, but the fact that all he saw was the darkest black known to man made him previously leery to explore his surroundings. When his mind started to drift away to the life he'd once had, he knew that he wanted to live. If he had to fight to the death, he would do it. Quietly, he rose from the rough ground and listened again to the rhythmic sound of water dripping. His heavy eyelids closed before he could pull them back open, and he began a journey that he hoped would be less painful than what he'd already endured.

With courage in his heart, he quietly walked toward the water. He assumed it was a small puddle, but he could hear more droplets falling. He followed the sound, and the noise grew louder. *Plink, plink, tap, tap, tap, plink.* He continued closer, until he felt his shoe submerge in it, and sure enough, liquid landed on the top of his head. Slowly easing back a step, he opened wide and waited. Waiting. Finally, a thick, warm, metallic tasting liquid dripped down, hitting only his tongue. Quickly, he realized this wasn't water. He yelled, "Fuck! Ptooey, ptooey."

Coughing and spitting for the next hour wouldn't have made this any better for him. His tongue was now forever stained. With whom, he may never know. He was just about to back away from the puddle when he heard it. Loud thuds echoed around him, causing him to stumble back in fear.

Pointlessly, he looked up, thinking that the noise was coming from above him. His heart leaped instantly when another thud came, and honestly, it only stayed in place due to his ribs.

Another thud. Then another. The air in front of his face warmed and smelt of rancid meat. Caging his eyes shut, he muttered to himself, "Like it fucking matters." It was dark already, and whatever creature lay ahead wouldn't be able to be seen; at least not clearly.

"Be brave, be brave. Fear is a poison. Just open your eyes and run," he whispered to himself.

His eyelids were sticky from sweat, but he pulled them apart nonetheless. As his eyes opened, a scream erupted from his throat.

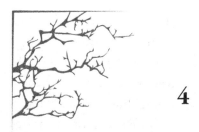

4

In the dead of night, Ben Drewitt's body shivered. The shivers didn't bother him as much as the pesky mosquitoes, who seemed to be at war with his biceps. Flicking them off was not even a real option. They came and went before he could even notice that another one had invaded. Despite his unwanted guests, the forest still took his breath away. It was an enchanting place that housed the fragrant smells of wild mushrooms with earthy moss, wildflowers and pine that smelt so strong you could feel the essence of the past holiday season.

Camping had become an integral part of his life growing up with his stepfather Harper, but when tragedy struck—taking his stepfather with it—Ben was hesitant to continue the tradition without him by his side. He was pleasantly surprised that although he felt that it was bittersweet to camp without him, he was still able to remember such fond memories, and ones that he knew Harper would have wanted him to continue. When Harper died, he had left him a leatherbound and tattered to hell journal that pieces of leather would flake off by just touching it.

There were random loose pages inside that seemed to have been added years later, but Ben had so far refrained from reading them. That was until this trip. This trip was the first time Ben decided to read the journal, instead of flipping through just so he could see his handwriting one more time. As he turned the aged leather journal in his hands, the fire crackled. The first part he read was a little tidbit about a girl he had liked when he was in school in Whinnville. A town that, to Ben's knowledge, was now a ghost town. Ben thought fondly about the ghost stories Harper used to tell him about where he used to live.

As a small child, the stories scared him, but when he grew into a teenager, he found humor in them. He would even sometimes take the lead on the stories when they would camp with friends. Skipping through page after page, he came to one that seemed oddly familiar. Ben placed his hand on the page and stared intently at each word. The inscription was close to forty years old and read: *In the summer, the darkness came and swallowed the town up, the town that was my home, and took my good friends and family along with it. The darkness will be back again to claim another town, but when that will happen, I don't know. If you are reading this, please take my words in seriousness, so that you may do things differently than I.*

Chills ran up and down his spine and his body shook along with it. His brain was a whirlwind of questions. Ben's finger marked his place in the journal as he held it closed in his lap. Ben muttered to himself about how old Harper must have been when he wrote that, before returning to the page. He took a deep breath and focused back on his words.

Ben had just found where he'd left off on the page when his fire disappeared just as quickly as a power outage would cause electricity to cut off. The flames were doing well, he had just placed his dinner over them, but yet they had vanished. There was no wind tonight, and the clouds hadn't produced any rain, yet here he was, plunged into almost complete darkness and in total shock. Sweat beaded on his forehead and began to drip down quicker than you could say, "DANGER."

As Ben sat there holding the journal, he felt paralyzed. His body had reacted like it had on a previous trip when a bear had come into their campsite. Although in this situation he doubted that staying frozen due to an unknown source that could snatch fire without leaving a trace would help him, he still stayed still. Quietly, he pocketed the journal and allowed his brain to problem solve, while the rest of his body waited. He knew his tent was right behind him, and for the first time, he prayed to God... Mother Nature... whatever powers would listen; he prayed it was still there.

Quickly, he stood up from the log he was sat on and accidentally bumped his thigh on it, before turning towards his tent. To his amazement, there it stood. The plastic texture crinkled against his hand as he fumbled for the zipper. Finally, his fingers grasped the tiny piece of metal and unzipped the tent faster than he had ever moved. Diving in, he bumped into one of the corners and thought about how small his tent was feeling at that moment. Ben wished that his tent made him feel more protected from whatever lurked outside, but instead it made him feel like a trapped animal. He rummaged around to find his flashlight, but his boot got caught on his sleeping bag and made him face-plant the floor. Although he had landed on something hard that would leave a bruise soon, when he realized it was his flashlight, he gladly picked it up. *Click, click, click.* Nothing. Absolutely nothing.

Frustrated, he tried to turn it on again. *Click, click, click...click...click.* His palms were sweating increasingly from his body's response to his urgency, which didn't help him one bit. He might as well have been holding water from the river. In anger, he chucked it to the other end of the tent. It bounced off his backpack, and to his complete shock, it flashed to life. Shining brilliantly straight into his eyes. If he didn't know any better, he would have thought someone was playing a cruel joke on him, but no one poked their head out to surprise him.

He grabbed the flashlight and slowly moved toward the opening of the tent. Peering his head out, he placed the flashlight in front of him. There wasn't much to see. The animals must have all fled because like the light, all sound had vanished as well. Only his rapid breath and the cold breeze that blew against the tent could be heard. Turning his flashlight to look both ways before he left the tent, he tried to examine the fire pit. No sign of footprints except his were in the circle.

Rubbing his chin, he pondered what could have happened. Nothing he thought of could've done that, so he remained apprehensive of his surroundings. Then a whispering sound moved between the trees that was faint enough that he probably wouldn't have noticed it if he weren't on high alert. He began to run frantically in the opposite direction to where the sound came from, while looking behind him. Then *BAM*, he ran right into a tree.

The impact caused him to fall onto the wet ground, and the sound repeated. His thoughts became discombobulated for a few seconds, before he dared to push himself back up and run. Grabbing his flashlight, he shook as he tried to get up, his legs buckling from the crouching position he'd managed to get to. Again, the sound came, but this time he realized that it was just the wind blowing through the trees. Annoyed at himself, he tried once more to push himself up.

"Yuck," Ben whispered. The ground was sticky and had a rotten odor. It was the type of stench you couldn't quite place and normally turned out to be a piece of food left in the car. He tried to wipe his hands on his jeans, but they were covered in a thick, sticky sludge that smelt like gone off chicken. Perplexed by it, Ben started to think that maybe it was honey, but he knew of no honey that could smell like that. Then he wondered if honey could expire and that led his mind to a whole load of strange questions.

After all his questions that had no answers, he concluded that it couldn't be honey. Being in the forest, he thought it might just be a lot of sap. From his experience with sap, it was sticky as hell and sucked to get out of anything. He shined his now stuck to him flashlight on the ground, and saw it wasn't the color of sap. At least not any sap that he had encountered.

All around him was sticky, or so it felt. His hands were covered with it. He decided to try once more to get up from the ground, and hopefully find a way to get the sticky substance off. If anyone was watching him, they surely would think that he was doing some strange dance ritual. Though it felt more like playing Twister to him. At this moment, left hand on green, right foot blue, left foot yellow. Finally, after several minutes of jerking his body away from the sticky stuff, he managed to pull his body up by grabbing a tree's trunk. His hands were stuck to it like an adorable tree frog holds on tightly to a branch.

After several hours, he gave up on trying to escape the tree. He hoped that the sun would come, and this whole night would be thought of as just a strange night he once had. His eyes grew heavy, and he thought that he would soon sleep, but the silence kept him awake. It wasn't the type of silence you'd hope for as you fell gently to the dreamland. Instead, his body was working on adrenaline with so much fear that his brain had no way of comprehending it or calming down any time soon. Pathetically, he stayed glued to the tree like a tree-hugging, loving hippie until dawn came. This was by far the longest night he had ever endured.

When the sun finally started to come up, there were no birds chirping, no leaves crunching from small critters; nothing. It felt as if the forest had died in the dark night, right along with his sanity. With the pale early morning light, he was able to assess the sticky situation. Whatever was on his hands was definitely not sap.

Waiting for the light had dwindled his adrenaline, and he started to feel a tingling, burning sensation on his palms. Quickly, he pulled his boots free from the small puddle below, and pushed against the tree, while trying to pull his hands free. He managed to free one. Examining the substance, he thought it was black at first, but when he moved his hand more into the ever-brightening light, he realized it was actually purple and almost iridescent at certain angles.

He checked his surroundings and saw the shiny purple ooze appeared to be dripping down the tree, coming from beyond his view.

He wanted whatever it was off his hands, but wiping his free hand didn't seem to help enough. He didn't have much to work with, but he did have saliva. His only idea was a pretty gross solution, but one he hoped would stop the slight pain that was forming.

The dripping feeling of his own saliva made him gag a bit. Finally, after a disgusting amount of spit that he honestly didn't know he could possibly produce, both his hands were free. He leaned down and rubbed dirt onto them and wiped it off on his jeans. To his surprise, his hands were red with what looked like small boils on his palms. Not big enough that anyone would notice by just glancing at them, but enough for him to feel his heart racing again.

His tent was still where he'd left it, looking as if it had an air of melancholy. The leaves above it now dripped with that purple ooze, just like the other trees he passed. He walked with caution, wary of the new addition to the forest. How it had gotten there and why were questions he hoped would be answered soon. As Ben made it back to his tent, he avoided the purple ooze by hopping over areas, until he finally managed to pack up his tent. Hopeful to leave the whole experience behind him, he walked away from the campsite without looking back.

His journey back home felt like he had just taken a month-long vacation. Even the mosquitoes had disappeared, and he was left with nothing. Silence still. That ever-frightening bit of nothing. It was quite remarkable that something as simple as deafening silence could create such chaos in his mind. The more he walked, the more paranoid he became, causing his head to look around him every few seconds like he was a felon on the run. His eyes grew as wide as the size of a full moon when more ooze was around him. As he said in his head, "A fucking plethora of ooze."

One of the best things about the forest here was seeing the waterfall. When he first arrived yesterday, he had sat at the edge of the water and let his feet grow cold in it. It brought back happy memories, and ones that he would never want to be altered, but what lay before him now was something out of nightmares.

The water was no more. No clear beauty of liquid that housed many different types of fish that you could easily spot. Instead, hundreds of fish were washed up on the side. They were covered in the gelatin-like ooze. The smell was unbearable. Even though they couldn't have been dead for longer than a few hours, they smelt of rotting flesh. And if you happened to be one of those people who would just about puke from the smell of fish, this would have been your death sentence.

There was a group of fish laying in one gooey bubble, and he couldn't quite fathom what his eyes were seeing. The purple mess seemed to be eating away at their flesh. Eating might not have been the right word. Loosening? Melting? Melting was more accurate. The whole upper half had no flesh, just bones. The lower half was filled with saggy pieces of flesh and blood dripping down. It was hard to tell at first that it was blood, since it was covered in whatever the out of this world purple goop was.

One fish was laying on a rock and had the goop only on its tail. Its eyes were what burned into his brain. As though they'd seen what did this. Its eyes were frozen in time with a look of shock. The type of shock seen in movies when the best friend turns out to be the bad guy.

Had the fish seen this stuff before, or what it was that caused this? The tips of his fingers started to burn. Some of the purple goop of death was still clinging underneath his dirty nails. Scraping vigorously, he managed to get a few nails goop free. His thumb was burning the most, but he couldn't manage to get all of it out.

He stared on the ground for anything that could help him. He reached down, picked up a tiny twig and broke it so that it would have a point. He started bleeding as he scraped underneath. He decided it would be for the best to go back over his other fingernails too, just in case. Some of it was still pretty sticky, so he rubbed some dirt underneath and pushed the twig through. His nails were all bleeding, but the burning had stopped. It had worked, and he didn't care that his fingers would be tattered and scarred.

He carefully crossed the river, holding several low hanging branches along the way to help him balance on the larger stones above the flowing water. He managed to get across with only a small amount of the acidic purple goop on the soles of his shoes. Across the river was no different than his camping spot. The trees dripped in the purple atrocity. Like a child, he would have usually been fascinated by the luminous shades of purple that dripped down into giant raindrops. Luckily, his inner child was a lot more cautious at the moment.

The last bit of woods remained relatively untouched. Some trees had little to none of it on them. He wondered briefly why these trees were untouched. Maybe there was a reason that the trees on this side had been given a chance at life still, but he didn't think that it would be the most genius thing to stick around to wait and see. Instead, he continued on and cautiously watched his every step. His trust in the forest had been severely compromised now. Thinking optimistically, he hoped that he wouldn't always now think of the forest in a gloom-ridden way.

Ben was now less than half a mile from the edge of the woods, and he was starting to feel quite paranoid that this was a trap. Normally he would see other people walking into the woods right here.

He remembered one small child, probably around two, tripping over a fallen tree. She had been so determined to climb over it. Her parents watched her cautiously, but let her try. Of course, like with most new things little ones try, they get hurt. She scuffed up her knee a bit, not much blood, but she cried when she looked at her parents' faces. You could tell they tried so hard to not make a noise and scare their little adventurer. Despite the little girl having minor injuries, it was a happy memory to see others enjoy the forest as much as Harper and Ben did.

Finally, he could see the parking lot, and he let out a sigh of relief. Ben's yellow '69 Chevelle was the only car in the lot. A car that gave him pride. Even in this dark time, he still smiled at it. The feeling of dread inside him was becoming unbearable, so he ran to his car, pulled his keys out, threw himself into the driver's seat and tossed his bag in the back.

He had never looked in his rearview mirror as much as he was doing now. You could say paranoia had got the best of him. You could say it was near eating him alive. It was only a few miles from the campground to town. There were so many trees on both sides of the road. All untouched. Not one car was on the highway. That had to be a first too. But he still kept checking his mirrors like something might pop out at him at any moment.

Exit 206 was painted in large letters with a one mile warning on a slightly splintered piece of wood. The black lettering had faded to gray, and the people in the town complained that they needed a fancy metal sign like most other towns had. Ben had to disagree. He enjoyed the uniqueness of the sign and felt a new paint job would be all that was needed. But he barely took notice of it today as he raced past.

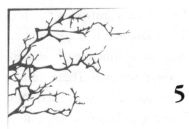

5

As Ben pulled off the highway, he saw a quick flash in his rearview mirror. His head jerked to look over his shoulder, almost swerving off the road in the process. When he saw nothing but leaves from the trees gliding in the wind, he shrugged it off as just a bird. He slowed to take the next left onto Vine Street and accelerated again as soon as he made it out of the turn. Many houses lined the street, all with their own uniqueness, which was something that Ben had preferred compared to the tract homes that were in almost every town around his. He couldn't help but look at them differently as he drove past them with a pit in his gut that they were all empty.

No dogs started barking as they usually did at the loud roar of his engine, no kids were out playing on their scooters, and not a single car was exiting any of the driveways. The whole neighborhood seemed vacant, and he wondered if all the houses felt as lonely as he was feeling.

Cranking his window down, he slowed to barely ten miles an hour and listened. In this situation, he thought that the sound of his car would surely give a heart attack to anyone who happened to be left. The noise of his engine normally brought smiling faces or even looks of appreciation, mainly from older men who remembered having a car just like his, or ones who wished they had one, but today's setting might evoke fear or a way to safety.

Ben was only four blocks away, and after several minutes of listening to emptiness, he decided to haul ass down the last blocks. For a moment, he forgot about the situation and smiled at the sound of his roaring engine. Turning left onto Fir Street, he came to a screeching halt in front of his home, 358. His street was no different than the others—a ghost town. When Ben cut the engine, he let out a breath that felt heavy, like he had been running, and turned to look up and down his street. No one to be seen and nothing to be heard except for the occasional wind blowing past.

As he closed the car door behind him, he stood staring at his lavender front door, almost hesitant to enter. He had contemplated getting back into his car and driving far away, but he fought against the urge and walked up to his door. Sliding his key in the lock, it opened with no hesitation and he pushed the door open, flinching at the possible sight that may have led before him, only to find that it was exactly as he had left it. Ben's face softened and he quickly locked the door behind him.

A stack of camping books were neatly placed on his coffee table with crease marks, his couch pillows as disheveled as they had always been, and a pair of hiking boots that still had dried dirt caked on the sides were next to the couch. Despite the sameness, Ben had an uneasy feeling in his home. He could feel it deep down, and he wanted to blame his home for being the problem, for what had changed, but it wasn't the home— it was him.

He let his backpack fall to the side of the coffee table like he could care less what was inside and continued past the living room to the kitchen. Placing his hand on the fridge, he sighed and opened the door. There were several glass bottles that stood on the top shelf that read Enerjuice—an organic energy drink, each with appealing liquid colors. The one he grabbed was a fruit blend berry flavor. Even though for the last several weeks that had been his favorite one, he would still place other types into his cart on his grocery trips, knowing full well that he wouldn't be drinking those flavors any time soon. Surprisingly, he didn't want any of them now, even his favorite. What he really wanted was a cold beer to help calm his nerves, but he knew that wouldn't really help anything. He didn't believe for a second that this was the end of the nightmare. No, he needed his strength to survive whatever was coming next.

Taking a sip of his Enerjuice, he walked over to the couch and grabbed his backpack. Placing it on the coffee table, he pulled out Harper's journal. Before he opened it, he chugged down more Enerjuice like he was hoping it would turn into beer, and took a deep breath. His remaining adrenaline made him fumble over the pages that all now appeared to be useless information. Some of the entries made him chuckle out loud as he skimmed them, but he quickly turned the pages to make it to where he had left off earlier. After around ten minutes had passed, he was starting to believe that he was mad. The page he was searching for didn't seem to exist, but he knew what he had read, and he found it not likable that the words had left on their own accord.

Frustrated, he closed the journal and set it down next to the stack of books. Despite his need to find out if what Harper had witnessed as a child was relevant to his situation, he had to step away and refocus. Gazing around the room, he got up and walked over to the curtains. He opened them slowly, hoping that he would see someone, anyone, in the street. Hoping that he would be proven wrong that the neighborhood had been turned into a ghost town. Sadly, Ben peered out at the still empty street that had proved that ghost town was once again the word he would use to describe his once happy neighborhood. Despite his car normally looking out of place due to all the minivans and eco-friendly cars that were quite common here, it now looked almost foreign. He backed away from the window and let the curtains fall back into place.

As he gathered his thoughts while pacing back and forth, he kept glancing out the window. He was hoping to see something or someone. He was hoping that everyone wasn't dead or covered in that purple goop. It was a frightening thought to imagine. He decided to drive to the center of town, but before that, he thought that his next best option would be to call the local police. If anyone knew anything, it would be them. He reached into his pocket, pulled out his cell phone and dialed 911. Anxiously, he waited for someone to pick up, but it just kept ringing. Eventually, he gave up and decided to look up Crater Village's non-emergency police line. It was the next town over, and where his mother lived. If anything strange was going on there too, he wanted to know. The phone rang again, but this time a man with a husky voice answered.

"Crater Village Sheriff's Department, what can I help you with?" the voice said confidently.

Ben let out a sigh of relief and said, "Hi... hello. There is an issue here in Harthsburg. We need everyone over here now. Everyone is missing in my neighborhood, and I don't know what could have happened—"

"Okay, hold on," the cop interjected. "Why do you think everyone is missing?"

"Well, the streets are quiet, I haven't seen anyone leave their house, or even any kids playing outside. You must believe me! I just came back from a camping trip and the forest...the forest..." He couldn't get his tongue and brain to cooperate because he knew how crazy it sounded. Gulping, he continued on to say, "The forest has something in it that's killing all the fish. The other wildlife—"

"Is this a prank call or something?" the cop said annoyed.

"No, no... you have to believe me. Something strange is happening," Ben yelled.

"I'm going to need you to calm down for a second. Unless you have knocked on everyone's doors and know for a fact no one is home, then you don't actually know that everyone is gone. Now, tell me, have you knocked on every door?" the voice said sarcastically.

"For fuck's sake, man, just listen to me," Ben hollered into the receiver.

"What did you say your name was again?" the cop said angrily.

"I didn't," Ben said through gritted teeth.

"Why don't you settle down and maybe go get a check-up at your doctor's office. Then you can call me back if you still believe that everyone has just vanished."

Ben didn't say another word, instead grimacing into the receiver as he clicked the big red end button, before chucking his phone clear across the couch. Feeling a sense of defeat, he placed both his hands on his face and rubbed it. His eyes looked down and on the top of his shoe he saw a small piece of the sticky purple goop. Instinctively, his body tried to move away from his shoe, but, of course, since it was still attached to his foot, it did nothing but make him stumble into his coffee table.

Quickly, he plopped down onto his couch and carefully unlaced them. He held on to the inside of his shoes while walking to his dining area that had a small sliding glass door, leading to his backyard. He placed them down in the grass, and then hurried back inside and shut the door as though he thought at any moment the goop would grow legs and attack him. Luckily for him, the goop could not. Peering out the sliding glass door, he pondered if he should look up a number for an environmental scientist, but he doubted that any would be nearby. He saved the idea for later. He grabbed his keys, Harper's journal, and his other pair of hiking boots from next to his couch and laced them up.

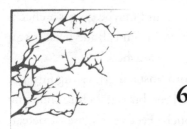

6

The Chevelle barreled down the several blocks into town. He was very close to the outskirts, but was still only about five minutes away. Pulling onto the main road into town, Clover Boulevard, he saw life, but not the life he was hoping to see. A raven landed directly on the hood of his car, staring blankly into Ben's eyes. Ben kept his eyes on the raven until it casually took off and flew behind him in the direction of the forest. He hoped the raven wouldn't be flying that far only to find the forest full of death. He was comforted by seeing the raven, despite what most people believed they brought. It meant he wasn't the last one left.

The donut shop was to his right—a bright pink building with a mural of donuts swirling around with rainbow sprinkles falling on them—but the air didn't carry the scent of freshly baked donuts like it normally did in the mornings. It was still early enough that they would be open for another couple hours. As though Maggie, the shop owner, never made it in, the lights were off and the sign still said closed.

Ben had lived in Harthsburg his whole life, and he knew if Maggie couldn't come in, one of her three sons would. Ben tried to think of a time when the shop was closed, but he couldn't recall one. It was quite a famous donut shop due to the exciting and original flavors that Maggie had come up with over the years. Tourists who thought of themselves as "foodies" would even come in to post on social media that they had eaten there. Ben fondly thought about the time when she had come up with a donut that had sugar with a blueberry sauce drizzled over the top of it, that was covered in some sort of delicious graham cracker chunks. Sadly, it was a limited time donut, but she had known Ben since he was a baby and would occasionally make a batch just for him. He thought about how unfair it would be if she was dead. Maggie's kind smile and plump body flashed into his mind, but instead of her being her normal self, his mind's eye envisioned her covered in the acidic purple ooze. Her eye was melting out of its socket. She was trying to scream and beg for help, but no one could hear her as the goop slipped into her mouth and down her throat.

Ben squeezed his eyes shut and blinked several times, while smacking his face to rid his mind of such horrible thoughts. He thought instead that there was no proof she was gone, and that maybe she was hiding somewhere safe. Really, that's what he was hoping for everyone, and that when he would find them, it would almost be like a surprise party. Everyone would pop out of hiding after hearing him call out for them, and then they would jump up happily, but of course without the party hats and kazoos.

The town gave off the same empty feeling as the residential area. Cars were left unattended, shops were empty, and his Chevelle was the only thing making any noise. He came upon a light green compact car that was familiar. It was parked next to the mini-mart and had a faded bumper sticker of the rock band The Peculiars. They weren't a huge band, but they definitely had a cult following. They had played a few summers back in Harthsburg, and Ben quite enjoyed them. He pulled up next to it, put his car in park, and tried not to think of all his friends that could be missing. He tried with all his might to not let his mind imagine them like it had Maggie.

After exiting his car, he decided to try his luck on foot. He first went around to peek inside the windows of the compact. It had been deserted, just like the other cars on the street, but he assumed someone had been in this one not that long ago. A single coffee cup was in the cup holder that had a logo from Williams Coffee Co.—a coffee shop just a few blocks before the mini-mart. Whoever owned the car had definitely favored that coffee shop because they had several empty cups scattered on the floor.

Even though a red illuminated sign said open in the window, the mini-mart was abandoned. The automatic doors slid open, allowing him to step inside. He felt awkward walking in with no one else around, almost like he was a thief or would be accused of being one. The aisles were all empty, but as he went down aisle seven, he found a clue. As though he was a detective, he crouched down to examine a single loaf of bread that was lying on the floor next to a shopping basket. No purple goop was on the loaf, so it wasn't much for him to go off. He continued to linger down each aisle, but nothing else spoke to him.

Slowly jogging out of the store, he crossed the street. Once he'd made it across, he stood on the sidewalk and sensed a change in the air. It almost felt like someone was watching him—that feeling that causes the tiny hairs to stand up on your body. He looked over his shoulder and only saw the empty street. He spun around to look down a side street, but all he saw were empty cars and some leaves that blew into the street.

Walking back towards the mini-mart, he saw a small orange flower. He couldn't help but smile at it, but then he noticed something. Kneeling to get a closer look, he saw that some of the petals were missing, but not just that, the tiniest drop of goop was directly underneath where the petals were missing. He stumbled back and sprinted to the only safe haven he could think of—his car.

Apparently that energy drink hadn't helped because his eyes were heavy. He couldn't blame the drink though. It's not like the back label read, "Perfect for those of you who love staying up all night in pure terror, and then spending the next day in terror as well." He would have to re-read the label, but he was positive it would not be there.

He locked his doors and pulled out his phone to call his best friend Theo. His introvert self struggled making true friends, but Theo was one of the few. As the phone rang, Ben's fingers tapped against the steering wheel nervously. For a moment, he thought that his friend had answered, but when he realized it was his voicemail, his heart sank. He wasn't giving up just yet, so he called once more. This time, when it ultimately went to voicemail, he left a message.

Trying not to sound too worried, he spoke into the receiver, "Hey, Theo, I'm really hoping you're out of town or something. Please call me back as soon as you can. It's been a few weeks since we've hung out, and there are some strange things happening. Hope you're okay." Ending the call, he closed his eyes and gently bit his thumbnail. A nervous habit that he rarely partook in as an adult.

Instead of just sitting alone in the parking lot, Ben turned his car back on and drove to Theo's house. When he arrived, he felt his stomach churn. Cautiously, he stepped out of his car and refrained from shutting the door just in case. He followed the cobblestone path to Theo's door and turned the handle. The door was locked and everything looked in place from what he could see through the window. It didn't stop him from pounding on the door and calling his name though.

When Theo didn't answer, he walked away and got back inside his car, about ready to have a breakdown. As though his body couldn't take it anymore, his eyes closed.

He awoke with a jolt, thinking no more than twenty minutes could have gone by since he'd passed out. When he looked at the clock, he realized an hour had passed. He also saw a single text and one missed call had come through. "Eliza," Ben muttered to himself and smiled at the name.

He read the text first where she'd wrote: "Ben, I know we haven't spoken in quite some time, but please tell me if you are okay. Something has happened. Please, please text me back, or call me. I am safe with some co-workers."

He'd gone on a few dates with Eliza a while back and had never forgotten about her. She'd wanted to end things with him and Ben was hurt, but he'd respected her wishes. Ben was happy that she was safe and felt a twinge in his heart that maybe she still thought about him too.

He decided to text her back: "Eliza, I am alright. I haven't seen anyone in town. Where are you?" He waited for a response, but when he didn't receive one right away, he felt that he was too late. His heart pounded as he decided to call her. The phone rang and rang, and when she didn't answer, he placed the phone down, feeling his heartbeat rise again. But then his phone started to ring. He reached for it and answered, feeling happier than he ever had before to hear someone's voice.

"Hello?" he said.

"Ben?" the voice replied.

"Eliza, it's so good to hear your voice. Where are you?" he asked with both comfort and worry in his voice.

"It's good to hear yours too. I'm actually hiding out at work. A few other co-workers are here too. Maybe you should come join us?"

"Yeah..." Ben rubbed his chin and looked around outside to see if anyone or anything was near him. When he didn't see anything he continued, "What's your address?"

"387 Crane Street. It's the Paper & Things LLC. building."

"Wait... that's where you work?" Ben said confused.

"Yes, why?"

"Do you know someone named Theo? I'm looking for my buddy and can't seem to find him, but he works there."

"I know a Theodore. I'm assuming Theo is for short?"

Ben started the engine and began to drive down the road, turning the speaker on his phone on. "Yeah, it is. Is he there?"

Eliza sighed before saying, "No... no... I haven't seen him."

Ben glared at the road and told Eliza that he would be there shortly. They hung up and he sped through town until he made it to Crane Street. He pulled into the parking lot of Paper & Things LLC. and saw that there were several cars already parked there. Quickly, he parked and cut the engine. Closing the car door behind him, he peered into the glass doors of the building. No one was on the first floor that he could see and when he tried to pull the door open it was locked.

As he pounded on the door, he yelled, "Eliza? Eliza? Are you still here? It's Ben."

While he waited for a response, he searched around the brick building and gazed up at the top floor windows. He saw no movement and decided to get back into his car and call her. The weird thing was that out of all the places in town, this was the only one where he could feel energy. Energy that only comes from interacting with other human beings, or animals at the least. It felt familiar, and he was beginning to not feel alone, even though nobody had answered the door. Just as he was about to close his car door, Eliza dove into his arms.

"Ben, you made it!" she said with tears running down her face.

Her state of mind must have been just as broken as his. Ben embraced her longingly. Her floral perfume drained his thoughts of the present into the past, causing a tidal wave of memories to ripple through his mind. One memory in particular flooded his thoughts—the last date they went on where Ben took her to the park for a movie night. Each Saturday every summer, the town would put a projector in the park, playing a different movie each time. The air would always smell like popcorn and cotton candy, and people would sit on blankets in the grass. Ben brought a blanket and was sat with his arms wrapped around Eliza as she snacked on cotton candy. As he remembered more of the day, he reminisced about how beautiful she'd looked and how her hair had had two small braids that connected at the back to a small dragonfly clip.

Overall, he'd thought it was a great date. He'd even ended up kissing her forehead when he'd dropped her off at home, telling her he would call her. Even now, he couldn't recall what movie they'd seen because he'd been so transfixed on her. They'd whispered and laughed throughout it, but when he'd called the next day, she'd seemed different. Eliza had told Ben that she'd thought it would be best they just stayed friends, and even though that'd hurt him greatly, he'd respected her wishes. Sadly, he hadn't been able to cope with just being her friend, so he'd removed himself from her life until he could be only that to her. He still wasn't quite there yet.

Snapping back to the present, he gazed down at Eliza. What a sobbing mess she was. Like a parent would lift a small child, Ben gathered her into his arms and carried her over to a little bench that sat outside the building. She didn't protest it, so he held her tighter. A few people stared down from the large windows at their reunion. Ben noticed the people staring and felt relieved that more people were still alive.

"Shall we go inside?" Ben asked.

Eliza got up and grabbed Ben's hand to lead him in. She locked the door behind them, and they began walking up the stairs. Ben noticed the strange smell that wafted out of the building when the doors opened. He decided not to ask about it, but instead focused on his steps as they walked up the rickety stairs. When they made it to the top, the rest of Eliza's co-workers were staring at them. They smiled at Ben, but only Gerald walked up to him to shake his hand and introduce himself.

"Everyone, this is my friend Ben. Ben, this is Audrey, Henry, Janet, Claire, Alex and Wyatt." She pointed to each one as she said their names, but when she got to Wyatt's name, she said it almost like she would have rather refrained from saying it. He thought they all looked a bit somber.

Ben waved his hand at them nervously and wondered if Audrey was the girl that Theo would talk to him about. He knew that he was casually dating a girl named Audrey, but he had yet to meet her. He felt comforted and overwhelmed at the same time, knowing that at least he wasn't the only one left alive. Gerald approached Ben again and asked if he could shed any light on the situation.

Eliza placed her hand on Ben's shoulder and whispered into his ear. She told him that Audrey had seen something that he needed to know about, but she wasn't willing to tell him herself. Ben turned his head from Eliza and pondered how to answer Gerald. It was the whole reason why he had come to this building and he couldn't wait any longer to know what had happened to his friend.

"Actually, I was wondering if I could speak to Audrey first. I came here looking for my friend Theo. Eliza told me that she knows what's happened to him." Ben looked over at

Audrey, and her eyes welled up a bit as she faltered over to Ben and began to explain.

If Ben was being honest, he wasn't as shocked by what Audrey had seen as he should have been because after seeing what was in the forest, he knew it had to be something otherworldly. As Audrey finished telling him her story, he raised his hands up and pushed his wavy brown hair away from his face. He shook his head, not able to look anywhere but at the slightly dirty blue carpet. Audrey placed her hand on his shoulder and wiped a single tear away from her cheek. She thought about apologizing to him, but she knew that wouldn't do anyone any good.

As Audrey walked away from Ben, he looked up and asked, "Where was he when you saw him get taken?" His mind was racing to an idea; a clue.

Audrey turned back to him and replied, "Across the street from the mini-mart."

Somehow, Ben had known it before she'd said it. That purple goop had to be tied to the disappearances. Eliza stood by Ben and grabbed his hand again. She looked up at him with her big hazel eyes, contemplating if she should say what she wanted to. Ben realized the look she gave and was about to ask her what she wanted to say, when Gerald cut into the moment.

"Ben, we would really like to know what you've discovered, if anything at all," he asked with slight irritation.

Ben took a deep breath and began to speak, "It's a bit of a long story, but it all started last night. Late last night. I was camping in Harthsburg National Forest. Suddenly, my fire went out, and in a panic, I grabbed my flashlight and began to walk. Despite having my flashlight, it only helped a little because it was like it wasn't just dark, it was like the moon had been swallowed whole. I ended up falling down, and when I tried to get up, I was stuck."

Eliza's mouth dropped open, but she quickly closed it again to let him continue.

"I couldn't see what was on me until the morning." As he looked up at the group, he paused for a moment. The whole group looked hungry for his next words, but also so distraught by what little he had already said. "What was on me was something I can't really understand. It was some sort of purple, iridescent ooze. It was super sticky and took me forever to get off my hands. I was definitely allergic to it. Well, either that or it has something toxic in it." Ben raised up his palms to show the red boils on them.

Everyone gasped, and Eliza looked away before touching them with pain in her eyes.

"When I packed up and began my journey back, I found that the goop was all over the tops of the trees and all in the waterfall. The crazy thing is the fish were all dead from it. It was melting their scales off."

Wyatt muttered "melting" loud enough for everyone to hear, and he looked like he was about to faint.

Janet raised her hands to her face and yelled out, "What the fuck is going on?" She paused before proceeding to say, "I mean, seriously, what are we doing? We are holed up here, knowing that people are being taken by something that can fly, and now..." She pointed at Ben, showing that she'd obviously forgotten his name already.

A bit deflated, he said, "Ben."

She continued, "Thank you. Yes, Ben here says that some goop is killing things? Is everyone who saw something on drugs?" She gazed to her other co-workers, hoping for them to agree with her, but none of them even gave her the slightest bit of a nod.

"Okay, you can stop right there. Janet is your name, right? While I understand that I am a stranger and all, what I saw was real. I've never done drugs in my life, and I can tell you that the horror I faced is not something that I would have shared unless it was really important. I came to find my friend, and if we can all work together to get through this, that would work better than accusing us of lying. I would leave your false opinions to yourself from now on." Ben was so angry that his body was shaking. Eliza started rubbing Ben's thumb with hers to help calm him. Luckily, it worked.

Janet seemed to have calmed down too. She stared down at her feet like she was ashamed of what she said. She replied to Ben, "Fine, I believe you." It wasn't an apology, but he accepted it for whatever it was.

"Have any of you reached out to the police?" Ben asked, hopeful. If they wouldn't listen to him, maybe they would listen to someone else.

Gerald furrowed his brow and scoffed. "We called, and not just one station. One officer I spoke to asked me if I also wanted to report a missing unicorn," he said angrily, before continuing to say, "I only hope that if they get enough of these calls from other people in hiding, that they will stop thinking that someone is just prank calling them."

Ben rolled his eyes at the comment the officer said to Gerald. He wondered if they had spoken to the same guy.

Since Gerald thought it was best for them to stay in hiding for now, everyone either talked quietly or sat alone at their normal work desks. Ben wandered off with Harper's journal tucked tightly underneath his arm.

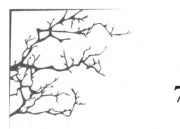

7

S **eptember 28, 1976:** *It was just another day, another gray and forgetful day—or so I thought it would be. My school is just a few short blocks away from my home, and let's be honest, it's my senior year and I'm not that concerned with making it to class on time. School is easy for me. Too easy. No one challenges me, and college can't come soon enough. Despite my intelligence, my teachers are not impressed. I get it. As a teacher, I would be pissed too about students who ditch. Then again, if I were a teacher, I wouldn't be so boring. Some people think I am just arrogant. Maybe they're right.*

I grabbed a couple of my favorite fiction novels; I was ready for the day. Into the woods I went. The forest was aflame with autumn. The trees boasted their new colors, and leaves had begun to fall, landing in the tall grass.

I plopped down next to my favorite tree—a large cypress that had bits of moss growing along some of the branches. I pulled out one of my books. It happened to be written by Felicity Dix. It's a novel about two kids lost in another dimension, that I'm so far really enjoying. About three-fourths of the way in, a girl came up to me. She startled me and I very clumsily dropped my book.

The sun hit her face just right and cast a yellow glow all around it. I asked her what she was doing there.

She smiled at me and told me she came to find me because she wanted to ditch class for once too. We talked a bit and laughed. Normally, I would go to class for my third period—history—but we talked so long I never went, and neither did she.

Right before I was about to leave, she grabbed my sleeve and spun me around to her. We kissed. A lot. I hope to speak to her again.

October 30th, 1976: *Taylor and I have been going around together for a couple of weeks now. We decided to go to a party tonight for Halloween. She insisted we dress up. I decided to dress up as a knight, and even had a fake wooden sword. Taylor wouldn't tell me what she was going as. I got to Dave's around 6 pm, and there were already a ton of people there dancing and drinking spiked punch. Two hours went by, and I still hadn't seen Taylor anywhere. I even asked some masked people to tell me who they were. I thought that maybe she had just stood me up, so I left the party. Dave told me he would call my house if she showed up. I've been waiting all night and no call from her or Dave.*

October 31, 1976: *Taylor is missing. Her parents are having a rough time and I can't explain the shock I'm in. I really hope she gets found soon, but the police say they have no leads. If they can't find her, I will.*

THE OFFICE REMAINED fairly quiet, with no one having any real idea of what to say or not say. Whispers came and went between two co-workers at a time, until nothing else needed to be said. Ben sat alone and away from the pointless whispers that were occurring in the other room. All he did was read. He was reading Harper's journal, and he had been holed up in the conference room for several hours already. Gerald seemed to be stalling, and Audrey couldn't help but want to get the hell out of the building. Everyone was becoming restless and hungry. Audrey had an urge, or to her a need, to get out and find Theodore. She thought about confiding in Eliza what she was planning on doing, but she feared what her friend would think; but after standing around doing nothing for so long, she was done with waiting.

Audrey walked to the center of the room with new courage, and said, "If anyone wants to come with me, I am going to go look for Theodore and anyone else I can find."

Oh, the stares she received. They all looked so confused. But Audrey thought to herself, "Do they seriously want to stay here for who knows how long? I sure as hell don't. The silence just makes me want to leave even more."

Then the door to the conference room swung open and Ben walked out, holding the tattered journal in his hands. He walked towards Audrey and said sincerely, "Audrey, I'll go with you. I want to find him too."

As though exhausted by both of them, Eliza closed her eyes. Though she still decided that she would join them. Audrey knew she wasn't thrilled about it, but she was obviously smitten with Ben, despite the fact she'd never heard her even mention him before. Which was surprising, as Eliza and her always discussed their relationship details, and try as she might, she couldn't even remember his name ever popping up. Audrey decided that she would ask her about how she knew him at a later time, when their very world wasn't in peril.

Audrey eyed her fellow co-workers once more to see if any of them would volunteer to join them. When none did, she said, "Okay, we're going to go out and will return soon with whatever we learn. Does anyone have a phone charged that could receive a call from us?" She looked around the room and Gerald quickly volunteered, putting his number into each of their phones. He said that he would make sure his phone was charged, and for them all to be safe, even considering giving each of them a hug—something he had never done before with a co-worker. He settled on a nod.

As Eliza looked at Ben and Audrey with imploring eyes while they walked down the stairs, ready to leave the safety of the building, she asked, "Where are we going?"

Ben and Audrey looked simultaneously at each other. It was clear neither of them had a real plan, but they were sure they would figure something out.

They walked down the many creaking steps back down to the first floor, feeling like the small sliver of security they felt they had was about to part ways from them at any moment. Audrey lifted her head up to the sky when she cautiously opened the glass door to the outside world. Then reality struck a chord, leaving them all speechless for a moment, while they wondered if leaving truly was the right decision. Ben's car sat in the parking lot same as he left it, but he had this unnerving feeling that something would be in the car, or at least watching them like they were a worm waiting to get taken by a bird.

"Ben, do you think we should go back to the forest? Maybe we can find out more there, since it seems like that is a pretty occupied area of strange." Audrey's left eyebrow rose when she said that last bit.

"I'm not sure we are prepared enough to go there. We have a lot of things to consider first. There's the strange goop, animals dying and the fact that there are flying creatures that could snatch us. It was quite terrifying, and I'm not sure I'm ready to go back yet." Ben looked at Eliza when he said this, and right away Audrey knew he was trying to protect her. He might have actually been scared, but Audrey could tell that wasn't what was holding him back.

"Eliza, what do you think we should do?" Audrey asked, hoping that her input would be to go to the forest, but she knew that would be a long shot. The forest was their only real lead, and Audrey thought that if Eliza was too scared to actually look for their friends, she shouldn't have come. Her response was slow.

"I don't think that I have much say here. Out of us, I'm the only one who hasn't seen anything. I arrived to work early, before knowing what was happening in town. I'll listen to whatever you or Ben have to say."

Audrey was surprised by Eliza's answer, but she refrained from saying anything about it. Ben got his keys out and asked, "Should we just take my car?"

"My car is still at the mini-mart, so we can't take mine anyway. Eliza, I'm assuming you don't mind?" Audrey peered at her friend.

"That's perfectly fine, Ben."

Ben smiled and unlocked the door, causing the metal to creak—a noise that Ben could never grow tired of, no matter how many years had gone by. Ben stuck his head in instinctively to make sure nothing was hiding in the backseat to eat them later. Nothing jumped at him and he gave a sigh of relief, before allowing Audrey and Eliza to get in the car.

Ben slid into the driver's seat and didn't even bother buckling his seatbelt for the first time. He turned to Eliza, who was presently having a flashback down memory lane as she sat down on the dark leather seat. She gently danced her fingers across the seat and grinned faintly. Audrey noticed, but she doubted Ben did, since he was more focused on locking his door and making sure all his mirrors were still adjusted properly. Audrey had climbed into the back and was admiring how cared for the car was. It was spotless on the inside and almost pristine on the outside.

Ben looked to Eliza and Audrey before asking, "Why don't we go back to my place? I actually have some of that goop on one of my shoes. I would like to see if anything has happened to it. It might help us understand more about it."

"How far is your house, Ben?" Audrey asked politely.

"Not far," Ben and Eliza said in unison.

Audrey rolled her eyes but nodded, while waving her hand at Ben to get a move on. As Ben started the car and drove away from the now desolate 387 Crane Street, she stared out the window to look up at the third floor where she had hoped to see Theodore that morning. Softly, her eyelids fell and her mind drifted to the night before.

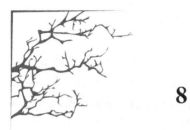

8

The smell of tulips carried in the wind, and let's face it, it was all Theodore had been able to smell for the last several blocks, after he had purchased a bouquet from a rustic flower stand some streets before. He had also unsuccessfully wiped the smile from his face that he had already relentlessly told himself to get rid of; part of him was happy that it had stayed. He had considered renting a car to pick up his date, but he felt that he needed some time to calm his nerves. It was an uncomfortable and unfamiliar feeling.

Theodore had arrived at exactly six o'clock at the now almost green clock tower. Being as old as the town, its light gray stones had become infected with moss in every new crack it had gained over the years. He greeted the old tower like a friend from another time; another world. For a moment, he stared in awe at the beautiful stonework, and even at the infectious bounty of green that made it seem like the tower was truly alive.

His right hand fell to his side and repetitively tapped at his thigh. The clock's arm moved to five past six and his smile finally started to dwindle, but of course now he ached for it to return. He imagined Audrey coming around the clock tower to meet him with her bright smile fixated on him, but the clock was still ticking and he stood there with only tulips to comfort him.

Audrey was known for being punctual to work and he had assumed that a date would be no different. Unless, he thought, she had changed her mind. A painful thought that crept into his mind, just as the moss had crept into the tower's cracks. No, he wouldn't let his happy thoughts turn to decay. He forced a grin, while he gently closed his eyes to smell the orange tulips.

A subtle breeze blew past him, causing the tulips to slow dance in his hands. He thought about the first time Audrey had finally accepted his invitation to get together after work. It was not a date she said three times prior to leaving the office with him, but he didn't care. He just wanted to be able to see her for longer than normal.

Theodore squinted up at the giant clock, whose ticking was now aiding in his uneasy feeling. The rusted brass arms showed him it was 6:13. His fingers tapped harder against his thigh. A number that he never thought of as anything bad, until now. Now it was the time that he was close to giving up.

He couldn't stand still anymore and began to walk around the clock tower. When he got to the side, he realized that Audrey was already there in a dark blue dress. Although, she wasn't waiting for him at the wrong spot. No, she was there standing and then walking away, and then walking back. Theodore hoped that she would make up her mind soon, but more so, he hoped that she wasn't regretting that she'd agreed to go on a date with him.

After peeking at her a while, Theodore decided to just go to her. He allowed his smile to escape again, and very happily shouted, "Hey, Audrey!"

Startled, she looked up, her mind immediately easing at the sight of him. She walked towards him and embraced him in a hug, while saying, "Oh, I'm so sorry I'm late. I couldn't decide what to wear." She'd lied and Theodore knew it, but he didn't care. He only cared that she had come.

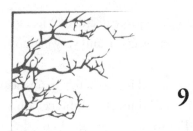

9

As if someone, or in this case something, was following them, Ben scanned the road like it could cease to exist at any moment and he needed to remember every detail of it. It didn't take them long to get across town and make their way into the now desolate suburbs. Eliza started to reach to hold Ben's hand, but she quickly decided against it. A large part of her wanted nothing more than to forget about the situation and make up for lost time.

When they pulled up in front of Ben's modest house, Ben cut the engine before glancing at Eliza like he was lost in a memory. A memory that they both shared. But Eliza failed to see his gaze while she brushed her skirt down like she was trying to get out imaginary wrinkles. If she have seen, she may have actually reached out for his hand this time.

"Well, we made it," Ben said with a small grin.

Ben got out and gazed over his shoulder, before cautiously closing his heavy door. He strangely felt the need to be quiet, even though his car would have already alerted the whole town of their arrival as he drove through it. Audrey didn't pick up on his caution and closed the door like any other day. Ben winced at the sound of metal crashing into metal. Eliza drew her eyebrows together at his reaction and closed her door gently. He took notice and tilted his head to her as though he were a gentleman from a past time.

Ben unlocked the door and ushered Eliza and Audrey inside. As they entered, Audrey scanned the room, realizing that it was more put together and decorated than any bachelor pad she had ever seen. That was saying a lot because Theodore was also a pretty organized man, but this was a new level. As if Eliza felt comfortable here, she plopped down on the sofa and waited patiently for what they would do next. Ben eyed Audrey and told her to make herself at home. Apparently, like Eliza already had.

When Ben disappeared into the back of the house, Eliza and Audrey both jumped as he shouted, "What the hell?"

The pair shared the same confused look, rose from the couch and ran in the direction of his voice. When they found him, he was squatting on his small patio that was right outside his kitchen. He was holding a shoe, but it looked absolutely normal to Audrey and Eliza. Ben continued examining it, despite it showing no new imperfections.

"There was purple ooze on it just a few hours ago," Ben said, while rubbing his forehead in disbelief. "I don't understand where it could have gone." He paused to wave his shoe around. "None of the material is melted... no holes... nothing. I don't understand." Ben continued to turn the shoe over in his hands, completely perplexed.

"Maybe it wasn't on your shoe in the first place? Or it fell off?" Eliza tried to console him.

They looked down at the grass for anything that resembled what he had described earlier. Eliza noticed a small bead of purple goop, knelt and asked, "Is this it?"

Ben and Audrey followed her finger to where she was pointing. At first, Ben seemed unconvinced, but then they saw the tiny drop of goop that was causing the grass to curl up and stick together. One piece of grass was combined with about ten. All of them hunched over to peer at it. Even Ben, who had seen the forest, still stared in confusion at the little goop. It was also very possible that he was still in shock. A feeling that he was unsure he could ever shake.

Audrey's heart started to race as she thought about the fact that if that small of a drop of goop could do that to grass, what could it do to a person? She didn't want to consider that Theodore could now be melting away, just like the grass. She stood up straight and walked back towards the door.

"I don't understand. Why didn't it melt my shoe first?" Ben asked.

"I'm not sure, but there must be a reason. Should we try to do an experiment and see if we can figure out the differences?" Eliza said enthusiastically.

"Maybe if we had time for it, but honestly, I think we just need to find where everyone's been taken to," Ben replied as he continued to stare at the grass.

"I agree," Audrey said as she looked up to the sky. Hoping to see anything that would make her feel a sense of normalcy.

Eliza nodded her head.

"Let's go back inside," Ben suggested.

They shuffled inside and Eliza headed towards the living room with Audrey following close behind. Ben stayed in the kitchen and asked, "Do either of you want something to drink?" He opened his fridge to look inside. He had a water filter attached to his fridge and not much else except a few Enerjuice bottles.

"Sure," Audrey hollered back.

As Audrey sat down on the couch, she shuffled through the books on Ben's coffee table. Eliza sat down next to her, but she was staring off into what seemed to be a place much further than the wall. Then Audrey spotted Harper's tattered journal laying on the coffee table. It looked so out of place from the other books that were stacked neatly. She had wondered what Ben was reading back at the office and she knew that this had to be it. With the current state of it, she wondered if it was a book that he had read several times or if he just collected very old books. Audrey picked it up and carefully flipped it open. Right away, she knew that it was a journal due to the handwritten scribbles and dates. Curiosity took hold of Audrey, even though she knew that it was not hers to read; her eyes couldn't help but continue to look.

NOVEMBER 1, 1976: *Taylor is still missing. The police are still saying they have no leads, but several people went missing that same night. I think they all must be connected and I am determined to find her. I'm going out to find her. The forest is the one place I know she might have gone before going to the party. That's where I'll start.*

THE FOREST IS A NIGHTMARE. It is filled with strange purple orb sacs and I fear that whatever this is, is not good. I found a cave in the forest that had more of the purple sacs all around it. I was not able to go inside. I will have to find a way to get through the strange sacs. I fear that Taylor is in that cave. Whatever this is could not possibly be from this world. I saw a poor squirrel when I was venturing through the forest with its brain showing. Its skin was sliding off and it was covered in the purple stuff. I dared not touch it and avoided it like a beehive. It is almost 8:00 in the morning. I've left a message at the police station for them to call me back because no one answered the three times I've called since I've returned. I have been up since 4:00. My mind felt at least partially awake all night though. I slept next to the phone just in case the cops decided to return my calls. I hope that they are all out searching for everyone that is missing. My phone never rang.

THE TOWN IS EMPTY. I've walked several miles and the silence is daunting. My parents are gone as well. No note was left or anything. I grabbed my wooden sword and decided to go back into the forest. It was the only thing I could think of doing.

BEN WALKED OVER TO the couch with both a glass of water and two Enerjuices balanced in his hands. He almost dropped them when he realized what Audrey was reading.

"Audrey!" Ben said it loud enough to startle her. She moved the journal so fast that part of it ripped.

"Oh, shit. Sorry, Ben, I didn't mean any harm. Have you read all of this?" She seemed upset—by what she had read, not that she was reading a personal journal without permission.

He sat next to her on the couch and let his irritation go. After Audrey handed Ben the journal he said, "I haven't read much yet, but I think it might be able to help us. It was my stepfather's. He left it to me when he passed." Ben closed his eyes like he could feel the initial pain of his loss all over again.

"Ben, there is some serious shit in here that is talking about stuff like we are going through now. Did you know about what happened in your stepfather's town?"

Eliza watched them both silently like she was observing a fly wandering around the room.

"He told me stories and mentioned when I was older that his hometown was now just a ghost town." Ben pushed his hair out of his face and continued, "I know now that the stories he told me as a child were probably all true."

"Then we definitely need to finish reading it," Audrey said firmly.

Ben agreed but was hesitant to let the others read it. It was personal and something that he hadn't planned to ever share with anyone.

"Alright, I'll read it aloud, or I can read through it and tell you what it says," he replied. Part of him thought that they would want to read it themselves, but he waited for Eliza and Audrey's input.

"I think you should read it out loud; it will help us all to hear it and maybe we can understand what is going on," Eliza replied.

"Ben, what did you read?" Audrey asked.

As Ben held the journal in his hands, he looked down at it like he was seeing a ghost. Ben looked up and explained to them about Taylor, and how she had been Harper's girlfriend. Then Ben asked Audrey to catch them up. When she described the forest, Ben could feel his hairs standing on end and his arms protruded bumps that resembled a bare chicken. His mind was racing, wondering how closely their lives were intertwined. He wished that Harper was still alive to help him, guide him, or add a bit of comfort. Before he let the situation muddle his mind, he turned to Audrey.

"Where did you leave off, Audrey?" Ben handed the journal back to her. As her eyes scanned the pages, she stopped and pointed to the middle of a page.

"Here, November 1st was the last thing I read."

"Okay, let's continue reading then." Ben cleared his throat and started to read.

NOVEMBER 2, 1976: I have found most of the townspeople, including Taylor. When I went back into the forest, the cave

was still dripping with the purple orbs. I used my wooden sword and some branches I found to clear the opening of the cave. It was dark, but I had brought a flashlight. It illuminated the cave enough for me to get through it.

I realized that the goop was sticky when I attempted to get it off my sword.

Strangely enough, it hadn't done anything to my sword as it did to the squirrel. At least not yet.

The cave was hard to navigate, and it was difficult to not touch any of the purple orbs.

Finally, I came to a large room with a lot of water that reached up to my ankles. I could see people. They were all spread out through the cavern, quietly standing or sitting. At first, they seemed terrified as I approached them and shushed me before I even began to say a word. It was then that I glimpsed Taylor to the left of the cavern, and I ran to her. Several wounds on her shoulders and arms bled heavily, but she was breathing.

I could tell from her face that she didn't believe it was me. Her eyes were glazed over. It was as if she wasn't really alive. But I was eventually able to convince her to follow me out of the cave. A few others followed as well, but some refused to leave. I decided to not plead with them because I was so desperate to get Taylor out. Once out of the cave, the others fled as if a spell had been broken. One man who was limping called out to me to do the same and leave this town behind. I didn't dare ask what he had seen. As though she was in a trance, Taylor sat on the grass and started quietly pulling out strands. She was looking at me, but it felt more like she was looking through me. It was unsettling, but I had to believe that she would overcome this.

I scooped her up and carried her to my car. I had every intention of leaving right then and there, but I couldn't. My parents were missing and so were my friends. I couldn't just leave them behind. I told Taylor to stay in the car with the doors locked; that if anything happened to just leave.

I went back to the cave and decided to head to the right this time. I hoped that my parents would be somewhere else in the cave if they weren't where Taylor was. As I traveled, my nostrils ached from the rancid smell. I covered my nose and mouth with my sleeve and held up my flashlight. Dead bodies were sprawled out, covered in the purple orbs. Their flesh was hardly there. I could see the insides of muscles and cheekbones. Even someone's fingers were all melted at the knuckles and weren't even attached anymore. My courage was beginning to wear thin, and I couldn't help but vomit.

No one I found was alive and I couldn't bear to keep looking at the melting bodies. I ran to the other side of the tunnel where I had found Taylor, and I called out to the remaining people who had refused to leave the first time, begging them to come with me to safety. Three of the remaining people responded and came with. The rest stayed silent; unmoving. I didn't know any of them, but I was glad that they'd followed me.

Taylor was still waiting in the car when I got there. She was in the driver's seat. The others took off, and one told me to keep an eye on the sky because that was how they took them. I asked what he meant, but he had already began to run through the woods.

November 5, 1976: *Taylor is doing a little better after leaving Whinnville behind. We made it to a new town called Harthsburg. The hospital here has healed her wounds, but* *wants to know how she got them. They were as astonished as I was when they saw the huge gashes in her shoulders. It looked as though a meat hook had torn into her muscles.*

The nurses looked at me as if I had done it, but Taylor held my hand the whole time. I tried not to leave the room unless she was sleeping. While she slept, I would usually go and eat, but I still felt like I needed closure about my parents and friends. I found a library nearby and hoped that I could find any information that would match what Taylor had described to me.

Taylor had told me that whatever took her was a large winged creature. She recalled that it had fur on its body and made her think of a dragon with how its body structure was, but not as large as what she would have imagined a dragon to be. Taylor went on to say that she thought there was a family of them, and that they produced the sticky purple orbs from their mouths. Taylor said she was able to hide in the cave's crevices when she would hear their loud thuds. While she'd hide, she would watch the creatures douse the other captives in ooze.

In my research at the small library, I could find nothing even remotely related to the things Taylor had described to me. I hoped that more people would come forward, and we could find what did this.

March 5, 1977: *I'm at a loss... I'm sure that my parents were murdered by those things. I've thought about going back to Whinnville to see if anyone has returned, but I'm not ready. Taylor has been doing better, and we have been trying to get our lives back to a new normal. Harthsburg is a nice town, and we've even found some of our friends who survived and made it here. I still haven't stopped researching, but so far I have found only useless information.*

August 23, 1977: *I found something. The book is called* *LOST MONSTERS FOUND* *by Alexander LeBelle. The eighth chapter is called Devourement. Devourement is believed to happen every couple of decades. The research suggests that these flying beasts are of magical essence. The purple sacs seem to be of importance, but all the lore found surrounding this is mixed. Some villagers from the early 1800's believed they were to drain the life force from living beings and they would take it to survive. Others that dated back to the 1660s stated that they (The Wings of Death, as they called them), used the purple orbs to save their food in.*

However, the author of Devourment had a much different theory. He theorizes that the purple orbs come from another planet and take samples from Earth that the beasts take back to their planet with them. The idea that these "beasts" are aliens, and that they care so much about our dull lives here on Earth, seems like a stretch to me. I doubt that these violent beasts are some otherworldly scientists, here to collect specimens to send back to their home planet.

When I tried to talk to Taylor about the book I had found, she asked me to stop looking for the beasts. She said that she just wanted to move on with her life. I understand how she feels, but I have to know what they are.

DECEMBER 14, 1977: *Taylor and I broke up. She wants to be with someone that isn't distracted by the past. I'll admit I am a little bit obsessed. She had let me read the book I found on*

the creatures and I would excitedly tell her all that I'd learned; what new theories I had. My obsession with these beasts broke her and ruined what we had. I wish I'd paid more attention to her, and not lost so much of myself to the beasts that had taken her.

August 20, 1978: Taylor is still going to the same college as me (Finnerville University). I was worried she would want to leave to get away from me after the school year, but surprisingly I see her in between classes sometimes and smile or wave at her. She kindly reciprocates. I still feel for her, but I know that love will never be found again. I am still searching for the monsters, and I'm not sure if I can stop.

November 18, 1978: Yesterday, I went back to Whinn-ville for the first time. My heart shuddered as I stepped onto Arcadia Street. The houses still stood, but no one remained in them. When I got to my house, it felt eerily uninviting. I hesitated to go inside at first, but once I did I was only greeted by dust and spiderwebs. The inside was left exactly as I remembered it. It was hard to believe that almost three years had passed. Dust was piled on the windowsills, couch cushions and the fake plants that my mother kept in the living room. Previously, I had left everything behind and started anew, except for my Chevelle. While here, I needed to reclaim things that had been important to me or my parents. I grabbed my yearbooks, pictures, my dad's Polaroid camera, a watch he used to wear a lot, my mother's favorite necklace and some other random items. As I was about to leave, I spotted a family picture on a side table from when we last went fishing. The picture made my mind flip a switch and the mourning finally began. I had need-ed to be strong for Taylor and had always thought we would find my parents and other friends, but at that point it hit me that none of them were coming back. If any of the others had made it out like the ones I had helped, they were long gone and living a new life. I let myself cry before leaving.

December 2, 1978: *I met a bitchin' lady. Her name is Gwen. She is in my economics class. Tomorrow night, we are going to the drive-in.*

"OKAY, YOU CAN STOP reading. I think that's all for the monsters," Eliza stopped abruptly and handed it back to Ben. Ben took it gladly because he also didn't want to read about any intimate details between Harper and his mother.

"Why didn't he ever mention the name of the monsters, or how long... oh, what was it called... Devourement lasted for?" Audrey asked.

"We should probably look for that book he wrote about. Maybe he left things out that would help. My mother lives in Crater Village. She might even know who Taylor is, since they apparently went to the same college." The gears were moving fast, and if Devourement happened that quickly before, they knew that they were already running out of time.

"Do you think that Taylor would want to help? I mean, she told your stepdad that she didn't want to talk about it anymore. She wanted to be free from what happened to her. This might open old wounds that she swore to forget," Eliza replied.

Ben agreed, but they had few options, so few that he would put his empathy aside if it meant saving his friends. "We have to at least try. I fully understand what you are saying, but unless you can give me a better option for the short amount of time we have, we are going to have to find her, if she is even still alive," Ben turned to Audrey. "Audrey, do you have any reservations with this plan?"

Audrey bit her lip and said, "He's right, Eliza. We have no other leads or options. If we want to save anyone, even if it's just a few people, we need to find Taylor and that book, or at least another book with the same references to Devourement."

Eliza, feeling outnumbered, replied, "Okay, let's go then."

"Alright," Ben said, walking to the front door. Opening the door, he let Audrey and Eliza head out first. He glanced back inside, almost wishing that he could wake up at any second and this all be just a dream.

"You comin' or what?" Audrey called out to him from beside the car.

Ben nodded his head and rolled his eyes, he locked up his home tightly before turning his back on his home. He was confused with himself for doing so, given that no one was around to steal his things.

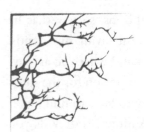

10

You could say he was just an ordinary man with an ordinary and slightly dull job. Wyatt would say he was anything but. Wyatt had lied about many things in his life, like his age, places he had been and even things that he had seen. Despite what some of his co-workers thought, he did see Archie Daniels get taken. It was true that he had just started working at Paper & Things LLC. about a month ago, which only added to their skepticism of what he actually saw. What his co-workers did know about him really only pertained to his feline, Alexandra, who he would annoyingly add to people's conversations by telling them what she did the other day. Other than that, he was just known as the guy who could crunch numbers.

After Eliza, Ben and Audrey had left, there was a clear difference in Wyatt's behavior, yet no one seemed to notice, since they were all dealing with their own realities. No matter what Gerald said, his co-workers continued to pace around the office, bite their nails, walk past the windows in horror and even sit on the floor while holding their legs to their chest and rocking back and forth.

Quiet as a whisper, Wyatt glided over to the large window that no one dared to look out anymore. As he stared out of the wide window with his feet planted in place, his eyes calmed and a slight grin rose up his cheeks. He took several minutes pretending that he was alone, at least in his mind, before he placed his hand on the cold glass and turned away, taking his grin away as he did so. Wyatt, who was still looking quite sickly but remained calm, left the room. He dared not to make any eye contact with anyone, and no one noticed his departure but Gerald. He took note of him leaving the room, but refrained from saying anything.

He headed towards the bathroom that was just around the corner. Upon going down the hallway, he realized how badly lit the area was. An observation that he hadn't remembered before. Nonetheless, he pushed the door open and let it swing back behind him. The floors had random scuff marks and the mirrors still had streaks from the last time they were wiped down.

He walked over to the mirror and stared at his soon-to-be decaying body. While he examined the dark bags under his eyes, he couldn't help but glare at the person who reflected back. He thought to himself about what a pitiful mess he had become, before he raised his left eyebrow and snickered like he knew a secret that no one else did. A secret that he was now about to let flow out of him like a waterfall.

Wyatt placed one hand on the mirror and his other in his pocket, taking out a small brown cloth bag from it that he placed on the counter. He slowly dipped his fingers in it, and when he pulled them out just as carefully as they went in, a dark residue stained four of his fingertips. Wyatt eyed the powdery substance with a fondness, before placing his fingertips on the mirror and drawing a circle out of X's with a crooked star in the center.

With one deep inhale, he placed his hand over the sigil and his lips began to move, rhythmic and familiar. After the moment passed, he took his hand away. The sigil turned to an iridescent purple hue and shined like a dim light. His eyes stared back at it, clearly pleased with what he'd done. He walked slowly out of the bathroom and made his way back to the others.

Not much had changed since he'd left, but Wyatt knew that soon it would. He slunk down in his usual chair and stared out the window. Within seconds, a cluster of wings peeked through the red sky. Wyatt tried not to smile, but his heart was singing. The first window broke, causing not only shards of glass to spiral several feet away, but a cold gust of wind that stunned everyone in the room. The disbelief was quickly followed by screaming, and Wyatt's co-workers began to run as fast as they could to the stairs. Gerald even stayed back and shouted for the others to run to give them a chance, but his bravery made him the first one to be lifted out of the window like a rabbit being plucked by a hawk.

Wyatt stayed seated as each co-worker took flight, leaving behind a small trail of blood that was sure to never get cleaned. When Henry, the last of them, realized that a set of claws had sunk into his shoulder blades, warm liquid seeped down the front of his pants. Shock shivered down every cell of his body, along with confusion, as to the betrayal of his co-worker who sat quietly amused. Henry was quickly pulled out the window, flying high above the buildings, possibly never to be seen again.

Sitting up slowly, Wyatt breathed in the air like he had just gone outside on a weekend morning to enjoy the sunrise.

He placed his hands together at his lips and let out a laugh. Nothing was left for him to do there, so he walked away from the now-gaping hole that used to be a window. Out he went, away from the building. He got into his car and left as though this was just any other day in the dull life of Wyatt.

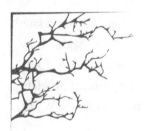

11

Ben drove through the deserted streets that just the other day were full of life. As they sped through, Eliza rolled down the window to feel the wind dance through her fingers. It wasn't long before the houses disappeared in the distance and Ben slowed down slightly as he swerved onto the freeway. The sign for Crater Village was almost too hard to read as they whizzed past, but Audrey was just able to make out the town name; not how many miles it was still away though. She wondered how she had never paid attention to the sign before, even though she had driven that way on many occasions to meet out of town friends and one of her cousins.

The drive to Crater Village was a mere half an hour that was sure to be cut in half by the way Ben was driving. The few minutes they'd already been on the road already felt too long, but somehow also too fast. Ben started to think of all the things that could happen to them, and none of his thoughts ended happily.

To calm his mind, Ben rolled down his window and turned the radio on. They all held their ears, except Ben who swerved, when loud static came out. Quickly, Eliza and Ben reached for the knob to turn it down. Eliza managed to reach it first and hit the input button to play the CD he already had in it.

The first song came on and Eliza quietly sang the lyrics. As she sang, Ben realized this was the first time he had ever heard her sing. He couldn't help but smile, but he dared not say anything in case he embarrassed her. Instead, he reached out his hand, hoping that she would place hers on top of his palm. Eliza slid her hand into his, while she continued to sing.

Audrey rolled her eyes, but even she couldn't help but sing along. Ben looked in his rearview mirror to confirm what he was hearing. Sure enough, Audrey was singing loudly. Another voice joined in— it was Ben's after he'd finally given in. Ben thought in his mind, "At least we can still smile, even if we are on the verge of extermination."

Echoes of laughter and slightly out of tune singing glided away in the breeze quickly behind the car, until Ben exited the highway and started into the quaint town of Crater Village. A town best known for hosting the best apple pie festival around. But there weren't many young families here, or working singles for that matter. It was more common for retirees to move there. Harper and Ben's mother had moved to the picturesque town nearly ten years ago and had enjoyed the simple life it offered.

"I'm going to check at my mom's work first. She usually works Wednesdays," Ben said loudly, as he turned onto the next street.

Eliza and Audrey peered out the windows, taking in the cottage style houses, well-trimmed bushes and the array of shops that made up the row of brick buildings. Ben's mother worked about a mile from her home at a craft store. When she was younger, she sold quilts for a living, but as she aged, her hands had gotten too frail to carry on. She was able to continue her passion through others when she took the job at the craft store; she had enjoyed giving tips to new quilters, even if she couldn't personally make them anymore.

They arrived in front of a large hand-painted sign that read Yarn-tastic & More! in cursive, that had a big ball of green yarn and slightly faded knitting needles next to it. A few cars were parked out front, but Ben couldn't see his mother's. He knew that didn't rule out her being there—she was an avid walker and sometimes her boss Denise would give her a ride home if she chose to walk in. Ben parked and told Audrey and Eliza that they could just stay in the car in case his mother wasn't working today. Neither of them minded, so he got out and opened the door to the store alone. A little bell above the door rang when he walked in, and Denise, a tall, curvy woman with graying hair, came out from the back and gave him a big hug.

"Hey, Denise, I was wondering if my mom is in today? I have something important that I need her help with," Ben said with as much restraint as he could muster. He tried to peer in the back and hoped that she would ignore that he'd came unannounced. Denise peered at his wandering eyes and gave him a worried look. Ben knew then that he needed to relax more, but the only thing he could think to do was smile. A very awkward smile at that, which probably made things worse. Denise had always loved seeing Ben and adored the relationship he and his mother had, so seeing him act so peculiar was alarming to her.

"Yes, she is, Ben. She was helping me in the back to sort through some new inventory. Is everything alright?" she said, her eyes narrowing as she patted his hand.

Ben kept on his fake smile and replied, "Yes, I'm fine. I just need her help. Nothing for you to worry about." He felt guilty that he had just lied to her, but he assumed that this was an acceptable time to lie.

"I'll go get her, honey." Denise hustled her way to the back, and Ben's mom quickly appeared in her place.

"Ben, what's wrong?" It was clear to Ben that Denise hadn't fully believed him once he saw his mom's concerned look. Gwen quickly wrapped her arms around Ben and squeezed him tightly. Even though a hug was much needed, in times like these it can cause someone to release all the emotions they had tightly caged up. Ben was no different and politely cut the hug short. Gwen outstretched her hands on Ben's shoulders and examined him to see if he had any physical injuries that she had not seen at first.

"Mom, I'm fine." Ben chuckled. "I'm not hurt or any-thing like that, but do you think you could come back to your house with me for a bit? I need your help with some-thing, but would rather not discuss it here."

"Yes, Ben, of course. Let me just tell Denise first, and I'll go grab my purse."

Ben's mom patted her son's shoulder and hurried to the back. When she returned she smiled at her son and nodded towards the door.

Eliza had already moved to the back seat with Audrey when Ben and Gwen made it to the car. Gwen eyed the Chevelle with fondness and thought back to when it was

Harper's. Harper had given it to Ben as a graduation gift when he turned eighteen. Ben was more than ecstatic when he received the keys that day.

"Who are they?" Gwen nudged Ben playfully. Ben's cheeks flushed, but he still grinned at his mom's reaction.

Ben opened the front passenger door and said, "Mom, this is Eliza and Audrey—a couple of friends of mine." Then Ben turned to Eliza and Audrey and said boastfully, clearly happy to call her his mother, "And this is my mom Gwen." Audrey and Eliza both gave Gwen a warm hello as she entered the Chevelle.

The short car ride consisted of Gwen wanting to know what was going on and Ben asking her to be patient with him. He wanted to wait until they got to her house to discuss anything, but Gwen was worried sick as to what could have caused Ben to get her from work, and with two strangers nonetheless. Eliza and Audrey stayed silent in the back, hoping that she would relax once they arrived at her house.

They arrived at a little cottage that had green vines growing up the sides and a plethora of wildflowers that sat nicely and trimmed near the front entrance. Bees flew around the flowers, happily pollinating them. It was a small but perfect house that Harper and Gwen had bought when Ben moved out aged eighteen. Gwen wanted a new place to signal their change in life, one where she wouldn't dwell on being an empty nester. She considered the cottage her dream home. Ben hoped that even with Harper gone she still found joy there.

They walked up the wooden steps that led to the front door. As Gwen searched for her keys in her purse, she remembered that she had placed them in her sweater pocket. Gwen reached into her baggy, aquamarine knit sweater. It was a miracle that the keys hadn't fallen through, since she had a few tiny holes that had formed from years of wear. Ben was always astonished that it was still intact since she had knitted it a few years after he was born.

As it usually did, the house smelt like lavender. Every time Ben smelled lavender, it filled him with childhood nostalgia. Gwen spent the early summers cutting fresh lavender that she would make or bake into various things. When he was a kid, he was almost annoyed with the smell, but now he welcomed it.

A small brown entry table stood to the right of them that had a loving picture of Ben and Harper playing in the yard together. Ben lingered on it for a moment. Even though Ben was not raised by his biological father, he'd still had Harper who'd raised him just like his own child. When his mother had first met Harper, she was already dating Ben's biological father Robert. Gwen got pregnant in college and Robert only stuck around until Ben turned three, not that he was around much even then. After he left, Gwen and Harper finally got together, and Robert moved far away. The last time Ben heard from his father was when he was five. A postcard was sent in the mail that read, "Happy fifth birthday. Dad." Even though Ben was only five, he had wished that he had just not bothered to send anything at all and was glad that he never reached out again.

Harper had a somewhat rocky time trying to transition into fatherhood. Ben always thought it was because he was worried that Robert would crawl back to his mother. Shortly after Ben turned six, Harper and Gwen tied the knot. It was a small wedding, but one that Ben was happy to attend. After the wedding, Ben and Harper spent a lot more time together, and Harper adopted him.

"Please make yourselves at home, ladies," Gwen said as she pointed over to the chairs and couch in the living room.

"Thank you, Mrs. Drewitt," Eliza replied, before plopping down on the couch.

"Do you want some water or tea?" She looked at all three of them with an uncomfortable smile.

Ben chimed in, "Some water will be fine. I'll get it, Mom." Ben walked over to the kitchen that was just a few feet away from the couch, but Gwen waved him away as she took his place. Gwen stood on her tiptoes to grab the glasses. She had thought about moving them somewhere lower now that Harper wasn't around to reach for her, but with such a quaint kitchen their wasn't a better place for them. Gwen took her time placing each one on the counter before turning around to fill them up with water from her fridge.

Ben joined Audrey and Eliza on the couch. Quietly he bit at his thumbnail. Shortly after, Gwen came into the living room and placed the glasses on the coffee table, before sitting down on her purple wingback chair. They all thanked her and took sips of their water. From the fact she was lightly tapping her foot, Ben knew just how nervous she was.

Deciding not to waste any more time, Ben cleared his throat.

"So... Mom, I was wondering if you knew anything about someone named Taylor who Harper knew? I believe you all went to the same college?" Ben felt wrong asking her about her passed husband's old flame, despite the importance of it.

"That is a strange question. Why would you be interested in Taylor?" She wrinkled her forehead and crossed her arms.

"I can't really answer that, but I need you to trust that I have a good reason for asking. Mom, I need to know what you know about Taylor, and if you know where she is now. I can't explain everything right this second, but it is very important. Also, did you keep any of Dad's books?" Ben was really pressing his luck because he knew his mom wasn't someone who enjoyed getting half the story, and this was more like a tiny breadcrumb.

"Ben, should I be worried? This seems so out of the blue, and I'm not sure what to think." She was stalling, and Ben knew she needed more information, but he wasn't willing to give it.

Before Ben could say any more, Audrey chimed in, "Gwen, I know this all seems so confusing, and I wish we could explain this better to you, but we don't have much time to sit and chat about this. I hope you can understand and know that it will help us greatly."

Gwen took in every bit of what Audrey said and thought about not saying anything until one of them came clean about the whole situation, but instead she just sighed. Then she placed her head down, and raised her hands up in defeat, before saying, "Okay, Taylor was one of Harper's girlfriends when he was in high school and part of college. They kept in touch here and there, but nothing constant. I see her sometimes out in town, and we cordially talk for a minute or two."

She took a sip of her water and slouched her shoulders a bit. "As for Harper's old books, I have a few on the bookshelf in the hall. You can look and see if you can find whatever you're looking for." Gwen stared at her son, her eyes full of pain. Ben had had no intention of causing his mother any discomfort, and he hoped that when all this was over, she would understand.

"Taylor lives here?" Audrey gasped.

Gwen's eyebrows raised at Audrey's reaction. "Yes, she lives in a more secluded part of town, out in the woods. As far as I know, she lives out there alone. I haven't seen her in a while though."

"Do you know her address?" Ben asked almost too eagerly.

"I'm sure Harper had it written down in his address book. I can grab it for you," Gwen replied somberly.

"That would be great, Mom!" Ben tried to say encouragingly, but Gwen seemed more dismayed by his enthusiasm.

Gwen rose from her chair, swiftly walked out of the room and down the hall, before disappearing into one of the other rooms. When she came back, she was carrying a small blue notebook. Without saying a word, she shuffled through the pages. She stopped and carefully ripped out the page she had stopped on and gave it to Ben.

As though he could feel Harper from the inked page, he ran his finger across it. He thought about how many things he missed that he never thought he would until Harper passed, like the handwritten birthday cards he would receive from him. Ben had saved every single one of them, and made himself a promise to reread them once he returned home safely. One lonely address was on the paper that read: Taylor Grim, 657 Elderberry Lane, Crater Village, Weston 96272.

He folded the paper and placed it in his pocket, before giving his mother a kiss on her cheek. "Thanks, Mom. I'm going to look for some of his books, and then we will have to be on our way," Ben said, already at the bookshelf.

Audrey got up to help look for any books that would be helpful, but Eliza stayed planted on the couch. A part of Ben thought that she was hopeful about their survival and was taking this opportunity to get to know his mother. It was a nice thought, but one that he wasn't sure if he felt as optimistic about as she did.

Audrey sat down on the wooden floor and began searching the bottom shelves for anything that remotely mentioned monsters. Ben took the top shelves and scanned every one with careful attention. One dusty black book stood out to him. It had gold lettering on the spine that read: *The Ancient Ones by Clive Wright.* Ben quickly scanned the preface; it discussed legends of creatures that came from dark magic, which he assumed could include what they were looking for. He dusted it off and put it aside to take with them, just in case. He kept searching for any more books that could prove helpful.

Then Audrey shouted, "Here it is," as she held up the book by Alexander LeBelle.

"Good eye! Any other books that might raise a flag?" Ben asked quietly to Audrey.

As she stood on her knees to search the next shelves, she sighed and said, "Not that I can see. I think we should go find Taylor now."

Ben nodded his head and picked up the other book. Ben walked over to his mother and put his hand on top of hers, before saying, "Sorry to cut this short, Mom, but we have to get going. I promise I will call you tomorrow at the latest."

He said it in the most convincing way possible. Honestly, he wasn't sure if they would still be alive tomorrow, but he was hopeful. Ben gave her a hug, and Audrey and Eliza both said their goodbyes, before all three exited the house.

12

Ben viewed their goodbye as a bittersweet moment; one he hoped wouldn't be the last. They piled into the car and Ben took out the now creased piece of paper from his pocket. He handed it to Eliza, who looked over the address, and without Ben having to ask, she pulled up the address into her GPS as they pulled out of the driveway. Gwen stood on the porch and waved them goodbye with tears in her eyes. Ben's heart leapt, but he simply waved back to her, and shut his emotions in a little box that he'd keep closed until it was safe to open.

"Your mom is lovely," Eliza said softly. Eliza could tell Ben had a mask on, and she wasn't going to try to see beneath it. There would be a time for that in the near future.

"Thank you," Ben replied, as he reached to hold her hand. "Hopefully, when this is all behind us, we can go over for dinner or something, and you two can get to know each other better."

"I would really enjoy that." Eliza beamed.

"Then it's a date." Ben smirked.

The back seat seemed oddly quiet to Ben, so he gazed in his rearview and saw Audrey's eyes darting from line to line, completely consumed in what she was reading. Ben wanted to thank her for delving into the books, but he refrained so that she could stay concentrated. The more they knew, the better their chance of surviving and hopefully finding Theodore and possibly other friends. Or, at the very least, killing the sons of bitches so they couldn't return.

Elderberry Lane was further away than they would have liked. Once they made it out of town, the road was filled with twists and bends. The winding road would take over twenty minutes to drive down. The trees made an ever-expanding blanket that consumed the ground on both sides of the road. Pine needles caressed the blacktop, causing a beautiful symphony of lovely aromas. As Ben drove over the pine needles, his mind couldn't help but wander. Harper and Ben had never camped in Crater Village, but they had talked about planning a trip for it, and now that trip would never come to fruition. No signs were present to address the winding turns, and Ben would quite suddenly have to turn the wheel hard, while pressing his foot on the brake. He thought about slowing down, but if they could get to Taylor quickly, it might save more lives.

Ben started to go into a new turn at only fifteen miles an hour due to the sharpness of it, when Audrey screamed, "LOOK UP, LOOK UP!"

Panicking, Ben looked up and swerved the car hard to the right, causing them to run off the road. As the car moved faster and faster down the sloped earth, the tires crushed wildflowers, and barely missed a brown hare that hopped away just in time. A tree was waiting for them just a few feet ahead. As though the tree was angry with them, its branches were tilted just the right way, sloping down and then arching to its sides like a cross parent does with their arms when mad.

Ben rode the break, but the slope of the forest made it hard for him to gain control back. At last, they came to a screeching halt that caused the Chevelle to crash into the tree. The instant the car collided with the tree, their bodies flung forward.

As he tried to make sense of what had happened, Ben's pulse kept rising. He raised his head and looked next to him at Eliza. Her head was tilted down and he couldn't tell if she was breathing, but he couldn't see any injuries on her, so he hoped she would come to soon. Ben then turned to the back seat and saw Audrey shaking her head gently, before raising it. Seeing that Audrey was okay, Ben turned his attention back to Eliza. With his hand gently on her shoulder, he repeated her name until she slowly opened her eyes. She moved her hair out of her face, revealing a small, black tattoo on her neck; one that he had never seen before.

"Is everyone okay?" Ben asked. Finally, Eliza lifted her head and nodded. Audrey, instead of answering Ben's question, decided to ask a more concerning one.

"Did you guys see that... that thing?" Audrey said loudly, while she rubbed her head where it had hit the passenger seat.

"I saw something flying, but I didn't get a good look. Especially after I lost control of the car," Ben said with a tinge of annoyance towards her. Although, he admitted to himself, that if she had have said it calmly, he would have still probably done the same thing.

"Ben, you're bleeding," Eliza said as she turned his face towards her so she could get a better look.

He raised his hand to his forehead, gently touching where he felt pain. When he moved his hand back down to where he could see it, he had blood on his fingers. "I guess I am. I don't think it's anything serious," he said, while peering at himself in his rearview mirror.

"Let me help you with that. I should have something in my purse," Eliza replied.

She bent down to grab her purse that was down at her feet. A few seconds later, she pulled out a packet of tissues. Eliza reached over and placed one on Ben's forehead to stop the bleeding.

"I think I'll live," Ben said jokingly. Audrey snickered, but Eliza just rolled her eyes and continued to pat his forehead.

"Eliza, did you see it?" Audrey asked in a serious tone.

Eliza looked back at Audrey and shook her head. "Not really. The car swerved before I could get a proper look."

As her body shook, Audrey peered out the window and said, "I saw it." Her eyes remained transfixed on the sky, before she took a deep breath and continued, "That thing's teeth were dripping with that purple ooze, and for a second I thought it smiled at me." She shivered.

"Should we be worried that it isn't in Harthsburg?" Ben asked.

Eliza calmly looked out the window and replied, "I don't think that it will be taking people from another town."

"Why would you just assume that?" said Audrey.

Ben nodded his head like he wanted to hear her thought process as well.

"Well, according to Harper's journal, they only stayed in one town. Maybe they only stay in one town at a time, and this one we saw was following us, since we are from Harthsburg. Or it could be that it lost its way?" Eliza said, hoping that they would stop staring at her like she was spouting things that were far-fetched.

"Well, I hope that it's not following us. Audrey, what else do you remember?" Ben asked.

"Its eyes... they were as yellow as sunflowers. It felt like it was looking into my soul." Audrey paused. "Before we crashed, I did find something important in the other book you grabbed."

"What did you find?" Eliza asked.

"They are magical beings that can only survive off magic, but it mentioned that a powerful enough person could harness their magic," Audrey said, shuffling around to find the book. It happened to be slightly lodged underneath the passenger side seat. Audrey was able to pull it free, and her hands raised triumphantly with the book *The Ancient Ones in them*. "I'll have to find the page again, but it spoke of creatures that they referred to as Twilight Breathers," Audrey said, turning page after page. Eliza flinched.

"Here we are. It says: 'They come at twilight and consume all night.' The purple ooze is a magical essence that is used for what the author believes does two things," Audrey announced, raising two of her fingers. "They use it to reproduce and eat. It doesn't fully explain how it works, but I'm assuming that the Twilight Breathers haven't actually been studied. Could you imagine someone capturing one and being able to find out exactly what it is?" Audrey contemplated.

"So, we are dealing with some sort of creature that comes to kill living things so it can mate or just get a snack? I'm assuming that they don't come here every time they are hungry, or we would know way more about them," Ben concluded. Although, he was feeling more confused than before. None of it made sense to him, but that didn't change the fact that they were here carrying away and devouring everyone in town.

"I'll keep reading. Do you think we are going to be able to drive to Taylor's still?" Audrey sighed.

"Wait in here. I'll check out the damage to the car. Eliza, do you think you can start reading through the other book?" Ben asked.

Eliza held her hand out to Audrey, who handed the book *The Ancient Ones* to her. "All set," she replied, showing the book to Ben.

As Ben stepped out of the Chevelle, he held his breath. Not that holding his breath would've prevented anyone watching from knowing he was there. The grass was tall and had a plenitude of tiny wild mushrooms that sprouted around the tree before him. The car had a crack in one headlight and some scratches, but nothing that would prevent it from running again. Ben was about to hop back into the car when he spotted something across from him.

Eliza must have seen his gaze dart across the grass because she called out to him from the small crack in her window. Ben couldn't look away from the area where he was searching, and he already felt as though he was several yards away. Eliza's voice sounded as though it was fleeting. An invisible tugging sensation came from deep inside Ben. Whatever was in the woods wanted Ben to come to it, and he couldn't resist the call. As he followed, he felt the crunch of a cluster of mushrooms stick to his shoe with his next step, causing the gills to turn to a crumbling mess.

Audrey cranked down her window and started shouting Ben's name, but Ben could only hear a whisper calling after him. It was probably just a woodland creature walking through the woods, he thought, but he couldn't stop moving forward. Then he saw two large eyes peering out from the bushes that oddly caused him to calmly continue towards it.

His body felt indifferent; perplexed by the large eyes of the creature. The creature did not move. It stayed and waited, knowing that he would come. Ben could feel the energy of power; of otherworldliness. Just as Ben was about to reach for the bushes and push them to the side to meet the creature who was calling him, hands pulled him back toward the car. Sadly, they were a second too late. The creature touched him—a moment that even Ben wasn't sure really happened. He thought it must have been a tree branch that caressed his head gently before he was grabbed.

Audrey and Eliza dragged him off the ground and hurried back to the car. Quickly, they threw him in the back, without any concern for injuring him, and jumped into the car themselves. All the doors shut and so did Ben's mind. Audrey took the driver's seat, the engine already on. She put the car in reverse and held the gas like her foot was made of stone. Her head was turned back the whole time, hitting small plants and ignoring their flattened demise.

As they bumped around in the car without seatbelts on like they were on a bouncy castle, Eliza held Ben in her arms. Once Audrey saw they were about to reach the road, she turned the wheel with such strength that the engine roared and hopped onto the road again. Only with a little whiplash, they were back on track, and finally put their seatbelts on.

"What the fuck were you doing back there? Didn't you hear us?" Audrey wasn't holding her thoughts back. She was mad, rightly so, but Ben couldn't explain why he'd pursued the creature.

"I could. It was more like a distant whisper though; and I was feeling such a strong tug to continue toward whatever it was." Ben sighed. He could feel his thoughts tickling his brain. Something felt wrong underneath his skull, but he wasn't sure what. He felt like something was missing or moved around. Scratching his head, his stomach churned, but he was able to hold back the vomit that he felt bubbling up his throat.

As Eliza sat with Ben in the back, her eyes squinted at him. The head itching caught her interest, but she refrained from asking any questions or even telling him to stop. She rubbed his thigh and placed her head on his shoulder. As though she hoped this was all a dream, her eyes shut, and for a few moments, she cleared her thoughts.

"Where do I go next, Ben? According to that sign, there's a fork coming up soon." Audrey pointed towards a splintered sign post. "Do I turn toward Passage Grove or Sleepy Den?" She didn't take her eyes off the road, and she sure as hell didn't look back at him, not even through the mirror.

"Hold on, let me get my phone out and find my map," Ben said as he reached for his phone. He noticed red flakes of skin underneath his fingernails.

When Ben failed to find it right away, Eliza pulled her phone out and stated, "Okay, it looks like you turn at Sleepy Den. You will follow that for about three miles, and then it says there will be a small dirt road called Shady Hollow. Then one last turn to the left that will be Elderberry, where Taylor lives." Eliza hoped that she would remember what she said. Audrey nodded and continued without saying another word, like the words were already etched into her brain.

None of them spoke until they got to Shady Hollow. "Anyone have any ideas on what we are going to say to Taylor?" Audrey asked.

Ben contemplated who would be better at convincing her to help. He felt Eliza was a naturally calm person and Audrey was very blunt. But he decided that either of them would be better at talking to her than he would be. He felt it was pure magic that they could get through to his mom, and that if he had gone alone his mom would have made him stay there until he'd poured all his guts out. He knew the situation would have torn her apart and made her unbelievably scared.

Turning to Eliza, Ben said, "Do you have anything in mind? You are a calming presence. I feel like you and Audrey are much more help than I am at convincing people of anything."

"This will have to be more of an in the moment type situation. I think we will have to try to read who she is first. Once we can gather her initial response to us, we can follow what we think will work. I do want to say though that I don't think we should lie to her about our situation and the help we need from her, so no trying to trick her or anything," Eliza insisted. "What do you think, Audrey?"

Audrey gazed in the rearview mirror, before saying, "I agree with Eliza. We have no idea who Taylor is, especially now. For all we know, she could be in a terrible mental state still, but you do have a connection to her that we don't have. Since Harper was with Taylor, I think you should use that to relate to her, Ben."

Ben started to scratch at his head again. Eliza calmly moved his hand down to his side. "How about you both lead, and I'll add in to help?" Ben insisted.

Audrey nodded her head and continued down the road. The road curved again and this time it was an ongoing turn. To no one's surprise, Audrey handled it effortlessly. Ben wondered if she raced cars on a regular basis, or if she was on such an adrenaline high that she could maneuver the car just right given the situation.

Ben's brain felt like it was being tugged. He rubbed at his head, but couldn't feel anything that would be of any concern on the outside. Nothing protruded from it or even felt sore, yet he knew something was off. He thought back to his high school anatomy class and thought about the parts of his brain. After contemplating for a bit, he was sure his cerebrum was the source of the unusual sensation. The realization didn't make him feel any better, in fact, he wished that he would never have thought about what felt off. Whatever it was, was undoubtedly inside his skull, undetected from the world, and that made him feel claustrophobic. His breathing sped up and he scratched at his head like it was a normal thing to do repetitively.

Before his thoughts ran away to the land of hopelessness, he calmed his breathing and thought of Theo. He thought that whatever was happening to him couldn't be worse than what his friend was experiencing right now, so he would pull himself together until after they found him. Ben's eyes closed, and by the time he opened them, they were on Elder-berry Lane.

13

It was what you would expect from an off the grid type of place. They drove down a dirt road that made them bump all around from the rocks and dips. A small cabin came into view that had a boarded up window and seemed to be more of a spider breeding ground than anything else from the spiderwebs consuming every corner of the patio.

An old wooden rocking chair stood on the front porch that rocked as though a ghost was sitting in it. Audrey somehow immediately knew it couldn't be Taylor's house and drove right past it, toward a large house that stood alone at the end of the street.

Dandelions wrapped around the house like she was afraid she'd run out of wishes. Despite the abundance of dandelions, they didn't stand a chance against the sunflowers that towered over her yard. A large white porch peeked out from behind the flowers. A lonely old chair stood to the right of the front door with a couple plants on either side of it. This cabin seemed much more inviting than the one they had seen previously.

Audrey crept up to the house, knowing that Taylor might hear their tires on the dirt road. She decided to park away from the house just in case Taylor wasn't a fan of outsiders. Audrey put the car in park and quickly cut the engine.

Gazing at the house in contemplation, Audrey placed both her arms over the top of the steering wheel and rested her head down on top of them.

"You both ready for this?" Audrey said with a forced expression of optimism.

One by one, they exited the car and looked around like they were tourists that had just gotten themselves lost. The door wasn't far away, but they hesitated to go up the steps and knock.

The door swung open and a woman in a long, gray, floral dress came out and gazed unkindly upon them. To their surprise, Taylor had come to them. Ben's heart thudded and his brain felt like something was squirming inside. His hand rose again to scratch, but Eliza quickly caught it before he could.

Taylor swirled the wine in her glass and inquired, "Who exactly are you three?"

Audrey walked closer to the steps, but dared not walk up them. Although, she had wondered about going up and shaking her hand, but that had been before she'd spoken to them.

"Hi... Hello, are you Taylor?" Audrey asked.

"Who might you three be?" Taylor repeated. "I would rather know why you're here before I answer any of your questions." She sipped her wine, but kept her eyes on their every movement.

"Oh, yes, of course. I am Audrey," Audrey said as she pointed to herself. "And these two are Ben and Eliza. We have come to seek your help." Audrey wondered if her sales skills could help with persuading Taylor.

Taylor eyed each of them as Audrey put a name to each of their faces. She was hard to read, but they wouldn't have thought of her as the fragile soul tormented by her past that Harper had described. Unless over the years it had hardened her. As Taylor took her time to respond to them, her dress swayed in the breeze. She looked beyond them and tapped her index finger against her glass, causing her ring to clink.

Taking a small sip, she said, "Have you now? And what sort of help do you think I could provide?"

Audrey eyed Ben and Eliza. Before Eliza could say anything, Audrey replied, "Let's just lay it all out because we don't have much time. Here it goes... you are our only option right now. We know who you are because Ben is Harper's stepson, and we know about the disappearances in your town when you two were in high school. We know that you went through something terrible a long time ago, and it is happening again where we live. We could use all the help we could get, or any information you could give us, to stop this or at least save anyone."

Taylor's hand clenched around her wine glass tight enough that it shattered, and a mixture of wine and shards of glass hit the floor. Her face turned ghastly pale. Taylor's hand was bleeding from the glass breaking, but from the shock on her face, she must not have noticed. Eliza ran up the steps to catch her in case she was about to faint. Ben and Audrey followed Eliza, but Taylor had already edged away.

"You should not have come!" she said grimly.

"Taylor, we know that what you went through must have been one of the most devastating situations imaginable, but we need to find our friends and save them if we can. Please help us," Ben replied, while Eliza let Taylor put her arm on her shoulder.

Eliza walked her over to the lonely chair on the porch and had her sit down. Taylor let her eyes rest and touched her plants fondly as she reflected on the situation. The three of them moved cautiously back to the steps, hopeful that the space would give her room to process what they were asking. Eagerly, they watched her be comforted by her plants.

At last, she responded with a cold, "Join me inside."

Taylor got up and used her uncut hand to swing open the screen door. An eclectic room stood before them that looked to be a living room down the short hallway. Gray. So much gray surrounded them. All different shades and styles were carried throughout the room, with tiny bits of green and brown mixed into the overwhelming gray hues. Natural wood chairs that were stained gray, gray vases with green plants, brown books that sat on a metal shelf and a large tufted green couch with large gray decorative pillows. It was as though she was mixing industrial with Victorian and a splash of country.

Taylor motioned for them to sit on the couch, while she walked off to another room to care for her open wound. They sat down and looked around awkwardly, hoping that she would return shortly. When Taylor came back with a bandage over her cut, she calmly sat down across from them in an ordinary chair, that looked quite out of place in such an eclectic house.

"How many people are missing?" She was literally on the edge of her seat, her shoulders drooping and hands clasped together.

"We aren't sure, but it seems like most, if not the rest of the town, except for us and some people from our work," Ben said calmly, feeling his brain tug again.

Ben was trying his hardest to not think about what was going on inside his skull, but his thoughts kept going back to it. As though his brain was trying to separate from him. He thought about how he wanted it out of his skull. He knew that it made no sense to think that way, but the uncomfortable feeling was draining him, and he just wanted it out. Taylor started to reply, but Ben could only hear his own thoughts.

"Well, that definitely sounds like what happened to me all those years ago. It was the day before Halloween when it took me. I was walking through the park on my way to a party to meet Harper when I saw something. There were a few Halloween parties going on that night, so I thought someone was just trying to scare me. I became mesmerized with it though. I felt this urge that I needed to go to it, and I wish I'd never followed it because once I got to it... it wasn't human." She paused to look away, before continuing, "It was a MONSTER. Like a mad dog foaming at the mouth. Its teeth dripped with purple ooze. It didn't speak to me, but I could feel its warm, rancid breath on me. Though, for some reason, I wasn't frightened. If anything, I felt the opposite. Like I was in a trance or something. And before I knew it, it grabbed me with its claws and lifted me into the air," she said, while reaching her hands out like claws. "My trance ended, and horror smacked me in the face. My own blood was dripping down my shoulders the entire flight. When I was thrown into the cave, I was all alone—at least, at first." Taylor looked away, out the window, as she recalled the horrors she'd faced.

When she looked back, she screamed, "What is happening to YOU?"

At first, they thought she was having a flashback, but then they followed her eyes to Ben. Audrey and Eliza looked at Ben with wide eyes and scrunched foreheads. When Ben realized they were gawking at him, he removed his hand abruptly away from his head and realized his fingernails were stained red and his hair wet.

"Ben, why are you scratching your head like that?" Audrey shouted.

As Taylor got up, she said, "I'll get you a towel." She disappeared down the hall and Eliza moved Ben's head down to her lap so she could examine the damage. She made a shrill noise and then moved Ben's head back to its rightful position.

"What is wrong with you?" Audrey said in a disgusted voice. Ben assumed she was more scared of him than actually disgusted with him. He couldn't blame her because he was already scared of himself and what was happening to his brain. Ben thought of how to respond to their questions, but he didn't know how to answer, so he ignored them and waited quietly until Taylor returned with the towel.

"Ben?... Hello?" Audrey snapped, but Ben remained silent. He was hoping that he would just become invisible to them.

Taylor came back with a towel and some peroxide.

"Ben, can you sit down on the floor, please?" Eliza asked.

Eliza took the peroxide and towel from Taylor, patted Ben's head with one part of the towel, and then drizzled peroxide over the open cut. When the peroxide touched his scalp, he winced as the stinging sensation started. It made Ben remember a time long ago when he was in grade school. He had fallen off his bicycle and scraped his knee badly. He'd poured so much peroxide on his knee that the bubbles fizzled down his leg, causing it to sting so bad that he couldn't help but laugh at his own pain.

Eliza made sure to not pour a lot at once, and he thanked her for that. Although, at this moment, it might not have made a difference. His body wasn't functioning normally, causing delayed responses. It wasn't until he could feel Eliza's breath blowing softly on his scalp that his nerves woke up.

His body felt like a defibrillator was shocking it. Standing up fast, Ben shook and ached from all the pain. Eliza held her hands up as though she was trying to say she didn't do it. Audrey and Taylor stood back from him, waiting for his next response.

"What has happened to you, Ben?" Audrey gaped at him.

Ben said hoarsely, "I... I don't know. When we went off the road, something was watching us. And like Taylor said earlier about how she felt a pull... I felt the same. Since I didn't get to it, I think I am having some weird side effects or something. My brain feels like it's trying to escape, and apparently my nerves are completely out of whack." Ben felt relieved to get everything out, but now another problem needed to be fixed.

Just as Taylor was about to speak, Ben started yelling, "FUCK, FUCK, FUCK! Someone look at my wound, PLEASE! It feels like I'm being burnt."

All three of them came over and had Ben kneel on the rug so they could get a better view. Speaking as calmly as she could, Audrey said, "Fuck, Ben. You have that purple ooze coming out of your wound. What should we do? Taylor, any suggestions?"

"I think the only option we have is to get the ooze out," Taylor said gravely.

"You mean to cut him open and then sew him back up?" Eliza shook as she said it.

"That's exactly what I mean. Otherwise, he'll die." Her matter of fact attitude made Ben gulp. His stomach churned, but he had no other choice than to let them do it.

"No, we can't just cut him open. We aren't surgeons," Audrey scoffed.

"Look, Taylor is right. We have no other option. Ben, do you want to live or not?" Eliza asked.

Before Audrey could protest, Ben nodded his head. "Can I get some alcohol first?"

Taylor stood up and rushed to the kitchen. When she returned, she had a small knife that she had heated on her stove to disinfect it, more towels, a bottle of brandy and a needle and thread. She also pulled out a tube of medical glue.

"You're prepared." Ben chuckled uncomfortably.

"Well, when you go through what I did, you're always prepared." She handed Ben the brandy and told him to drink up. He swished back a pretty big gulp and then immediately started to cough. Ben wasn't used to drinking alcohol, especially hard alcohol, but given the situation, he wanted to get down as much as possible.

"Eliza and Audrey, hold him down. This is going to be rough. Ben, take this towel and bite down on it when you need to. The brandy will be right here if you need more," Taylor said assertively. Without much hesitation, Eliza and Audrey stood on either side of Ben and held his shoulders down.

As Taylor prepared, she picked up the bottle of brandy and pushed it into Ben's hand. "Drink some more before I start."

Taylor poured more peroxide over his wound, before leaving the room. Ben raised his head in confusion as to where she was going. He almost hoped that she had changed her mind and was calling 911 to send a surgeon over, but instead she ran back over with a bright pink razor, a mixing bowl, scissors and a turkey baster.

Eliza pushed Ben's head back down and whispered in his ear, "Remember to breathe, and you can squeeze me as hard as you need to." Ben's eyes, now foggy, nodded with trepidation at her.

Taylor gazed at his head, not with disgust but with curiosity. When they saw Taylor grab the scissors, they held Ben down, unsure of what she would do first. Luckily, for Ben's sake, she only cut his hair as short as possible, before shaving a large enough area to get all the ooze out. She hummed the entire time she worked, and although Eliza felt very uneasy by it, she didn't question it.

Ben could feel the cold razor move over his skin, and when she shaved over the wound, his head twitched. The brandy was already helping to ease the pain, but he did not know how much pain he would actually feel once she tore down into the tissue.

"Can someone give me some more brandy?" Ben forced a smile.

Shakily, Eliza quickly tried to pour some more into his mouth, but a lot of it landed on the rug underneath them. Eliza apologized, but Taylor was concentrating so hard that she didn't even acknowledge her.

As Taylor raised the slightly blackened tip of the knife to Ben's head, she hummed a happy tune, and Ben thought to himself, "*Are all butchers this relaxed?*" Before she made her first incision, Ben's eyes shut faster than his heart could make its next beat. His chest was rising and falling rapidly. Ben wailed out in pain when the tip of the blade cut through the first layer of skin, and he knew at that moment that there wasn't enough alcohol in the house to save him from the pain that he was about to endure.

Taylor sliced through deeper and Ben could feel the blood running down through his hair. Part of him wondered if maybe it was just sweat he was feeling, but then Taylor lifted the knife. He saw his reflection in the shining metal; a bloody scene. His head was dripping with blood and purple ooze. Taylor wiped the blood off the knife before continuing, but seeing himself in the mirror of the knife proved too much for Ben. His vision went blurry, and before he could think, all he saw was black.

Eliza watched every incision with disgust. Not a word trembled out of her lips, but she wished that she could say something, anything to make everything go back to the way it was before the creatures came. Of course, she could do nothing, so she watched as Taylor worked and made sure she didn't do anything to kill him. After all, she didn't really know this person who was slicing into his head.

Audrey had a much harder time concentrating on what was happening. Her stomach was doing her no good and had already been churning since Taylor's first carve into Ben. As though Audrey was watching a scary movie, she found it hard to keep her eyes from gazing upon the now bloody mess that used to have Ben's skin covering it.

Taylor made one more long slice, which caused more purple ooze to drip out, along with his blood that was now looking quite purple as well. Once she had a big enough hole, she pushed the turkey baster in and sucked up as much ooze as possible, before squeezing it out into the bowl.

The turkey baster made the same sound every time Taylor stuck it back into Ben's flesh—like that of someone slurping down the last bits of soup. Droplets of ooze came down Ben's face. Immediately, before Taylor could get to them, Eliza noticed the ooze and grabbed a towel to wipe it away. She struggled to get it all wiped away due to the stickiness, but it was enough to not cause any damage to that part of his skin. Ben remained passed out, and Eliza hoped at least his mind was at peace and having pleasant dreams.

Once again, the sweet sound of humming flowed out of Taylor's lips as she dug the knife into his already mangled flesh. Taylor made another cut and pulled one flap of his scalp to the side like a chef would butterfly chicken. Audrey couldn't help but look over again the second Taylor peeled the skin to the side. She immediately regretted looking and gagged at the raw pieces of flesh.

Luckily for Audrey, Ben gave her a distraction when he woke up and spat out the towel, his voice turning hoarse from his screams. Audrey and Eliza held Ben down with all their strength, despite his efforts to escape. Tears flowed down his cheeks, and Eliza tried with all her might to help keep him calm by telling him to just focus on her voice, but Ben was only consoled when he passed out once more.

When Ben woke up again, Eliza and Audrey had to sit on his arms to hold him down. At one point, Audrey had sat on top of his torso while Eliza had spread her body to hold both his arms, since he'd kept trying to flail his legs at them. But Taylor wasn't fazed by his movements. Again, Taylor repeated cutting, sticking the turkey baster in, and wiping off any ooze that dripped onto Ben so he wouldn't be burned. Ben continued to pass out and wake up like his body was being controlled by a puppet master.

At last, Taylor sighed and said, "This will be the last cut, and hopefully I'll have all the ooze out then."

Eliza's eyes gazed at Audrey, and they both knew what to do without saying anything. Before Taylor drove her knife in for the last time, they pushed all their weight down on Ben as they breathed heavily, exhausted. Taylor's wide eyes made her look like a mad scientist as she tore through Ben's flesh. Ben wailed out in pain, but to their surprise, he had little fight left in him. His voice was barely audible, and the little bit of strength he had only lasted a few seconds, before his chest lifted and fell.

The turkey baster crept into his head once more, but no ooze was left. Instead, it filled with just blood. Taylor squirted the blood out into the bowl and grabbed the glue. Gently, she closed the flap of skin back over and carefully ran the glue in between the two pieces of flesh. More tears trickled down Ben's cheeks, and although Ben was in pain, Eliza was relieved to see the tears because that meant he was still alive.

"Just the sewing left." Taylor sang and continued to hum as she picked up the needle.

Her hands started to shake as she pulled the needle through. Audrey wondered if it was all her adrenaline catching up to her, or if her hands were just exhausted from working. Taylor made sure the stitches sat snug together, like a fly captured in a spider's web.

Without saying a word, Ben woke once more and pointed to the bottle of brandy. Eliza fumbled with the bottle and almost drowned him in it from shaking so much. Ben grabbed on tightly to Eliza and Audrey, hoping to find comfort in them. His eyes rolled around in his sockets, and they began to worry that he was about to die. Ben's forehead was dripping with sweat, and some specks of blood that were becoming crusty surrounded his stitches.

When Taylor finished sewing, she touched Ben's head with the back of her hand. Heat flowed into Taylor's hand like a warm summer's day. "He has a fever. I'm going to put everything away and wash my hands. There is a room just down the hall to the right where you can lay him down." Taylor pointed her hand in the direction, before running off to the kitchen.

Eliza grabbed his legs and Audrey grabbed under his armpits. Audrey walked backward down the hall and, sure enough, the room was on the right. As Audrey kicked open the door, she grunted and Ben tilted a bit, but they held him tightly enough that they didn't drop him. Darkness crept out of the room and Audrey strained her hand as she balanced Ben on her knee to find the light switch. When she found it, a large bed was unveiled with an even bigger hand carved frame behind it. Perfectly ironed blankets sat upon the thick mattress, embellished with a blood red design on the comforter.

Ben's strapping body made them struggle to get him onto the bed, along with the mattress height. They rocked him as though he was a swing and then let his body go. He landed on his back and Eliza climbed in next to him. As her head laid down on his chest, her eyes welled up with tears.

Eliza whispered between sobs, "I can hear his heart still beating."

Audrey wanted to comfort her and tell her that he would be fine, but she knew deep down that making such a promise could cause further heartbreak if he wasn't. She had no words to use in this situation, so she patted Eliza's back and kissed her forehead in the hopes that it would give her at least some comfort.

Shortly after, Taylor walked in with a damp towel, a cup of water, and one red pill. "Has he woken up at all?" she asked kindly.

As she tried holding her tears back, Eliza said, "No, he's burning up still."

Taylor shook her head and laid the cold towel across his forehead.

"If you can get him to sit up for a minute, have him take this pill." Taylor put a glass of water on the nightstand and placed the pill next to it. Before she left, she whispered, "It will help with his fever. If you need anything else, I'll be out on my back patio."

When Taylor closed the door and left them behind, Audrey realized that she had to use this time wisely. Audrey followed her out into the hall and called, "Wait, Taylor!" Taylor stopped and turned to her. "I have a question about how long the monsters stayed?"

"I was in the cave for a couple of days; I'm not sure how long they stayed in town. I know Harper went back later, but that was well over a year or so after the whole ordeal. He said that no one was there. Just empty. If I were you, I would take care of what you need to sooner rather than later though." Taylor turned to leave Audrey, but the conversation wasn't over for her.

"Did you ever find out how to kill them?" Audrey knew it was a long shot that she would know such a thing, but she couldn't not ask.

"The monsters?" she said perplexed.

"Yes, the monsters."

"Hell no. I left and tried to forget about the whole thing. Harper might have. He never stopped searching. I think he thought if he found out how to kill them, he could bring everyone back, but I don't see how that could be true."

Before Audrey could let Taylor leave, she asked one more question, "Did he tell you about anything else he found out that could help us?"

"He would share things with me, but honestly, I wanted nothing to do with it all and that's why we broke up. He became obsessed, and I have spent my whole life in therapy, trying to forget. If that's all, I'm going to go enjoy some wine outside," she said annoyed, before turning on her heel and leaving Audrey behind.

Audrey waited in the hall to collect her thoughts, none of which were good. Everything pointed to them failing to save anyone, and that there was a chance they could all die too if they found where the creatures were keeping their neighbors and friends. When Audrey returned to the room, Ben was awake, but he didn't look well. His eyes were open and his mouth drooped like a man on his deathbed. Eliza was singing a song that sounded like an Irish lullaby and stroking the side of his face affectionately.

"Eliza, did he take the pill?" Audrey whispered so she wouldn't startle Ben.

Eliza nodded and replied, "He was able to swallow it. If you could give us some time alone, that would be great. I'm just worried that this will be all the time we have left together."

Eliza rubbed her nose and teardrops fell from her eyelashes. Audrey walked over to her and gave her a hug. As Eliza squeezed her back, Audrey gave her a kiss on the head. When Eliza released from their embrace, Audrey left without saying another word. She felt heartbroken seeing her friend in such pain and hoped that this wouldn't be the last time all three of them would spend together.

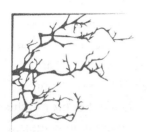

14

Audrey lingered in the hall alone with only somber floral wallpaper staring back at her. She couldn't help but think that this twist in their plan could cost Theodore his life. Her hands clenched at her sides, feelings of anger and sadness flooding her thoughts. As she glared at the wallpaper, she thought about punching a hole in it, but instead she redirected her thoughts. Her hands opened and fell at her sides, almost like she was lifeless. A single tear glided down her cheek, and as she wiped it away, she knew she would never give up on trying to save him. If she were a tree, the bark was surely Theodore, and she had no intention of losing her bark.

Her eyes flitted away from the wall, still with uncertainty of what to do. When she made it back to the living room, she couldn't help but look where Ben had laid. The image was still fresh in her mind—an image, she assumed, would never be forgotten. Despite the fact that Ben was gone from the floor, it was like she could see his imprint still, made easier for her to remember by the blood that remained.

She looked up as her mind tried to forget what had transpired. When she did so, she noticed a sliding glass door that led to the back where Taylor said she would be. Audrey could see her between the slits of the drapes, gently rocking on a chair with a new wine glass in hand. For a moment, she thought she saw another figure next to her, but when she peered closer, she only saw Taylor. Audrey blinked and her forehead scrunched when she looked once more. Now she was thinking she was losing her mind. Under her breath, she said, "Let it go, Audrey." She turned away and quietly slipped out the front door.

As she walked, the dirt crunched under her shoes—the sound felt so normal and so calming to her. A noise that wasn't screaming, or crying, or gasping or a deafening silence. A whirlwind of emotions flooded into her thoughts, and the more she thought, the more she focused on the blood that had dripped out of Ben's head. Before she could stop it, her stomach churned.

Her body hunched over and stomach acid spilled out, like she was a dog foaming at the mouth. It had been so long since she had vomited that she had forgotten the awful lingering taste and feeling like her stomach had just worked out for the first time in ages. When she was done, she wiped her mouth and glared at the ground. In reality, she wasn't mad at the ground, she was mad at who she felt she was becoming.

Kicking rocks to the side of the road, she decided to walk down it in hopes of clearing her mind.

A few minutes of walking later, Audrey spotted a pile of severely burnt branches off to the side. The odd thing was that they all belonged to a single oak tree that stood proudly behind the pile. No other trees surrounding it were burnt. She noticed that it didn't look as fragile as she would have expected a half-burnt tree to look.

Her fingers moved with the twirling shapes on the blackened bark, soot crumbling away with every touch. Audrey moved her fingers away from the disturbed bark and rubbed her index finger and thumb together, causing the soot to bleed into her fingers like dye.

As she moved away from the trunk, she gazed upon the remaining limbs.

They sprouted in a tangle of new thin branches and thick old branches that looked to be barely hanging on. Audrey knocked on one of the old branches that had survived the fire, and sure enough it had hollowed out. She assumed it was from insects or other animals that had taken advantage of its tragic soon-to-be demise. The more she looked, the more she saw how the new branches tried with all their might to hold up their elders.

Before she could leave and head back to Taylor's, Audrey felt the need to touch the trunk once more as though she was comforting an animal in pain. As her fingers glided against the roughness of the bark, she wandered around to the other side, and to her surprise, her fingers dipped into the ashen wood. As though a snake had reached out to bite her, her hand retracted from the tree and her body wobbled back.

When nothing popped out at her from the hole, she stared into the pit of darkness. It couldn't have been larger than a few feet tall, but it was just large enough for her to fit inside. A part of her wanted to hide out in it and have it cradle her like an infant child, but there was something damning about it that kept her from lingering on that thought. Slowly, she knelt and crawled into the void.

Once she'd disappeared into the tree, it was harder for her to see. Her hand dove into her pocket to retrieve her phone to create some light to illuminate the space around her. Her fingers worked quickly to turn the flashlight on. Her eyes adjusted once more to the new light, and when she turned her phone, her mouth gaped open.

A slanted tunnel stood before her that went down deeper into the earth. Audrey contemplated whether she should just go back, but this was too strange of a discovery to walk away from, and she was also avoiding going back just in case Ben had died in her absence. She hoped with all her heart that when she would return Ben would be very much alive.

The further she walked away from the opening, the mustier it smelt. She had wanted to walk though quietly in case someone was at the other end, but leaves crunched under her feet that must have blown through on windy nights. Her footsteps startled her every time she stepped on something, causing her to wince and her body to freeze momentarily. Every time she heard silence again, she would continue.

Audrey whispered to herself, "Just breathe. No one is down here. There might be some squirrels or something, but that's it." She repeated it to herself, but even she didn't believe it. It wasn't like trees grew tunnels. Someone had to have made the tunnel, but for what reason?

As she followed the path, the dirt-ridden ceiling gently brushed against her hair. She started to be able to see a larger area at the end of her light. When the tunnel curved, Audrey gazed above her. Her jaw dropped open when she saw a group of purple orbs that hung from the ceiling like sleeping bats. A curving row of them lined the tunnel, and the closer Audrey got to examine them, she realized that there was a reason why they weren't dripping. As though a spiderweb was underneath them, they stayed nestled in place until whomever they belonged to could come and take them. To Audrey's disbelief, instead of running, she began to count every floating orb. By the time she got to the end, she fell face first down several steps that she would have seen if she had only remembered to look at her surroundings. The last number she'd counted was fifteen before she'd plunged into the new space.

Her shaking arms brushed away her thick blond hair from her face. As her eyes adjusted to focus on the new light that glimmered through a dirty window on the opposite side of the room to her, a part of her wanted to believe that Theodore was here, and she would save him like a knight in shining armor. But as her eyes surveyed the room, she saw no one with her. Audrey turned back to look at the tunnel, before using the steps to pull herself up and gain her balance. She dusted what she could off her now dirty jeans.

A chair creaked outside as it rocked in the breeze. When she heard it, she knew exactly where she had ended up. The not-so-abandoned cabin that they'd driven by earlier now surrounded Audrey like a prison. Old photographs of people and strange creatures were pinned onto a colorless wall above a small desk.

The desk had splintered down the middle, but was still somehow able to hold several items on it without falling apart—two stacks of books, a taper candle, a cold cup of tea and scattered pressed flowers. Audrey ignored what was on the table as if it were invisible and scanned the many strange photographs instead. Since she didn't know what the creatures that took Theodore looked like, she wasn't sure if any of the pictures were one of the beasts staring back at her, but she concluded that none of them looked like they had wings.

Since it was unlikely that any of the pictures had captured one of them, she turned back to the desk. As Audrey's hand reached toward the top book, her fingers gently tapped the cover and a large brown spider ran out, clearly frightened by her disturbance. Her body jumped at the surprise, but not as much as she would have expected.

Not so long ago, Audrey had been quite scared of spiders. Thinking back to when she was about five years old, a spider the size of a large blueberry had fallen on her from its thread. It had perched on her cheek, and at the time she had thought that meant the spider wanted to kill her. She frantically hit her face to get it off, causing her hair to swish violently in front of her. In the end, she wasn't entirely sure if she had killed it or not, but she wouldn't have been surprised if she had caused the small creature to have a heart attack with her reaction. Now, she couldn't understand why the spider would have scared her, especially now that she knew a supernatural creature was hunting them. All her past fears seemed almost null. Pathetic in comparison.

Her focus diverted back to the books and she picked up the one on the top that had a red tattered cover and some wear to it. Gently, Audrey picked it up and read the title: *Powerful Beings: An Advanced Witchcraft*. Since her time was limited, she only scanned through the pages. Before long, she realized a pattern of stars were sketched in blotchy red ink on several pages.

Audrey wrinkled her nose while she skimmed the pages. She turned to a page that showed a spell to make someone cough up shards of glass. Her fingers stroked through more of the book, and after reading through some more of the spells, she concluded that they were all aligned with dark magic. Audrey closed the book, carefully put it back where she'd found it, and wiped her hands on her jeans as though she had to get the wicked off them.

The room was cold and the floorboards moaned in agony under her heavy feet. To her left, she could see a small glass table that was covered in instant film photographs. Audrey picked up a handful of the photographs and regretted it the second she saw the first picture. An animal—maybe a possum—was turning to melted goo. But the photograph wasn't in color. Despite the lack of color, she knew the possum must have had the purple substance on it, and that meant whomever took the pictures was also investigating it.

Each photograph was of other dead animals. She sifted through more and more until she stopped at a beautiful fox whose sad eyes stared back at her, its torso nearly a puddle. It was at that picture that Audrey felt sick again and filled with grief. As she stared into the fox's eyes, she couldn't help but think of how Theodore's eyes would look now. Would they be filled with pain and confusion like the little fox's?

Audrey hoped that all the pictures and spell books were here only for investigative purposes. Instead of putting the fox back to be lost for all eternity with the rest of the photographs, she put it in her pocket. She turned away from the pile and walked over to a very dark door that looked almost burnt with grays and blacks veining throughout it. The doorknob was an antique gold color that was likely an actual aged relic, unlike those home accessories that impersonate what came before.

The room had a small twin size bed on a simple wooden frame. There was an oversized quilt that held the colors of the night sky right before the sun transitions back to life. It was ripped and torn in a few places, but the mesmerizing shapes that resembled a star left it still feeling beautiful.

Against the wall, a dirty white vanity sat with a giant oval mirror that had yellowing on the frame. The mirror itself was quite clean, with no cobwebs or dust on the surface. A wooden bowl sat on the dresser, and when Audrey gazed upon the contents in it, she stumbled back. Purple goop sat in the bowl, along with what looked to be black powder of some sort. At that moment, she knew she had to leave. She was starting to think that whomever this home belonged to was not a kindred spirit, but someone full of darkness.

Audrey fled from the room, causing the floorboards to squeal in pain. Before leaving the house, she went back to the stack of books and read the spines more carefully. Two of the books had monsters in the title, so she grabbed them. Instead of going back the same way she came in, she decided to use the front door.

When she turned the knob, it stuck. She jiggled it with all her might before it finally gave way and the door opened. A chill ran through her when she felt the cold breeze hit. She stepped out, walked down the steps from the porch, and followed the dirt road back to Taylor's house.

Before she could go to the house, she had to hide the books just in case Taylor knew what was in that house. Just in case it was Taylor's house too, and she wasn't who she said she was. A large bush sat on the side of the dirt road several yards away from the cabin. She knelt behind it and pushed the books underneath. Once they were hidden, she ran back to Taylor's house.

She looked down at her phone saw an hour had already passed. The sun was now setting. An hour could mean that Ben was already gone, so she ran faster, hoping that she was wrong. By the time she made it back to the house, she was a sweaty mess and her mind was all jumbled. She wasn't sure what to tell Eliza, but she wanted her and Ben to leave with her this instant.

The house was quiet as she slipped back inside. To her relief, there was no sign of Taylor as she walked down the hall to where Ben was. Audrey looked towards where Ben had been operated on that was still stained with his blood, but she refrained from lingering on the horrid experience and continued to the room. Audrey raised her fist to knock on the door, but instead of knocking, she put her ear to it. When she didn't hear anything, she slowly opened it.

Eliza was laying with her head on Ben's chest; he was still.

"Eliza," Audrey whispered.

She looked up in confusion at Audrey with wet cheeks and reddened eyes. "Audrey, where did you go?"

"Just for a walk, but we need to go," Audrey said with urgency.

"Ben is still recovering." She looked down at him, and her eyes started to well up again.

Audrey interjected, "We should take him to a hospital." As she eyed the door, she whispered, "Let's go. I'll explain later."

Just then, Taylor walked into the room carrying a silver tray that had cups of water and a homemade loaf of bread on it. "Oh, good, Audrey, you're back." She smiled at her, and then looked over at Eliza and Ben.

"Thanks, Taylor, for all your help, but we need to get going now. We're running out of time, and if you want, we can let you know if we make any progress," Audrey said sternly.

"Is Ben going with you as well?"

"Yes, of course. We will take him to a hospital if we need to," Audrey replied.

"Well, I wouldn't do that. You can't explain to them what has happened," Taylor

replied slyly.

If Taylor wanted to argue, Audrey wasn't going to allow her to win. "True, but we can make something up if we need to. Or I can take him to his family to stay. We will let you know what happens."

Without letting Taylor get another word in, Audrey grabbed Eliza's arm and motioned to her to help with carrying Ben to the car. Eliza gazed at them both before she concluded that she would trust Audrey. Eliza helped pull Ben from the bed and carried him out the room the same way they had carried him in. Taylor didn't try to help. Instead, she watched as they slightly stumbled down the hall and out the front door.

As Audrey struggled getting the keys out of her jean pocket, Ben moaned groggily. When he went quiet again,

Audrey and Eliza gently placed him in the back seat. That is if you define gently as putting his head and shoulders on the seat teetering on Eliza's arms, and then Audrey running around to pull from his shoulders to get his whole body inside the car. Ben's eyes opened a few times, but when he saw where he was, he let his eyelids crash back down.

Taylor watched from her porch the whole time, and after Ben was safely in the car, Audrey stared at her for a minute. She contemplated whether she was capable of the evil that she had seen in the spell books, or if she kept them to prevent such darkness from happening. Her eyes left Taylor's with no more certainty than she had before as she got into the car. Audrey pushed the key into the ignition and sped away.

Eliza sat quietly in the back seat with Ben. She held him the whole way, his head resting peacefully in her lap. His eyes would occasionally open and Eliza could have sworn she had seen his lips grin up at her when she'd massaged the side of his head gently.

When Audrey reached the bushes she had hid the books under, she called back to Eliza, "I'm going to stop for a minute. Don't get out of the car."

Eliza looked confused and worried, but nodded.

Beyond the bushes, Audrey could see the oak tree. Its mesmerizing shape still had a hold on her, but the hidden door it held was enough for her to stay away. Audrey walked around to find the green leaves that housed the books. Crouching, she looked around to make sure no one was watching her. A bird chirped as it flew past, but to her relief, no footsteps crunched behind her. Audrey picked up the books and ran back to the car.

She threw the car door open and chucked the books to her right. Eliza said something, but Audrey couldn't quite hear her. Audrey's foot pushed down hard on the pedal, and as she drove, her mind focused on just getting them safely back to town.

As Audrey rounded the first sharp curve down the hill, she took a deep breath of relief.

They made it back to town without any distractions. But the town was quiet. Too quiet. After leaving their own deserted town, she had hoped to see cars driving, people going into restaurants, or at least on the sidewalks. It was now night, so she made sure to keep it in mind that that meant there would be less people out in a town like this anyway right now.

When they came upon a stoplight, a brightly lit gas station sat on the corner in view, with a man there pumping gas. Audrey couldn't help but lock eyes with him, and the more she stared, the more she saw Theodore's face looking back at her. As Theodore's face drifted away with the wind, she snapped out of the trance and realized the man looked nothing like her lost love. When she looked up at the light, it was no longer green and was now yellow instead. She made it through the yellow just before it turned a blinding red.

The highway was just a few minutes away now, but Audrey felt a tinge of indecision cloud her brain. She thought about them returning to Harthsburg, but then she wondered if the Twilight Breathers would return at night to get them, or if perhaps they were all done with snatching up people now. Another idea that she felt would be better for all of them was to return to Ben's mother's house. She would no doubt take care of Ben, and Eliza and Audrey could look over the books before heading out as the smallest search party she had ever heard of.

"Eliza, has he woken up at all?"

"He wakes here and there, but I think we need to take him somewhere where he will be safe," she said, her voice shaking.

"Do you think we could take him to Gwen's? I know she would take care of him, but she could decide that we can't be trusted and call the cops on us or something. We could also go back to Ben's?" Audrey replied indecisively.

"I think we should call Gerald. He might be able to help. He was in the military, remember?" Eliza was quite hopeful of her suggestion.

Audrey let her eyes dart around the area before she replied. "You could try calling."

Eliza pulled out her phone, found Gerald's name and hit the call button. Eliza put the phone up to her ear and listened to the constant ringing. She was about to put the phone down in defeat when the ringing stopped and a voice answered. Audrey only just heard the voice say, "Hello".

"Who is this?" Eliza asked sternly.

Audrey wondered who had been on the line when Eliza clicked end call and looked at her phone in disgust.

"Eliza, who answered?" Audrey looked back at her for a second, before returning her eyes to the road.

"It... It sounded like Wyatt's voice. But why would he have Gerald's phone?"

Goosebumps took over Audrey's arms. "I'm not sure. Are you sure it was Wyatt? What did he say?" Audrey asked impatiently.

"He said... he said... I'm not sure."

Audrey knew she was lying, but she had no intentions of making this day any harder by fighting with her. She decided to assume that it wasn't good. They were coming up to Gwen's street, and Audrey felt like that was where they needed to go.

"I think we should go to Gwen's. Do you think we could wake Ben up long enough to tell his mom that we were trying to help him?"

Before Eliza could speak, Ben cleared his throat. "I can manage a bit, but can you make sure I get some water soon? I feel like someone has poured cinnamon down my throat."

Good old Ben, Audrey thought. "Yes, of course, we can get you whatever you need."

Eliza squeezed his hand and beamed at him, and Audrey felt happy for them this time instead of jealous. They continued down the road until they arrived at Gwen's quaint cottage. Audrey turned off the ignition and the car juddered before it turned completely off. She tapped her hand against the steering wheel, hesitant to get out. But when Eliza opened her door and went around to help Ben out, it was clear that they were going through with this plan.

Audrey got out and hoped that Gwen wouldn't mind their intrusion. It wasn't that late, but for all she knew, Gwen could've been one of those older ladies who didn't stay up past seven. The outside light glowed brightly on the porch and fortunately there were still lights on inside that they could see through one of the front windows.

"Ben, are you able to walk at all?" Audrey asked, while Ben sat up on the back seat, holding Eliza's hand.

"My legs weren't cut open, so I believe I'll be able to walk just fine," he said sarcastically, coughing a bit.

Audrey rolled her eyes at him as they helped him gain his footing. "Is there anything you want us to tell your mom? I think she is going to be pretty freaked out to see us. I guess not so much to see us, but to see her son with a head wound," Audrey said with a closed smile.

"It's true. Your mom might blame us right away and call the cops," Eliza said in a serious tone. It was clear she wasn't in the mood for jokes.

"I'll think of something; but why did we leave Taylor's?" It was a question that Audrey wasn't ready to answer yet, and she wasn't sure if what she'd found was actually even linked to her. However, Ben stopped and waited by the passenger door, refusing to budge. He eyed Audrey like he was about to interrogate her.

"Okay, okay! I found something, and I'm not sure if Taylor is linked or is in danger as well. When I went for a walk, I found this burnt oak tree. It had a huge hole in one side, and I decided to go into it. I assumed it was just a hollow tree, but it had an underground tunnel that led to that abandoned looking house that was on Taylor's street; do you remember it?" They both shook their heads. "Well, there were lots of books on witchcraft in there and even some on monsters. That's where I got those two books I threw in the car when we left from. There were even photographs of melting animals and weird faces."

Audrey reached into the car to get the books. She held them up and continued, "I was thinking maybe the person was investigating the creatures too, but then I found a bowl that had ooze in it!" Audrey felt good that she had blurted everything out and that the secret wasn't just hers anymore.

"Taylor could be involved, but wouldn't Harper have stayed with her if she was interested in researching them just like he was?" Ben paused and gently put his hand up to his wound. "It just doesn't add up. There has to be more to what's going on in that house. Maybe in the bowl were things to banish the creatures or something, because if it is her house, then she is a great actress. I mean, you saw how she reacted to us when we told her what we needed help with. It would be a huge act on her part if she was involved in this."

"Wouldn't she have just let Ben die? Or she could have just as easily taken us to the Twilight Breathers," Eliza replied.

Ben and Eliza had good points, but Audrey felt in her gut that there was more to Taylor than what they'd witnessed. "You're both making sense, but I just want to be cautious."

Eliza looked up at Ben with restless eyes and said, "Can we go inside now? Then we can discuss what we are going to do."

Before Ben knocked on the door, he said, "Let me do the talking. She will more than likely not believe either of you two." He smirked at them both.

"Okay, mama's boy. We'll be backup for you then." Audrey smiled widely and Ben seemed to catch her playful tone, since he grinned back and rolled his eyes at her.

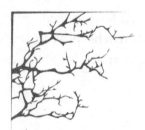

15

The door looked just as they had left it—a vibrant yellow with vines overgrowing around it like tidal waves crashing. Ben exhaled when he stared at the door, knowing that it was unchanged. It was a comforting sight. His body ached and his mind felt like it was being split in two. He thought to himself that the normalcy of life was an absolute bullshit idea of what reality really was. They had all lived their lives without monsters and now the harsh reality of what lurked in this world was slapping them ever so harshly in the face.

Ben knocked on the door. It was a pretty gentle knock, but loud enough that his mother would hear it if she wasn't upstairs. There was no answer at first, so Ben knocked again, louder this time, and yelled, "Mom."

Gwen, wearing a dark purple robe, threw the door open, making all three of them jump back. As though she was hiding out and had been found, her eyes were wide and her jaw open.

When she laid her eyes on Ben, her expression softened until she noticed his stitched up head. Gwen grabbed Ben and placed her arms around him tightly. As she did so, her wild hair blew in the breeze. Gwen glowered at Eliza and Audrey, causing them to both turn away from her rageful eyes.

Small tears slipped down her cheeks, but she quickly wiped them away. Eliza nudged Ben, who was in the dark about his mother's angry stare.

"Mom, can we go inside?" Ben spoke softly.

"Are they coming too?" She pointed a finger at Eliza and Audrey. Audrey almost scoffed at her, but she thought about how she would be feeling in this situation if she were a parent. She imagined that she would have had the same reaction.

"Yes, Mom. I know this looks bad, but I promise you, they are my friends and didn't harm me," Ben said confidently.

As they walked through the door, Gwen had Ben lean on her. Audrey closed the door behind them all and made the decision to lock it—mainly for her own comfort. When Gwen made it to the living room, she ordered Ben to lay down on the couch while she went to fetch him some water.

They both had lost their rights to that warm welcome they had received just mere hours ago, but Eliza had hope that once she heard what Ben had to say, all would be well again. Gwen darted her cold, furious eyes between Eliza and Audrey, before looking empathetically at Ben as she stroked his hair. Ben thought about swatting his mom's hand away, but relented when he remembered the danger that still lay ahead.

"Tell me what happened," Gwen said sharply to Ben.

Ben quickly averted his eyes to Eliza, who nodded encouragingly at him. Ben sat up and pulled away from his mother, before gulping. "Well... uh... I got hurt and..." Ben's eyes focused to the back of the room, while he forced his mind focus on any explanation that would be better than the truth. Gwen's foot began tapping impatiently. When Ben heard the tapping, he returned his gaze to his mother. "Well, as you can see, I'm fine, and Eliza and Audrey have been watching over me and helping me recover." His eyes squinted and his shoulders tensed, while he waited for his mother's response.

Gwen's eyebrows rose with suspicion. "Ben, tell me what the fuck is going on. You came here earlier in a hurry over something to do with Taylor, and then you come back like this. I don't care what is going on, but you need to tell me the truth and tell me now."

Ben stood up straight, his mouth gaping at his mother. It was apparent that Ben had never heard his mom talk to him like that before. Ben looked over at Eliza and Audrey and gulped, before twiddling his fingers nervously. Ben shifted his body and he bit his lip.

"Mom, something's happening in Harthsburg. I'm not sure what Harper told you about where he grew up, but what happened to his town is now happening to ours. Something took Theo and almost the rest of the town, and we are trying to find out how we can save them. I know I look awful, but my life was saved by these two women and Taylor." Ben stopped to catch his breath, but before he could continue, Gwen held her hand up.

"Wait, Taylor helped you? Have you three been there this whole time? What has she done to you?" She was shaking hysterically.

Ben cocked his head, eyed his mother and shook his head, annoyed that the only thing she'd seemed to hear was about Taylor. "Mom, did you hear anything I just said? Taylor helped me. We needed to ask her some questions to help us with what's going on in our town."

"I heard what you said. That horrid woman laid her hands on you and now look at you. All bandaged up and wounded. I should have never told you where she lives. I knew only bad would come of it. Ben, you tell me what kind of trouble you are in right now!" Gwen rose up like an angry bear and eyed each one of them like they were her biggest enemies.

Ben stared at her with a blank face, uncertain of what to say next. The only thing going through his head was, "*Run*." As she rambled on, Ben was losing faith in the situation and couldn't help but tune out her voice—something that he was not used to doing.

Reactions can't always be predicted, and Ben obviously hadn't considered well what the consequences would be to put trust in someone that his mother clearly despised. Looking at Ben, Eliza walked over and put her hand on his shoulder. He looked up kindly and put his on hers. Gwen stopped talking when she saw this affectionate display between them.

"Mrs. Drewitt, none of us are trying to be deceitful or secretive, but we are trying to protect you. That protection is mainly for your sanity. I will tell you what has been happening and how we have ended up where we are, but you must promise not to panic. We have little time for such reactions, and I would very much like to use the most out of the time we have left." Eliza's calm voice flowed out with such command that Gwen sat down and took a deep breath.

Eliza was dead serious about telling Gwen the truth and neither Ben nor Audrey thought to change her mind on it, even though they both felt that it could cause even more uproar from her. Gwen's eyes remained on Eliza and she quietly nodded her head for her to begin the life-changing tale.

Eliza started her story with the disappearances and how none of them knew what was happening until they'd spoken with Ben. She mentioned Harper's journal, but was cautious to not mention too much about her dead husband's past with Taylor and just how strong of a bond they'd had. Gwen didn't need details. She needed closure on the whole situation for her worried soul. It was easy to see that she loved Ben more than she would ever or had ever loved anyone else. Audrey hoped that she would want to stay out of this, but that seemed like a long shot given her devotion to her son and Harper. As Audrey contemplated how the night would go, Eliza's words became muddled in her mind and came and went like smoke.

Finally, Eliza ended her tale with, "And that's how we arrived back here." Gwen was on the edge of her seat by this time. She placed her plump hands on her hips and exhaled. They were all waiting; waiting for either a storm or a light breeze. Unlike earlier, it was hard to tell what she would say or do. Her eyes weren't full of rage, her arms weren't flailing around like a bird in flight, her mouth wasn't trembling or drooped open in surprise, but her eyes looked glazed over like a well-made donut.

Gwen's hands rose over her worrisome eyes and her head shook slowly like a light breeze nudges a leaf. When she peered out from between her fingers, she inhaled the air around her and slowly exhaled like she had just finished a meditation exercise. "Ben..." She looked at Ben like he was the only other soul in the room. "Shortly after we started dating in college, Harper told me about what had happened to him then. It wasn't something that I could believe at the time, and ultimately it caused our relationship to end. I thought he was a bit mad and wasn't going to be with someone who either had lied to sound mysterious or really needed some mental help. We didn't speak for a while, at least not how we had done before. I still cared deeply for him, but I got with your father—"

"Biological father," Ben interjected and rolled his eyes.

Gwen nodded her head and continued, "When things went sour with him, Harper and I reconnected. I had never stopped loving him, but like I said, it was a hard thing to believe. When we got back together, he never brought up what had happened to him and I never asked. At least, not until Taylor moved here. It was quite strange when she showed up after she had moved about two thousand miles from here to Brindestone after college. She'd never spoken to your father during that time, so I'd assumed we would never hear from her again."

Ben cut in, "When did she move here?"

"I was getting to that. Harper told me she would be moving over here about five years ago. She'd told him that she missed her friends from here, but to my knowledge, none of her friends lived here except Harper. It would have made more sense if she'd moved to Harthsburg, but she came here and since then it wasn't the same between Harper and I. On a regular basis, she would have lunch with him or they'd go for a walk and talk, and not once was I invited."

Her eyes darted to the floor and again she took a deep breath, before staring back into Ben's eyes. "When he would come home from seeing her, I could always tell something was stirring in his mind, but he didn't tell me freely what it was. I noticed that he started to spend most of his time on the computer in his study, and books were being bought constantly."

A small flicker of a smile started on Gwen's face like she had thought of a fond memory before it dwindled away, and she continued. "As you know, he always liked to read, but these were much different than his normal reading materials. He would stay up late and go back and forth between large history books and the computer. He was consumed for weeks. I didn't know how to address this new obsession, and he never mentioned to me what he was doing. Instead, one day when he went out, I looked through his internet history and at the books he was reading." Gwen paused, shook her head and took a sip of her drink like whatever she was going to say next was a lot to handle.

Audrey wondered what she was drinking; since she clicked her tongue, she assumed that it was something sweet and tart like lemonade, or perhaps even something alcoholic.

"What did you find out, Mom?" Ben asked. Eliza and Audrey were both thankful he did because they were hanging on by a thread. Neither of them had thought she would know much about what had happened before, and Audrey felt like they had made a huge misstep in not talking to her first. She almost felt guilty that if they had, then Ben might not have had to be cut open like a fish getting ready to be filleted.

Gwen's eyes wandered to the bookcase, before she took a breath and answered her son. "It was all the same. A creature that was referred to as an Eltrist or Twilight Breather. They have been known to take people from a specified area. The creatures are pack animals and live off flesh. But that wasn't what caught my attention." Her body shivered as her thoughts started to jumble.

"Go on, Mom," Ben said softly, placing his hand over hers.

Gwen looked up into her son's eyes with pure worry; a worry that surprised her. It was easy to worry about everything that pertained to her child before, but this was the type of danger that she had only seen in movies or books. It had never crossed her mind that there were real things that lurked behind the shadows, or perhaps behind the stars, which would have an unspoken power over all of them. It was as though she felt like they were all ants just waiting to be crushed into nothing.

As her head slowly drooped, Gwen shook it in disbelief. Clearing her throat, she muttered, "He had a tab open that had details on how to summon them." Her face turned pale, just like it had the first time she'd read about what Harper had been looking at. "I couldn't understand why someone would want to summon something that would feed off of us, but when I dug deeper, I found out why."

Eliza's eyes were practically bulging out of their sockets with fear.

"Twilight Breathers produce a type of liquid that when consumed, along with other ingredients, will grant a person immortality. They only produce the liquid when they are feeding or mating, but there's a catch. The person who gets granted immortality still has to take the potion every so many years to keep their immortality." Gwen shivered again as her body went into shock. Her mind started to remember everything she had read before, and even though it had scared her before, she'd never truly believed that they were real until now.

"Gwen, did you find out why Harper was researching them again? I know in his journal it mentions that he was quite obsessed with finding out what they were and how to kill them, and it seems like when he met you, he stopped," Audrey asked delicately.

"Yes, in fact, I confronted him one night. I pretended I was curious about it so that he would feel comfortable talking with me. I had just taken out a piping hot cherry pie from the oven." Gwen smiled fondly. "Cherry pie was his favorite, and I knew it would put him in a good mood. I asked if he would join me out in the garden to eat it, he agreed, and I casually asked about the book on his office desk. It was about monsters, and I knew he wouldn't suspect much from me asking about something in plain sight. As soon as I asked, he dropped a cherry from his spoon, and I thought that I was about to come to a dead end. Instead, I laughed and hoped he would too. He did, and then told me a little bit about what he was looking at. He made it seem like he was just really interested and that his talks with Taylor had nothing to do with it. I knew he wasn't telling me the whole truth, so I

asked him about Twilight Breathers specifically. He was startled by the name and quickly asked how much I knew. I told
him not much, but that I needed to know what was going
on."

An upset habit Gwen had acquired over the years was
twirling her wedding ring around, but she was seldom ever
upset enough to do it. Now, she couldn't help but stare at the
aged gold as she let it glide between her fingers. She moved
it enough to notice the tan line beneath it. She allowed her
mind to settle on it—to remember the wonderful memories from prior to this day—and she hoped that when she
returned her son's gaze, she would have forgotten all about
what had just occurred, and that no flying creatures existed
waiting to consume them. But, of course, when she finally
lifted her head, Ben was sat across from her with his head still
stitched up. She quietly sighed and bit her lip.

Ben thought about how hard that must have been for
his mother to see her husband becoming consumed by what
she saw as fiction. He knew that the fact Harper had spent
so much time with Taylor didn't help with the pain she had
and still was feeling. Ben had never known about their rough
patch, which made him feel uneasy. He would never have allowed his mother to go through such pain alone.

Gwen rubbed her hand on her neck before saying, "He
said that he had gotten a lead on the creatures who took away
his parents. Harper made it clear that he knew I wouldn't
want to know because of our previous discussions. Instead of
talking to me, he would go to Taylor. She filled his head with
ideas on how to find them and encouraged him to go after
them again. He was confused about why she wanted him to

keep looking, but he searched anyway and we ended up staying up until the next morning discussing what he had found out. We finally fell asleep and when we woke up, I decided I was going to help him. Finally, I believed him about what had happened, and I wanted to be the one to help. I told him to come to me instead of Taylor. Well, when that happened, Taylor surprised me by coming to me."

"Wait, she came to discuss her relationship with Harper?" Ben said angrily.

Gwen picked up her glass again and took another gulp. As she placed it back down on the table, she nodded her head without delving more into that part. "Taylor was mad. She told me that I had no right to discuss anything about the creatures with Harper and that I should leave. I couldn't understand why she would be so angry, especially since I should have been the one getting angry. I mean, she was spending more time with my husband than I was. She never even spoke to me about it in the first place. Now when I see her, it's always a fake smile and hello, but really, we hate each other."

Gwen looked around the room and then got up and walked over to the bookshelf. Her fingers walked across each spine, dusting off the row by blowing on it, before shaking her head. She left the bookcase and went upstairs. They could hear her footsteps above them on the wooden floor. She shuffled back downstairs to join them again, her hand holding a small book. It couldn't have been more than fifty pages long. Her hand shook as she handed it to Ben. The cover had an obscure photograph of a winged creature with ooze dripping from its mouth in black and white. The title said *Eltrist* in bold letters. The author's name was too hard to read as it was really worn down.

"Mom, what is this?" Ben opened it and the font was about the size of a poppy seed. She pulled a tiny magnifying glass out of her pocket and placed it in Ben's palm.

It had a small crack on the right edge, a beaded chain attached at the bottom to make a loop around your wrist and there was a silver casing around the glass.

"This is the most useful book Harper found on the Eltrist. It talks about the people who've encountered them and their word for word accounts. It was hard to find, but we found it in a new age shop that was run by a lady who referred to herself as a modern-day witch. She knew exactly what we were talking about when we described the monsters and called them Twilight Breathers. I imagine that since they are magical beings, witches or other people who dabble in things of this nature would have heard of them. I'm not sure if Harper ever found any closure from his research because one day after we had gotten this book he just stopped. He went back to his normal routines, and when I asked him about what he had found, he told me that he was done. He was done with searching for answers, I think because he knew it wouldn't bring anyone back. I'm not sure if the Eltrist can die or how, but this book may be the key for your town," she said encouragingly.

Eliza gazed at the book fondly and held her hand out to Ben, hopeful that he would pass her it. Ben almost didn't notice her small hand reached out to him, but when he did, he was hesitant to give it to her. Eliza's eyes were almost teary—a reaction that he wouldn't have expected over a book. A few moments went past while Ben tried to read what she was thinking, but before he could, Eliza changed her demeanor. Eliza cleared her mind and her eyes started to look more interested instead of longing. Ben hovered the book over her hand and finally let it fall into her palm. Eliza released her breath and she felt her heart skip a beat.

"Gwen, did you read the book?" Audrey asked inquisitively.

"Yes, I read parts of it. What these things did to people was horrific. Harper didn't push me to be involved like he was. He just wanted support and someone to listen to him, and that's mainly what I did. He never mentioned why he gave up though."

"Well, I think one of us needs to read the book. We need to find our friends. The quicker the better. Tomorrow, we need to go to the forest. That has to be where they are, like Harper mentioned in his journal," Audrey suggested.

In reality, she wasn't really suggesting. She would go to the forest with or without Ben and Eliza to find Theodore if she had to. Audrey knew that Theodore might already be dead, but even if he was, she needed to see it for herself or she would go mad with not knowing, just as Harper did. She couldn't imagine spending the rest of her life in anguish. Ben insisted that he would read the book, since he couldn't do much else until he got his energy back. Then he asked, "And what will you two do?"

"One or both of us could search for where a cave has been found in the forest. I bet some of the local kids have gone exploring there, and we could find some threads about it online. Do you want to look with me, Eliza, or do you want to do something else?" Audrey was sure she would say yes.

"Actually, I think I need some time alone. I need some fresh air."

"Where are you going to go?" Ben asked.

"I think a walk around the block will really help."

The room turned quiet; no one objected. Ben hardly had a reason to disagree that some time alone could help her mind feel more at ease.

When Eliza stood up, Ben followed her to the door. "Don't get lost, okay? I know this town is safer than most places, but it's getting pretty late."

Eliza nodded and stood on her tiptoes to kiss his forehead right below his wound. "Don't worry, I will be fine. I promise I won't be gone that long. I just need some time."

Ben nodded and watched her walk out the door and down the driveway, onto the sidewalk. Feeling uneasy, he waited by the door until he could no longer see her dark hair flowing in the wind.

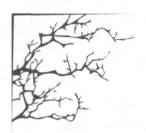

16

With each step she took, she could feel rage building. Her eyes were as wild as an owl's and she was as vexed as a caged animal. As she approached the next corner, she pulled out her phone. The light casted a glow on her face. She had no intention of bringing attention to herself, but she assumed that it wouldn't be hard to avoid people in a small town like this.

She pulled up her contact list and hovered over a name. The name, she felt, was taunting her. When she made it to the next street, she let her eyes shut and her fist clamped around her phone like a Venus flytrap. Slowly, she allowed her eyes to open again as she looked at the name. Before she could drive herself mad with contemplation, she clicked it.

And just like that, she had her phone up to her ear as she stood next to a white picket fence that hadn't aged well. She analyzed every paint chip and splintered post, while she waited for a voice. The ringing continued, but no answer came, and her phone eventually went to voicemail. Eliza growled and raised her arm high above her head to chuck her phone, when it began to ring. The light glowed once more, lighting up a couple feet in front of her. When she looked at the name, her lip curled.

She immediately answered and the voice at the other end of the line spoke before she had a chance. "Eliza," the calm voice said like she was in a dream; in another time.

Her voice failed to reply as her heart sped and the anger flowed out of her like warm butter.

The voice continued, "Are you there still? Have you figured it all out?"

A single tear rolled down her cheek and dripped from her chin. Her eyes glared off into the distance. "How could you do this?" she demanded.

"Well..."

"I trusted you; he trusted you; we all trusted you! Then you decided that we weren't enough?" Eliza screamed.

The voice sighed loud enough for Eliza to hear it. Loud enough for her eyes to grow darker than they already were.

"Sometimes people change sides."

"Don't talk to me like I'm a child! Do you even understand what you have done? What this will mean for my family?"

Her voice was now growing hoarse, and the house she was stood in front of turned on their porch light. She thought about throwing a rock at it, so the person would just mind their own business, but instead, she walked away. She counted each step she took, and by the time she was at fifty, the voice replied. Her legs stopped moving and her mind stopped counting.

"I do know the consequences, but the promise I have been given far outweighs what happens to everyone else. While I've enjoyed our time together, it was only a small chapter in my life. You are not my story; but I could make you a part of it, if you'd like?"

If Eliza's eyes could kill, it would have been in this moment. Luckily for her, the street was bare, save for a few moths that surrounded the street lamps. Her chest rose and fell with her growing thoughts. She didn't know what to do and she feared that she would never know. Anger was clouding her brain. With several deep breaths, she slowly calmed her mind.

"Let me make this clear, you will not be remembered in my story. If anything, you will be remembered because of the end I will bring to yours." Eliza hung up the phone.

The bright light stayed on for a few moments, before the words *Wyatt Call Ended* faded, along with her hopelessness.

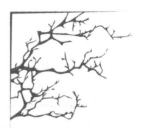

17

Quietly, Ben shut the door behind him and joined Audrey and his mother in the living room. Audrey and Gwen were sat next to each other, talking like old friends. Ben grinned when he saw that Audrey was comforting his mother. When Gwen saw Ben return, she sat upright and sniffled a bit, before putting her mask back on. Ben wasn't fooled by her fake smile, but he appreciated that she wasn't going to guilt trip him into not leaving in the morning.

Audrey began to think about what an odd situation she was in, but it wouldn't be as odd as when they ventured into the forest tomorrow to track down vicious creatures that hardly anyone had heard of. "Gwen, do you mind letting me use your computer?"

"Of course, dear. Follow me." She led Audrey down the hall to a small office. It had a nice woodgrain desk that had the computer and some pens in a little black cup on it. A small gray swivel chair was pushed under the desk. Audrey moved toward it and Gwen sat down. "I just need to type in my password. If you need anything, I'll be in the living room. I'll bring down some blankets for you to sleep on the couch with, and I can make up a bed on the floor for Ben and Eliza."

"Thanks, Gwen. You go get some rest and I'll take a nap as soon as I find what we need."

Gwen stood up, patted Audrey's shoulder and left the room.

Gwen approached Ben, who was sitting huddled with the *Eltrist* book in one hand and the magnifying glass in his other. His eye stayed squinted and looking through the glass when he looked up at her. Gwen snickered at how he looked, causing Ben to lower it and glare playfully at her.

"Honey, I think we should change your bandages before you fall asleep," Gwen suggested.

Ben rose his hand instinctively to gently poke at the wound that he was still having trouble believing he had actually endured. Gwen reached over and caught it, preventing any further meddling. Ben nodded and moved his hand back down to his side like an obedient hound.

"Yeah, I think that would be good, Mom."

"I'll just go grab some clean bandages then," Gwen said, patting his hand. Gwen was only gone for a few minutes. She poured peroxide on the crusty piece of skin and it turned squishy. Ben winced. She left it to dry a bit before she added some clean bandages—the bandages had little yellow ducks on them. Ben's head cocked to the side when he saw what was on them.

"Really, Mom? These are the only ones you have?"

"Oh, hush. They're all I've got and they work the same as any other bandage."

"Okay, Mom. Thank you." Ben chuckled, rolling his eyes.

"Anyway, I'm going to get back to reading."

"Okay, honey. I'll be in my room if you need me," Gwen replied with a shaky voice.

It was hard to ignore the fear his mother felt, but Ben nodded and returned to the book. Gwen left as she said she would, but not because she wanted to.

Before Ben continued reading, he grabbed the overly colorful knitted blanket that his mother had made almost a decade ago and placed it over him. The blanket made him feel safe, and even though Ben wasn't a child anymore, he felt as though he was as helpless as one. He needed all the comfort he could get. His hand caressed the front of the antique book like he could feel part of Harper's presence from it. Determined to save everyone, he opened the book again, took a deep breath and let the words lead the way.

Ben positioned himself closer to the hummingbird lamp on the side table next to the couch. The book was a collection of accounts of what people had heard or seen happen during the time the Eltrist had come. One paragraph spoke of a small village in Europe called Gravin, where much like Harthsburg, townspeople were abducted and sadly never found.

Another town called Vitma had a similar situation happen; however, they were able to save about half the townspeople by escaping at just the right moment. One man who survived believed they'd came to mate, and to do so the males would lay eggs protected by a sticky purple liquid and the females would later swallow them. The man was quite sure that the female would then become immediately pregnant and produce an offspring within six moons. Although the author had made notes that he agreed with the assumption, Ben thought it would be impossible for them to know such things. Especially if they were as vicious as they sounded. Yet, the author continued to say that right after the baby Eltrist was born, it would feed off the goop that the parents would place on small animals. The melted animals would be consumed, and then they would leave. The author said that it was called the creature plague of blood and magic.

Ben scrunched his eyebrows and almost mentioned what it was called to Eliza, but then he remembered that she wasn't there. Ben's mind drifted as he stared at the front door, hopeful that she would come through it shortly. To be honest, Ben felt like this whole thing couldn't be real. His mind was still set on being a skeptic, despite knowing what he had seen; knowing that something was out there looking back into his eyes just hours ago. And even with his brain being torn open, he still had doubts.

When the door remained unopened, he turned away and went back to reading. A moment later, Gwen came back downstairs and quietly placed a stack of blankets and pillows on the recliner, before smiling at Ben and tiptoeing back upstairs.

He muttered to himself that it didn't seem like they were just mating this time. The other book they had that talked about the word Devourement seemed more likely, since he hadn't seen any eggs when he was in the forest, but it was also possible that he was wrong about that too. He ached for concrete answers, but sadly, he was only left with more questions.

The aching pain from his wound was starting to give him a headache—one that he assumed was also caused from straining his eyes to read. Ben gently laid the book on the side table and got up to check on Audrey. While stood in the doorway, he saw Harper's face on the desk and felt a jolt of sadness. But before he could focus on it, Audrey poked her head up to peer at him from behind the computer screen.

"Oh, hey, Audrey. I just came to see how things were going," Ben said casually.

"Like everything with these creatures, nothing is easy." She looked painfully annoyed at the computer screen again before continuing, "I am trying to narrow our search to the right cave since there are more than one that have been found there. It's not the easiest thing to search, since I haven't found anyone suggesting that The Twilight Breathers or... what was their other name?" Audrey looked up at Ben to finish her sentence.

"Eltrists. I think that might be their actual name and Twilight Breathers was just given to them by the first humans who encountered them. At least that's what it seems from what I've read so far."

Audrey nodded her head. "It could be, but honestly, I could care less what they are called. We just need to find Theodore, and whoever else we can. This whole thing is fucked up, but I have hope that we can get through this. Is Eliza back yet?"

"No, not yet. I was thinking about calling her, but I want to give her the space she obviously feels she needs right now. It's a lot to deal with."

"I'm sure she'll return soon. I doubt she would want to wander around all night in an area she doesn't know."

Ben nodded and placed his hands in his jean pockets, so he wouldn't start itching again. "Okay, well I'll get back to reading and then probably take a nap. My mom brought down blankets and pillows. You can sleep on the couch when you're ready."

"Okay, cool. Thanks for letting me know."

Ben grinned awkwardly and then went back to the couch. His eyes felt heavy, but he couldn't sleep knowing that Eliza was still gone. Opening the book once more, he let his thoughts wander to only the words on the pages in front of him.

As he scanned page after page with no real insight, he thought about giving up until finally, he found something. Something that could save them. A few paragraphs that could change their fate. The author referred to the person who he interviewed as "The ancient traveler." No real name like the other unfortunate souls who had encountered an Eltrist, or a Twilight Breather as some referred to them. Instead, this mysterious person knew of things that the others did not.

The yellowing page read: "On the night of October 22nd, I was approached at a tavern in Weaver. The encounter was a shock and the closest I would come to understanding the Eltrist. A person in a long coat that flowed to just below their knees sat in the chair across from me. The stranger kept their black hood up and stared into my eyes. While keeping their eyes fixed on mine, they hollered to the barkeep for a pint. I had never seen this ancient person before in all my days, but could feel they somehow knew me.

I took a swig from my mug and then asked politely what he wanted. The ancient traveler chuckled and grinned. As I brood over that day, that grin still haunts me. It was almost like the stranger was thinking about how best to cook me in a pot of stew. Something echoed through my body that the stranger was not to be messed with. A lady came over and placed a pint on the table. I wanted to speak, but my tongue stayed silent.

The traveler told me that he had some information that would be helpful for the document I was working on. I asked him how he knew about what I was creating. The ancient traveler smirked and stated that it would be better to leave that a secret and that it was best not to question from where the information was received. I went with my gut and closed my lips tight.

The traveler offered me a brief interview on who the Eltrists are, and when I asked what was required in return for the information, the stranger simply said, "nothing." I was confused as to what the stranger meant, and when I asked for clarification, the response was simple, "Give me the name of a town that you want to be rid of."

My pulse rose and I could feel the danger of giving the name of a town that could potentially have some ill intent shadow over it. I decided to give a fake name: Riveron. The ancient traveler smirked again at the name and that is when the tale began, and my life turned upside down.

The traveler told me that they had become quite fond of the Eltrists and that they could even be ridden. The stranger warmly spoke of riding one over the ocean. That made me laugh uncomfortably. I knew that they were winged beasts, but I found it unlikely that they could be tamed. The stranger did not bat an eye at my uncomfortable outburst and continued on to tell me that the creatures enjoyed eating living creatures not of their world. "They cannot consume food the way we do though. They have to extract a substance that melts away the skin and muscles. This makes it so that they can slurp up the guts without taking any of the bone. The gooey substance they use creates a magical essence to devour what they need to live off, and they come back and consume it once the bits are melted off the core."

The strug was very important and was mentioned several times. The strug could do things to powerful beings that allowed them to walk the Earth way past their expiration date. The ancient traveler didn't delve into this any further but changed subject and continued on. "They come to eat, reproduce like any other creature; amongst other things, of course."

Devourement was the time they needed to feast as a sort of ritual. That was why they continued to come back every decade or so, as opposed to never leaving. The strug could stay hidden in their fur until they needed more food later.

Mating was not needed to enter this world, but they found Earth to be a safer place to do so, since they were quite vulnerable when reproducing. When they mated, they would use their strug to get ample amounts of nourishment to provide their new offspring.

They could also enter this world by a "calling." The "calling" was executed by an outside force to use the Eltrists' strug for their own means. If someone really wanted their strug, they could call them to this world, but with a severe consequence. Death would befall an entire town. The ancient traveler told me that if you were willing to pay the price, you could have immortality. I asked how that was possible. The response was, "Strug, a sacrifice, blood and a few words. Even immortality has its limitations and requires nourishment sometimes."

My thoughts whirled around in shock and confusion. I had more questions now that I knew the truth, but I wasn't sure if I could handle the answers.

I sat there staring in utter angst. I had started my research to find out how to stop the killing of so many people and animals from around me, but this gave me the sense that it was not the Eltrists who necessarily needed to be killed, but the conjurer or conjurers. I asked if anyone had ever killed an Eltrist. The ancient traveler told me that perhaps one could be killed, but who would want to? After that reply, I was left alone in the tavern with only my thoughts."

Breathing in deeply, Ben placed the book down after he'd marked the page by leaving the magnifying glass poking out of it. Just as he did, the front door opened. He couldn't help but jump at the sound. It wasn't that it was loud, but that it was unexpected. Eliza was standing in the hall with reddened eyes and puffy cheeks. Before Eliza could say anything, Ben got up and reached his arms out to her. He knew she was having a hard time with everything, and he wanted her to know that he understood how she was feeling.

Eliza reciprocated, but only she knew how she felt, which made everything a lot worse. She let herself cry for a moment more, before pulling away. Silently, Ben led her back to the living room and put the blankets on the floor.

Eliza was done with talking for the night, but then she noticed Ben's new bandages and couldn't help but erupt into laughter.

"What?" Ben frowned.

"It's nothing really... just love those little duckies." She giggled a bit more, before slowly stopping.

Ben rolled his eyes playfully at her. He thought about telling her about the book, but instead he asked her to lay next to him. Eliza obliged and set an alarm on her phone to wake them in a few hours. Ben left one light on in case Audrey decided she was done with the computer and felt like napping too at any point.

It was easy for Ben to fall asleep. He fell asleep long before Eliza did. Too much lingered in her mind, and more started to form when she saw the book sitting on the couch beside her. Quietly, she reached over and grabbed it. She almost lost the page he had marked, but was able to catch the magnifying glass in her palm with her index finger in the page. Her heart raced as she parted the pages and read what he had read.

When she was done, the magnifying glass went back in the book and she placed it back on the couch, wishing that she had just left it. Eliza cleared her mind as well as she could before closing her eyes. Luckily, her body and mind were too exhausted to fight against sleep this time.

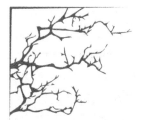

18

A loud musical tune woke Eliza from her slumber, but she woke up smiling, knowing that she had slept next to Ben for the first time in a long time. She turned off her alarm as her eyes slowly opened with ease.

As though she was in a fog, her eyes had trouble adjusting to the room around her. Her smile quickly drifted away like a kite being taken by the wind—the only thing she could think of was grape jelly to describe what she was seeing. Even though Ben was still next to her, his silhouette was hard to make out. The grape jelly was not the normal dark hue that you would see walking down the grocery aisle; this was much lighter. Like peering through a suncatcher. However, if she had to guess what it would feel like to be covered in jelly, this was certainly what she would imagine. When she tried to move, her body even bounced in slow motion.

Frightened, Eliza moved her arms to shake Ben awake, but her fingers could barely leave the bed. In fact, they would not go past the comforter, and when she realized she was trapped, her fingers started to claw at the jelly-like substance. Her fingers began to burn and her fear felt like it was about to swallow her whole. Her body was trapped, but she had to keep trying. Finally, after what felt like hours, she made a small hole that led her to Ben's face.

Ben's eyes remained sealed shut and his body unmoving. Eliza reached to caress his face for the last time, but as soon as her index finger grazed his cheek, his eyelids shot open. Except his once cinnamon colored eyes were now nothing. All that looked back at her was a pair of hollowed-out holes. Holes that oozed with the jelly. Eliza opened her mouth to scream, her lungs instantly filling with the sticky substance. Despite her lungs filling, she kept trying to scream.

Ben didn't respond to her movements. He laid there like a dead corpse. It was clear that no one was coming to save her, so she closed her eyes. The burning sensation started going down her fingertips to her shoulders, and then to her lungs. She gasped like a fish out of water until the pain reached her head and down to her toes.

It was clear her death would be painful, but not as painful as knowing that they had failed to save even one person. The pain responses sent to her brain caused her body to go into shock, and she hoped that it would make her faint, but instead, her brain allowed her enough consciousness to watch as her flesh melted off.

Eliza used all the energy she had left to fight to be closer to Ben. She moved what was left of her limbs to Ben's side. Tears clustered around what would have been her eyelashes. As the last bits of her melted slowly away, Eliza looked down to her lower half. Her stomach, torso, thighs and toes were all just a puddle of muscle and bones.

Ben was nearly completely gone now, so Eliza went to close her eyes, but no eyelids remained. She wondered why her eyes weren't already taken, but knew it could be as punishment. For the first time in a long time, Eliza prayed to any and every god or universe to make death come quickly. Finally, the moments she had left were about to be gone, and she welcomed eternal sleep like the moon greets the stars.

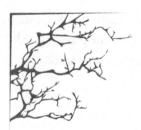

19

A loud musical tone blared out and Eliza jumped up in fright. Quickly moving her hand over to the left of her pillow, she grabbed her phone. As she jabbed the button to turn her alarm off, she stared around the room until she saw Ben. She sighed with relief when she saw his fully intact body before her.

Underneath her wild hair, her once bright hazel eyes now looked like night had overcome them. A dark forest encapsulated her and Ben had no way of knowing if what he saw was misery or rage. At first, Ben thought that she was regretting waking up with him, but a moment later, she brushed her wavy hair out of her face and scooted closer to him. Gently, Ben put his arms around her like a bat sleeping. Eliza's face nuzzled his chest as she calmly said, "We need to get up and go."

Eliza looked almost stoic as she rose—a definite change from the day before. Ben thought about how he would do anything to go back to before any of this happened, but all he could do now was hope that Eliza's heart wouldn't become hardened by everything. Their fate was about to be sealed and Ben knew that stalling wasn't going to change any of it. Given a different reality, he would still be lying next to her at his house and he would have snuck downstairs to the kitchen to make her French toast. Instead, they were about to risk everything for the life of a friend and anyone else who might still be alive.

Ben looked into Eliza's eyes, speaking without words that they would get through this. Eliza nodded, her face still stoic. Ben sat up and looked to see if Audrey had made it to the couch. It was empty, save for the book.

"Audrey!" Ben whispered down the hall. When she didn't reply, Eliza got up and walked to go get her.

Eliza lingered in the hall for a second more than Ben felt comfortable with. He got up and stood beside Eliza, half expecting something to be wrong with Audrey. All they could really see was sandy blond hair splayed out on the keyboard. Ben smirked, which lightened Eliza's serious demeanor a bit.

"You wanna wake her?" Ben suggested to Eliza. He clearly didn't want to be responsible for waking her himself.

"Yeah, I'll do the honors." She snickered. Eliza shook Audrey's shoulders softly, and then a little harder. Finally, Audrey's eyes started to open. She looked at Eliza's face in horror.

"AHHHH! Get back! Get back!" Audrey screamed, waving the keyboard at them. Eliza slapped her face without thinking.

"Audrey, it's Ben and Eliza. Listen to me!" Eliza grabbed her shoulders, noticing a strange symbol on her arm.

"Ben, look!" She pointed to it as she tried restraining her.

It was a circle with an inner star and x marks around it. It looked like it was drawn on.

"Grab something to get it off," Eliza yelled.

Ben grabbed a tissue from the desk and dipped it in the cup of water that was sitting on the desk. As Eliza held her arms behind her, Audrey threw her legs around as Ben began scrubbing the mark off. As the mark faded, Audrey stopped and slumped to the floor.

Eliza knelt in front of Audrey and said softly, "Audrey, do you remember us?"

Audrey nodded her head before it lolled down, along with her shoulders. When she was able to control her body again, her eyes darted around the room in confusion.

"Eliza, Ben. What happened?" she asked.

"You just started freaking out when you saw Eliza. Where did you get that mark that was drawn on you from?" Ben replied.

"Oh, I drew it on myself to remember it. I found it on one of the threads. It said that it was drawn in one of the caves and people believe it was drawn by a witch." She took a deep breath and stood up slowly with the help of Eliza. "I figured if we could find the cave with that symbol, then it might help us find where everyone is. It seems like our best bet."

"Why don't you get yourself ready? We can talk more in the car," Eliza said, while she rubbed Audrey's back.

"Yeah, that sounds like a plan. Give me ten minutes." She walked down the hall to the bathroom.

"Eliza, could you help me gather some stuff from around the house that we might need?" Ben asked.

"Sure, what do you want me to grab?"

"In the kitchen, in the top cabinet above the counter, there are traveling water bottles. Grab at least three and fill them up with the water in the fridge. My mom usually has some clean rags under the sink that could come in handy too."

As Eliza rose from the couch, she nodded and walked to the kitchen. Ben quickly went on a search for flashlights. He knew his mom had at least one in Harper's office. She tried to keep them in separate places in case the power ever went out.

Audrey stepped out from the bathroom and asked Ben if there was anything she could help with. He asked her to go to the hall closet to grab one of Harper's duffle bags.

Ben lingered at the bathroom door and decided to head to the medicine cabinet. He eyed all the usual items inside like his mom's green toothbrush, an almost empty deodorant, but there was nothing here that was useful. As he started to leave, he remembered that there was a first aid kit below the sink that Harper would take with them on camping trips.

The mirror caught his eye before he could reach down to grab the kit. He had yet to look at himself since before his camping trip. The bright yellow ducks on his head caused a slew of giggles. Upon further examination, Ben's laughter came to a halt as he saw the dark bags under his chestnut eyes and his deep brown hair now greasy and bloodied. For the first time, he didn't recognize who stared back at him, and he wasn't willing to find out who he had become just yet, especially since today was sure to transform more than his appearance.

Ben left the bathroom with his head down and his mind heavy.

Eliza was placing the water bottles, rags and some cooking knives into the duffle bag that Audrey had found. Gently, she wrapped each knife in a rag.

"Good idea. We will need some weapons just in case," Ben concluded as he handed over the supplies he'd found. As Eliza placed them in the bag, he gazed around the room, hoping they hadn't forgotten anything.

They could hear Ben's mom snoring upstairs. Ben decided not to wake her, but he wrote her a note and hoped that it would bring her some relief that he was there that morning.

Ben leaned over to Eliza and kissed her cheek. Instantly, she smiled and blushed a bit, but her radiance faded just as quickly. Her face hardened and she parted her lips and said, "Ben, I think we need to stay focused. If things go how I hope they will, we can give this another chance."

Ben knew she was right. There was no debating that their heads needed to be clear and focused on the right thing. "You're right. I'll get my head in the right place and we'll save who we can today." Eliza turned away from Ben like she wished he would have said something else. In all honesty, he wished he had, but today was not a day to overthink. Ben didn't take offense to her body language, but he was grateful when Audrey stood between them.

Audrey looked like she was ready for anything. Her fearless nature was perfect for this situation. Almost too perfect. Like she was preparing for some mythical creature to rain down and try to kill everyone. Heck, after knowing what was going on, it could very likely happen, Ben thought. If he had to bet, Audrey would for sure survive this. She had her blond hair up in a ponytail and a bright red umbrella in her hand that had a silver metal point at the end. It was one of those ones that made a bubble when you opened it. It wasn't raining out, so Ben wondered why she had grabbed Harper's umbrella in the first place.

The umbrella had been bought in Ireland by Ben's mother. Her and Harper had gone on a trip there after Ben had moved out. Harper had said that they would be fine with a cheap umbrella that he'd gotten from a discount store, but after a couple of days of rain, his umbrella had broken.

The story went that Harper and Ben's mother had been walking back to their hotel after going to one of the restaurants in Dublin for dinner.

It hadn't been raining when they'd first left, but after about five minutes of walking, it had become an all-out downpour. Harper had taken the umbrella out of his pocket and placed it over them. Sadly, after less than a minute, the wind had picked up and blown the umbrella up, showing all its insides. Of course, this made it quite useless. Ben's mother had started to wail with laughter and Harper had soon joined in. After that, they'd bought a much more durable umbrella. It was a cute story they would remind Ben of any time he was over while it was raining. They would look at each other and snicker. It did seem like a funny situation, but probably one you would have had to be a part of to find the humor in over and over again as they did.

"You two ready?" Audrey asked, eyeing both of them.

They replied, "Yes," at the same time. Audrey shook her head approvingly and walked towards the door.

Audrey pointed up the stairs and whispered, "Should we say goodbye?"

Ben shook his head and whispered back, "I think I've given her enough stress. She needs the rest and I've already left her a note."

The three of them walked out the door, knowing that this could be the end. Ben lingered outside for a final glance at his loving mother's home, who he hoped with all his being he would see again. Before he knew it, he was starting the engine of his car, about to change their lives forever.

20

As he ran, every aching bone told him to stop, but after a while, he saw a tiny light shining in front of him. A bit of hope ignited a spark in his body to continue on, but the closer he ran to the light, the more discouraged he became. The light didn't grow much larger and was only about the size of a dollar bill, which clearly showed him it was not a way out. His body stopped abruptly at the light that was coming from the ground below him. It was not what he had expected to see—a phone. It had a long crack down the middle but looked like it was still working, at least to some extent. The growing amount of missed calls and texts had caused the phone to illuminate like a beacon.

With shaking hands, Theodore scrolled through the phone to find who owned it, but he didn't recognize anyone messaging or calling the stranger. He instinctively turned on the flashlight button and turned around to see if anything was lurking behind him. To his relief, he saw nothing but stone. The battery flashed red, and he knew before it would be too late, he had to call someone, anyone, for help. Aching the whole way, he made it to the side of the cave and leant up against it. He thought about letting his body sink to the cold ground, but doubted he would have the strength to get back up.

With his heart rate slowly going down, he relaxed. His throat was on fire and it screamed at him for water. All he could do was ignore his needs and hope that whoever he called would answer. When he dialed the last person who'd called the phone, the bars on the phone went down to none. His heart sank. He felt around his pants pocket to see if he still had his phone, but nothing was there.

His head lolled to the side, pressing hard against the black stone. The ridges hurt his cheek, but the cold outweighed the pain. The cold calmed his body. He turned the flashlight off and put the phone on battery saving mode. He saw no one else in the cave and wondered why the creature had allowed him to run away. Surely, there was no way that he would have been capable of outrunning it.

His eyelids fluttered the more his head rested. He strained to keep them open, before ultimately pulling his head back up. With his body shaking, he walked and walked and walked. The more he walked, the more his heart raced, his breathing became heavier, his throat sorer and his mind more uneasy.

Up ahead, he could make out what looked like a large body of water. Little ripples moved in the liquid, and he tried to move faster so he could drink from it. He pulled out the phone and turned the flashlight on. When he approached it, he saw that the water was not clear at all. It was filled with a purple liquid and what he saw would bring him nightmares for the rest of his days. The phone fell to his feet as he forced his hands over his mouth to not scream and jumped back in terror. He stumbled to pick up the phone and shine the bit of light it illuminated.

Like a curious child, he turned back to the grisly sight to make sure what he'd seen wasn't his eyes playing tricks on him. Unfortunately, his eyes had told the truth of dead bodies bobbing around like apples in water. The gelatin-like substance left bits of muscle and bone next to its victims. There was no way to know how many people were in there, and he wasn't planning on sticking around to count. His stomach started churning and his body convulsed as he began to retch. Not much came out, since he hadn't eaten in so long.

Turning the light away from the tunnel, he saw there was another one to the left and decided to go down it. He figured that any other place in the cave would be better than this one. The cave was so quiet, but his feet stepping and heart pounding made him feel like he might as well have had an alarm with him.

He looked down at the phone to see if there was any service, but a small circle with a sideways line crossed through showed he didn't. He would have to go back to where he'd been to make a call, or keep checking to see if another area had service. He chose the latter. The tunnel was starting to warm up and his palms began to sweat. He was beginning to think that the creature didn't care where he went because this was its home, and if he wasn't ready to eat him or throw him in the pool of liquid, it would let him think that he could escape until then.

His legs stopped no matter how many times he told his brain to make them move, so he tried to work on relaxing his heart rate, but his body fell to the ground from exhaustion and his eyes shut.

A dripping sound woke him. He struggled to open his eyes all the way, but then he saw what was in front of him and his eyelids shot open. A creature with large pointed teeth and lots of saliva, or something like saliva, dripping down its jaw. It screamed at him in a guttural "GROOAAAW" type noise. Its eyes opened wide and he saw they were as yellow as a lemon. The irises weren't normal either. They were in the shape of an upside down triangle. He feared that those eyes would be ingrained in his memory for all his years, or more likely, the minutes to come.

The creature did not harm him, to his surprise, and in his loss of thoughts, he started to hear another noise. The sound tickled his ears and taunted his brain. It called to him. As much as he tried to fight it, his body moved without his want and his feet started to walk. From his torso to his head, he swayed and bent in the opposite direction. But his feet kept shuffling forward, despite his juxtaposition. His world was about to end, but apparently his bottom half wasn't told.

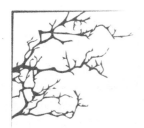

21

Gripping the steering wheel tightly, the engine roared, and before they knew it, the highway was already before them. The headlights casted shadows onto the jade leaves that speckled the dark road that was just beginning to see the sunrise. The cascade of green almost made Ben forget about the ancient creatures that had raised chaos in his town. But as the leaves settled, he came back to reality. He briefly looked to Eliza, who was reading one of the other books they'd brought. Maybe he was looking for hope in her eyes. In truth, he could have taken her intense calmness as that, but he was curious. He didn't notice the pain that carried in her eyes.

Audrey found Ben's body language odd. Odd in the sense that one of his hands wasn't gripping Eliza's tightly. When she looked at Eliza's face, she could tell that both of them were off, but she imagined that she seemed off too. They were all running towards danger, instead of fleeing from it like most sane people.

Ben brushed his hair back from his face and cleared his throat. Audrey turned away from looking out the window and raised her eyebrow at Eliza. "Before we get to the forest, I want to talk about some stuff that I read in that *Eltrist* book."

Eliza darted her eyes towards him and closed the book in her hands. She already knew what he was going to say before the words left his lips, but it wasn't something she wanted to hear. All she could think about was that another stone would fall from her internal bridge. Too many stones had already broken away, like her time was about to be up.

Ben paid no attention to Eliza's intense reaction. He imagined that her mind was going through so much that eventually, like his had, it would make it through the fog and reality would set in. "I found this interesting section in the book, where the author claims that he met with someone he referred to as the ancient traveler, who knew the creatures on a personal level almost. Apparently, the purple liquid is called "strug" and they use it to eat." Ben tapped his index finger on the wheel and sighed. "But that might not be the most important part. Apparently, the creatures can be summoned here by someone powerful enough and they can then use their strug to become immortal."

Audrey scrunched her face in disgust. "So, it's possible that a witch or something like that could have brought them here?"

Ben brushed his hair back as he said, "Yeah, I think that's pretty likely. It did say that they could come when they wanted, but usually didn't take out entire towns then. The author had this idea though that if you could just kill the conjurer, they would stop coming."

Eliza stared out the window like she was daydreaming about anywhere else. Audrey said, "So, we should find the conjurer?"

"Do we have any leads besides Taylor?" Eliza asked.

"Eliza, didn't you get a strange call from Wyatt?" Ben added.

"I did, but I doubt it was anything. It could have just been accidental."

"So, if someone did summon them here, that means we have to kill them. How do we kill a powerful and possibly immortal being?" Ben asked, curious as to what they could do.

"Well, we could always use methods that have previously been used to kill witches? An option would be to use fire, unless you have a better plan? I'm not saying I like it or anything, but someone is purposely allowing the Eltrists to murder our friends for their own personal gain," Audrey retorted.

"I don't think the witches who burned at the stake were actual witches. At least not the majority, so that doesn't really prove that it would work," Ben said.

"If they haven't taken more strug yet, they could be killed," Eliza chimed in.

"How do you know that they need to take more?" Audrey interrogated.

Without missing a beat, Eliza replied, "I read the page Ben had saved last night in the book."

Audrey relaxed a bit and thought that she shouldn't have questioned Eliza. She knew that Eliza wouldn't hide anything that would hurt her. They had been friends as long as Eliza had lived there, and she had no plans of dismantling that friendship now.

A sign larger than the town's read HARTHSBURG NATIONAL FOREST. The letters had been carved into the wood and a cascading waterfall was painted underneath. No longer did Ben smile at the sign like he had done for so many years, instead, when he saw it, he took a deep breath and bit his lip, knowing now that there was no turning back.

As Ben took a sharp turn to follow the winding road into the forest's entrance, Audrey began looking through the notes that she had made late last night. The symbol that she'd marked on her arm was drawn there. It could have been that the symbol was just random and a couple of punk teenagers had graffitied it on the cave wall, but that couldn't explain Audrey's strange possession.

She wanted to memorize the directions in case the worst happened and her phone got lost, ran out of charge or she wouldn't have time to look at it. As Audrey repeated in her head the directions, Ben pulled into what he would have assumed would have been an empty parking lot. They were all surprised to see a couple of other cars parked there. A small brown hatchback was parked at the far end, and Audrey couldn't shake the feeling that she knew who owned it.

"Eliza, what kind of car does Wyatt have?"

"I've honestly never seen him drive, but that is definitely Gerald's car," she said as she pointed to the brown hatchback.

"Gerald's? Does that mean he came to search too?" Ben said.

"I hope not, but it does seem that way, doesn't it?" Audrey replied.

The other car was a candy apple red SUV that none of them recognized, but they doubted it was a coincidence that it was here. Especially with how Ben had described the state of the park. One look at it would have had anyone driving the other way. They all took a deep breath; it was like for a moment they were all in sync.

Audrey studied the cars, but she couldn't decide what it meant. "Well, no need to prolong this any longer," Audrey opened her car door and got out, only to be startled by a sudden gust of wind. Dark green leaves danced around her and she shooed them away. Ben chuckled at her reaction as he and Eliza got out of the car too. His hands rested on the roof of the car, while his mind contemplated what to say to Eliza. She stared off into the distance, in the same direction as him, but she had much different worries on her mind. Before she turned around to face him, Ben took his arms down and closed his door.

For Audrey, she thought about what could be. If Theodore was found dead, then she would never forgive herself for not allowing him into her life. She wondered if he would even consider being together if they managed to save him. There was a very real chance he could end up as a completely different person after this. Audrey was quite sure that she had already changed, but to what extent, she wasn't sure of yet.

When Audrey saw Ben staring at Eliza, she jokingly said, "You lovebirds ready?"

Audrey was happy about what they had found with one another, but she couldn't help still feeling a bit jealous. She didn't want to hold her jealousy to any great lengths and let it devour her from within though. Audrey knew that if their lives were switched, Eliza would be happy for her. Probably not even jealous at all. Instead, she would say what she always said about people who had found the one. She would be overwhelmed with happiness for her friend and wish them many years of bliss.

Ben walked to the back passenger side of the car to grab the duffel bag and then popped the trunk open, gently brushing his slightly disheveled hair out of his face. There was a black backpack, random T-shirts, a towel and some tools inside. Ben grabbed the backpack and placed what was in the duffel bag into it. When he got to the knives, he handed one to Eliza, one to Audrey and put one aside for himself.

"We don't know if the knives will do anything to the Eltrists, but use them anyway. Let's try to save who we can and then get the fuck out," Ben gruffed.

Audrey let the cold steel of the carving knife gently scrape against her palm. Allowing the knife to tease her nerves before pulling it away, she knew that it would kill easily. She held her breath when she realized that it would kill easily if it were human, but without a doubt, she knew they weren't dealing with a human. As she locked away her dangerous thoughts, she let her eyes shut for a moment, before putting her brave face back on.

Eliza held a large silver chef's knife that she examined with uncertainty. When Audrey spotted her expression, she hoped for her sake that she wouldn't need to use it. Ben held an older looking and slightly rusted boning knife that was the smallest of the knives, but unlike Audrey and Eliza, he chose not to look at his weapon. He simply put it in his back pocket.

Audrey had almost forgotten about the umbrella she had taken from Gwen's. When she grabbed the handle, she smirked at it and stuck it into her hip belt loop, causing it to gently grace the ground as she took a step. The umbrella was long, but Audrey was quite tall, so it only slightly bothered her.

Ben slammed the trunk shut and slung the backpack over his shoulders. He looked at Eliza once more with a sense of longing in his eyes, before quickly looking away and asking Audrey, "Where to?"

Audrey was already looking at her notes, still making sure she was absorbing all the information she could just in case something happened to her phone. It wasn't like she hadn't seen a horror movie before, and she was thinking of all the what-ifs in her head.

"Alright, it says to take the Rockbridge Trail, which will lead us to the first cave. It's not on the trail, but it will get us as close as possible before we have to veer off."

"Is this the cave with the symbol you wrote on your arm?" Eliza asked.

"Yeah, I figured that one was our best bet. I still don't understand what the symbol could mean. Did you find the symbol anywhere, Eliza?"

"I didn't see it in the books, but with how it made you react, I'm going to go with it isn't a pleasant meaning," Eliza said solemnly.

Ben started to push them along the path by waving his hands towards it. "We can walk and talk," he said in a half-serious, half-playful manner.

It was hard to imagine what they'd find lurking in the cave, and they all were in more of a denial phase as they walked down the path. Audrey started to daydream about double dates with her and Theodore, and Ben and Eliza. She was imagining a warm summer's day in the woods on a camping trip. But then she thought about what Ben had witnessed in this same forest just the other day and the trauma it had more than likely caused him. Audrey begrudgingly let her mind drift back to the present.

The path was abundant with leaves and small pebbles that gave the simple dirt path a lot of personality. The three friends walked in silence as the only sound around them came from the crunching of the earth under their feet.

After about ten minutes of walking and only hearing footsteps and the wind from time to time, Audrey decided that she needed something to calm her nerves. A little bit of talking would help the suspense that was weighing heavily on not just her, but she assumed all of them.

"So, uh, what time did you get back, Eliza?" Audrey asked.

Eliza's fingers twitched as she replied, "I'm not entirely sure, but I don't think I was gone too long."

Audrey looked to Ben for him to confirm, but all he did was shrug his shoulders.

It felt like she was talking to one of the pebbles, so she dropped the conversation. To their surprise, Ben asked Eliza, "How was your walk?"

"Oh, it was fine. I didn't go too far, but it was a much-needed stroll."

Audrey scrunched her forehead like she wasn't convinced she'd had a good time walking alone in the dark. Ben too sensed Eliza was holding something back, but now wasn't the time to pry it out of her.

"Look over there!" Eliza pointed to the right and winced.

As Ben and Audrey turned toward where she was pointing, they saw before them the trees dripping in lavender hues strung up like lights. Audrey couldn't help but think that although it was lethal, it was also quite beautiful as it dripped slowly down. The subtle glow off it made the leaves glisten, and Audrey almost mentioned the beauty in such a dangerous thing, but she refrained as she got a surge of reality. A reality that she could be glamorizing the very thing that could soon or had already killed Theodore.

"Audrey, are we close to where we need to leave the trail?" Ben asked.

Audrey turned her gaze away forcibly, before responding, "What...? Oh no, we still have another mile before we go off the path. So... not really."

"Let's just be careful where we step now," Eliza stated.

"Right. We won't have to deal with the "strug" stuff if we stay on the path, by the looks of it." Ben had raised his hands and done the whole air quote sign with his fingers as he'd said the word "strug."

"I agree," Eliza responded.

The deeper they walked into the forest, the more strug appeared around them. The path remained a false sense of security. The majority of strug never touched the path and that eased their minds enough to continue.

A blue jay was led in the middle of the trail with a fate that was hard for all of them to witness. It appeared the bird had flown into the forest, only to have its wings cast in a lavender glow. Its chest would rise and then fall at an unprecedented rate, but in its eyes was acceptance, despite its body's reaction to the impending doom.

As its wings dissolved into nothing, the three of them gathered around the poor bird. There was no way of saving it. For the first time since being back in the forest, they all saw what danger awaited them. Ben grabbed a rock that was next to the path. He hesitated before smashing it down onto the bird's body. The blow killed it instantly. Eliza and Audrey said nothing, but patted his shoulder. Ben glared at the rock before tossing the rock to the side.

Quietly, Eliza stepped around the bird, and Ben and Audrey followed. Their lack of speech didn't change the closer they got to the cave. It was apparent that their moods had dropped after seeing the bird. The bird wasn't the last defenseless animal who they saw utterly devoured by the strug, and the deeper into the forest they went, the more frequent pools of strug were surrounding them.

Even the plants and trees had started to ache in pain. The leaves were all melted, followed by bits of the trees, leaving them partially naked. Their once outer protection had been consumed by the strug, and they awaited a slow painful death to the rest of their insides.

It was apparent that unless they could stop what was happening, their town would too make the list of "towns that disappeared by unknown forces."

As Audrey walked past the next pool of strug, her stomach started to churn, and painful cramps zoomed around her abdomen. Although Audrey was brave and willing to fight to the death, she knew that there was a very real chance that she would see things soon that would bring her nightmares for the rest of her life, if she even survived this. With a quick glance over her shoulder, she stared at her two friends, hoping that they too were just as afraid as she was. However, when she looked back, she saw quite the opposite.

Ben looked ready for a fight, and surprisingly, so did Eliza. Their faces looked set in stone. "See that large rock ahead?" Audrey pointed to a boulder that had to be about four or five feet tall with rough lines etched in blues and reds. Their eyes followed Audrey's hand to look at the rock. "This is where we leave the path."

"How much longer from here, Audrey?" Ben asked.

"Probably about ten minutes or less."

As they proceeded off the trail, Audrey could feel her fear bubbling inside her more and more. The only thing she could think to do was talk. Of course, she didn't want to talk about being afraid. No, she wanted to talk about anything that would keep her fear from growing any larger. So, as Audrey fiddled with a small hole in her pocket, she began a story that Ben hadn't had the pleasure of hearing yet, at least to her knowledge.

"Remember that day in April when we ditched work with Theodore?" Audrey asked with a smile.

Eliza beamed at the memory, and replied, "Of course I do. You guys both bribed me into it."

"That may be true, but that is exactly why you keep me around. I always make sure you have some fun in your life!" Audrey jokingly nudged Eliza's shoulder and she giggled in response, shaking her head.

"Okay, get it out. What happened?" Ben let out, snickering.

"I don't know, Ben. It might ruin the perfect image you have of Eliza. We wouldn't want to do that, right?" Audrey's smile was wicked. Wickedly happy.

"Oh, hush, Audrey. I didn't do anything that bad. I guess out of character a bit, but a girl has to break out of her shell sometimes. Right, Ben?" Eliza bit her lip and smiled playfully at Ben.

"Yeah, of course," Ben exclaimed, putting his arm over Eliza as he waited to hear the story.

"Well, Theodore came to me with surprise tickets to see that band The Peculiars. It was a last-minute secret show, I guess, and we convinced Eliza to leave work too. We all told Gerald that we had come down with a cold at the same time. Remember Gerald's face?" Audrey laughed.

Eliza let out a boisterous laugh before replying, "Yes, he looked so worried and sent us straight home. He probably thought that we had infected the whole office."

"So, we left and all met up at Theodore's place. He thought it would be fun to have a few beers before heading there." Ben's face squinted at her before she could say, "Don't worry, Ben, we called a cab to take us to the concert."

"Eliza here is not much of a drinker, but Theodore and I enjoy a beer together a few times a week. Anyway, that's beside the point. So, we had about an hour or so before the concert, and before we knew it little Eliza here has gotten pretty tipsy. That has to have been the only time I've ever seen you get a buzz." Audrey looked at Eliza to confirm her statement.

"Yeah and probably will be the last. Although, if we make it out of here today, I think a couple of drinks would be just fine. In fact, needed."

Audrey nodded. "So, we get in the cab, and Eliza starts singing. And I mean like in a loud, drunk girl singing way."

"I was serenading the cab driver!" Eliza joked.

Ben looked down at her and smirked.

"Theodore and I knew at that moment we were going to have a fun night." Audrey smiled so wide you would have thought it would stay glued that way. "The cab driver thought that Eliza was so "good" at singing that he didn't even charge us for the ride. Although, I assume it was because he thought you were quite gorgeous and funny. You know, he did slip me his number to give to you when we got out."

"What? You never told me that!" Eliza gave Audrey a playful pat on her back.

"Yeah, I figured I would save you the embarrassment, plus that guy was so not your type. He was probably in his late forties."

"Yuck!" Eliza said.

"What, you didn't want to date an older man who loved your singing talent?" Ben laughed. Eliza stuck her tongue out and pushed his arm away. He laughed a bit and then brought her back to him. She willingly accepted the embrace.

"So, we get to the concert and Eliza is still in her singing mood. Now, I knew that the only reason she let us convince her to come was due to her obsession with the band. I didn't know the extent of the obsession, but everyone in that room was soon made aware." Eliza rolled her eyes at Audrey. Audrey felt so much joy flowing through her that she'd almost forgotten they were very likely walking towards their demise; exactly what she'd been aiming for.

"The lead singer... what's his name?" Audrey asked, losing her train of thought as they passed a very dead rabbit. At least, what she assumed to be a rabbit because it's long ears and fluffy, white, round tail were all that remained.

"Peter," Eliza chimed.

Audrey shifted her gaze and continued, "Yes, yes, Peter! So, Peter noticed Eliza singing her lungs out in the crowd. Granted, she at least knew all the words, even if she sounded a little tone deaf." Ben chuckled hard at that, while Eliza hardened her eyes at the two of them but smiled all the same.

"Just as they were about to start playing their last song, they asked Eliza to come up on stage and sing with them. The only people who were annoyed with her were the girls who were jealous. Everyone else clapped and cheered." Ben gave a big smile to Eliza at that. "Eliza started to sing with them while holding an almost empty beer can. What was the song?"

"Forget the Lost Times," Eliza said.

"Oh, yeah. Great song," Ben replied.

"Great song," Eliza agreed.

"About halfway through the song, Peter got real close. He put his microphone right between her and his lips. Apparently, Eliza took that as an invitation."

With wide eyes and a smirk, Ben said, "Is that so?"

"She grabbed his shirt and pulled his lips to hers. The crowd, including Theodore and I, went wild! We were clapping and shouting. The best part though is that Peter totally accepted and brought her down like you see in those romantic movies where the couple is dancing and the guy sways the girl down and kisses her."

"Wow, Eliza. I didn't know you were already taken, and by someone half famous too!" Ben joked.

"Yup. Peter and I are actually together. Sorry, Ben," Eliza joked back.

"I believe Eliza ended up turning him down later though. Isn't that right?" Audrey recalled.

"Yeah, we went out a few times after, but my sober self didn't seem to connect with him that well."

"Well, that's a relief," Ben said, and in one swift motion, he took Eliza and draped her head down and kissed her with the most passion Audrey had ever seen.

"Alright, alright. Come on, you two," Audrey said, rolling her eyes.

Eliza opened her eyes at Ben, and Audrey couldn't help but feel happy for her. As Audrey watched the two, she felt like she was watching her best friend fall in love right before her eyes. It was the strangest of times, because if they were being honest with themselves, they had death sentences carved into them. But she thought that at least one or two of them should be able to enjoy these last hours, moments or seconds that they had left.

Ben smirked and pulled her back to reality. Eliza got her breath back and Audrey swore she saw a twinkle in her eye. "So, was it like that?"

Eliza shook her head. "No, that was a million times better."

A moment more was all it took for them to make it to the cave. As their footsteps stopped, so did their laughter. It faded away like the sound of a bird's wings fleeting. The menacing cave stood in front of them, dripping with strug. The trees that surrounded them were becoming no more than ghostly shadows.

Audrey stumbled back when she noticed the strug dripped down like melting icicles and there was no way to know when a drop would fall. The strug twinkled in the sun's rays and some had grass and dirt inside of it. At that moment, it was clear they had found the right cave—the cave that was surely housing their friends and neighbors who more than likely were wasting away into nothing, much like the animals they had seen on the way here.

Bravely, Audrey walked to the side to peer into the dark depths. Sure enough, etched in some sort of red ink, was a circle with an inner star and x marks around it, just like the one she had drawn on her own arm. The ink or paint used had dripped down, making the star's points look like they were bleeding. Just as Audrey was about to touch it, Eliza shouted for her to stop. Eliza caught her hand and moved her away from the symbol.

Audrey didn't fight her on it, and she calmly moved back to join Ben, who was standing a few feet away.

"I'm pretty sure this is the right cave. The strug and the symbol seem convincing. How do we want to go about this?" Audrey asked.

"Do either of you have cell service?" Eliza asked.

Ben and Audrey pulled out their phones, while Eliza grabbed hers from her back pocket.

"Mine is pretty weak. I think once we get inside, we won't have service at all." Ben's voice sounded hollow.

"Mine is the same. I don't think they will help us once we are in," Audrey said.

"Okay, then we need to develop some sort of plan for if we get split up," Eliza replied.

"Your mom has some markers she's let me borrow. They glow in the dark. I have four of them. I think we could make some markings going in, and if we get split up, let's all agree to follow the marks back to here. Unless we find a spot inside, we will adjust it to that location or get the hell out of the cave," Audrey suggested.

"That works. What do you think, Eliza?" Ben asked.

Eliza glowered at the lavender strug that lined the entrance of the cave. She nodded to Ben, but kept her eyes locked on the dripping orbs.

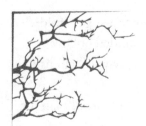

22

Alone. The only feeling Eliza could feel at the moment. Even standing next to her friends, she knew that if anything, it only made her feel it more. The type of alone you felt when you had a secret that would only make matters worse, so you swallowed it whole and hoped that it was as heavy as a boulder in your gut.

There was no time for hugs, words of encouragement or goodbyes. Eliza walked into the towering cave like she was being devoured. Out of impulse, Ben went to reach out for her to stop, but instead, Audrey caught his hand and yanked him into the cave to follow Eliza. While Audrey pulled, Ben looked up to see them barely escape a sticky piece of strug that splattered onto the ground behind them. With his heart racing, his back crept to the wall of the cave, hoping that he could keep his mind from signaling him to retreat.

His body successfully refrained, and Audrey helped him to move away from the jagged edges of the cave. Eliza was now several steps ahead, letting her knife lead her forward. She walked with purpose, making sure that each step was as quiet as her controlled breathing. Curiously, Audrey watched her continue ahead like she was watching a predator waiting to strike.

Their eyes struggled to adjust to the darkness, so Audrey turned on the flashlight on her phone. Eliza seemed to realize that she was walking too quickly and slowed her pace to join her friends in the light. As they rounded a turn, their shoes dipped into a small puddle and a chilly air crept around them. The puddle flowed down into the obsidian tunnel. It was apparent that it was water and not strug from the way it flowed, but it still caused Ben to cringe every time he saw anything but rock.

When the cave began to narrow, the air felt heavier, and a feeling of claustrophobia seeped into Ben. He had never really felt constrained from being in a tight space before, but then again, he had never felt so afraid of what might be lurking in front of him either.

To Ben's relief, a wide opening lay ahead, and he quietly sighed. However, when he looked around at the hollowed-out arches, his relief disappeared into the shadows. Audrey moved her light around and counted how many tunnels there were, while Eliza looked at the small stream that flowed beneath their feet. There were four new tunnels, each as dark as onyx and as unknown as the creatures they were trying to avoid.

Audrey looked away from the tunnels and bit her lip, before subtly saying, "shit" under her breath. Ben turned on his flashlight, stopping at a stalactite that was dripping water almost melodiously. Possibly in a trance, Ben's eyes transfixed on the droplets, and for a moment, he forgot the fear that had been pounding in his chest.

Eliza stated quite matter of factly, "We have to split up."

Her cold tone brought Ben out of his trance, and Audrey stared at him with her jaw clenched.

"You can't be serious, can you?" Ben asked, baffled.

"Eliza, are you sure you want to go alone?" Audrey spoke to her like a protective big sister.

"Yes, unless we all want to waste time by following the same tunnel that could turn out to be a dead end. I have a weapon, my flashlight and spotty cell service. But I'm hoping if one of us needs some help, a loud scream should suffice."

Eliza placed her hands on her hips and raised her head as though she were a queen dictating a hard but right decision. When Audrey stared back at her friend, she realized that something had changed inside of her. Eliza was never the one to take charge in most settings, but today Audrey stood in wonderment of her. She began to contemplate if she knew Eliza as well as she thought, or if something inside of her had finally caught fire. Whatever it was, Audrey stayed speechless for several moments; something that Audrey rarely did.

Ben took her decision as final and agreed with her, but that didn't mean he had to like it.

"It's a good plan, but I think we should have an hour tops. After that hour is up, we should head back here. We can check in, and if we don't find that we are all here, we will come searching. Keep using your markers too. It will be easier to find each other that way," he replied.

Audrey scoffed at Ben's reply and turned her back to them, before putting her head down to take a nice long breath. "Well, fuck. I guess I'm the odd one out. So, let's get this shit over with."

"Audrey, please don't be mad," Eliza replied sincerely.

"Nope, not mad. I just think this plan's a death wish. We would be stronger together than apart, but sure, let's journey alone into tunnels we've never been down before that could very well have Eltrists in them," Audrey said sarcastically.

"We don't have time for this, and we don't have time to journey through each tunnel together. If we can get one person out alive, that will be a win at this point. Taylor said we have to move fast. This is our best option, even if I don't like it," Ben said.

Audrey glared at Ben, but not in a pissed off way, in more of a you better be right or else we are all fucked type of way.

Letting her loose curls fall in front of her face, she shook her head. When she looked back up, she was more frustrated than she'd ever been before and replied, "Yeah, don't forget to mark where you go. Scream if you need us, or if your cell phone miraculously starts to work, try to call or text and hopefully one of us will get it. I'll do the same." Audrey stepped over to a tunnel that was on the right middle. "This one looks grand. I'll take it."

"I'll take the one on the left," Eliza replied, ignoring Audrey's eye roll.

"Ben, which one do you want—the upper left or the far right?" Eliza asked.

His hand rose to brush away his dark hair, but really, it wasn't covering his face. It was a nervous response. He panned his flashlight down both his options, wishing he knew what was at the end of each. Of course, he couldn't know which one was the better choice, but he couldn't deny the nagging feeling of which one was calling to him either. That calling made him want to deny it and go down the other tunnel, yet he wondered if the tug was due to it being the safer choice. The tunnel that would in fact save his dear friend, and even other townspeople.

For that reason, he made his final answer. "I'll go in the upper left one. Let's hope everyone isn't in that other tunnel," he said, brushing his hair away one more time.

Ben thought that if he'd chosen where the monsters were, at least it wouldn't be Eliza or Audrey who had to subject themselves to death by one. His heart raced when Eliza grabbed his hand lovingly and placed it on her heart. When her hand let go, Ben's fell almost in slow motion, like it was being carried down by a calm stream.

As though he was in a nightmare, he watched her walk into the tunnel without looking back. A jolt of raw fear clawed at his insides, but as the shocks of reality slowly drifted, his cold eyelids closed and opened. Audrey looked anxious and thought about approaching Ben one more time, but instead, she sighed and also disappeared into her own onyx tunnel.

Ben stood alone in the cave, more frightened than he thought possible. But after seeing his two friends depart without letting that fear cripple them, he knew he had to journey down his own tunnel. So, off Ben went, alone, and hopeful that he could be a hero.

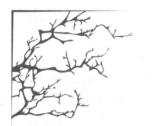

23

Her heart pounded, but not out of fear for her life. She knew more or less how it would end for her. No, her heart pounded with fear of what would ensue with the bond she had created with her friends. Her head tilted towards the ground, bobbing as though it was hardly attached to her neck. She aimlessly held up her marker and marked the wall as she went, like it was pointless to mark where she was going, but nonetheless, she continued to mark every several feet.

The flashes came and went of Eliza's dream. Almost inhuman, Eliza stretched her head back up, cocked it to the side and rolled it, while shivers ran down her spine. Ben's disfigured face was like a stain in her thoughts. No matter how much she shook her head, closed her eyes or tried to ignore it, the image stayed as clear as the first day she'd met Ben.

Her car had broken down in the middle of the highway. Luckily for her, it wasn't a busy time of day. Ben's was the first car she'd seen in the half an hour that she'd tried pushing her car out of the way, cursing the whole time. She was mostly unsuccessful in her attempts, but nonetheless, she still tried.

When she'd first heard his engine roaring behind her, she'd jumped. Almost afraid of any other sound than the wind blowing or the songbirds singing. The Chevelle had come to an abrupt stop. Ben had stared at her, almost mesmerized, as the wind had curved her dark hair around her face. Eliza had walked over to the driver side, and Ben, unsure of who she was, couldn't help but roll his window down.

As soon as she'd explained her car troubles, Ben had helped push her car to the side of the road and gave her a ride back into town. They'd talked like old friends the whole way and Ben had been quick to ask to see her again. Eliza had hesitated at first, but eventually agreed. Since then, she'd always felt an instant connection to him. She was hoping that her mind would haze into that first moment, but the nightmare stayed as alive in her mind as her own reality of walking alone in the cave was.

She kept blinking, hoping that her mind would grow foggy around the nightmare, but it remained for the next several minutes as she wandered down the dark, narrow tunnel.

It wasn't until Eliza found something in the middle of her tunnel that her mind cleared of Ben's horrific body. A thumb. Nothing more, just a thumb sitting in one of the side crevices. No purple goo was on it, so Eliza assumed that the rest of the body had now melted completely, leaving only this measly thumb behind. Instead of feeling fear, she thought about how strange thumbs looked. The mere stubbly size was quite odd as it laid all alone and fairly pathetic looking. Before she continued past it, she took a deep breath.

As she turned her flashlight up the sides of the tunnel and back to the center, a noise made her drop her phone, but she very quickly caught it before it hit the ground. Her feet stopped moving as though she was a scared deer standing motionless in front of a car at night. Her light was pressed firmly against her chest, her breath was held and she pushed her body as close to the side of the cave as she could. Her eyes closed as she listened for the noise to come again, but all she could hear was her own heartbeat.

After a few moments passed of listening to her heartbeat, she moved her light around and all she could see was the dark rock surrounding her. The tunnel was getting wider, but she didn't realize the path was coming to an end until she almost plunged to her death. Her feet clung to the last piece of rock that stood before a massive drop to a body of water. Frightened, she backed away from the ledge, causing pebbles to plunge. The sound of them hitting the water was as quiet as leaves falling to the ground in autumn. The only noise she could hear came from herself.

Before she could leave, she knew she had to make sure no one was down there. After all, it was the only reason they'd entered this dangerous cave. Cautiously, she crept back to the edge and faced her light to the bottom, with minimal cursing to herself. As she moved her flashlight around, the light refracted into the dark mass, but she still couldn't see anything resembling a human, or even an animal for that matter.

Still, she called out, "ANYONE DOWN THERE?"

Her voice bounced off the walls, making a harmonious sound. After hearing her echo finish, she waited patiently for any type of response. The water seemed still, and no noises responded back to her. She decided to go back the way she'd came and continue down the last tunnel that none of them chose.

The minutes that passed felt like hours and her eyes were sick of staring into the dark, but she knew that this journey wouldn't be a quick and definitely not painless one. Finally, she saw the last of her glow in the dark markings as she advanced back into the last place she'd seen Ben.

Neither Audrey nor Ben were back in the main part of the cave. A part of her had hoped they would have been there and ready to get the hell out, but since no one was, she stared at the last tunnel. Rubbing her cheek with uncertainty, she got down on the ground in the center and wrote with her marker, "*Tunnel dead end. Right next. -Eliza.*"

After wiping the dirt off her jeans, that in all reality she couldn't see well enough to even know if it was there, she cocked her head at the tunnel like she thought it would tell her something by just looking at it. When nothing seemed to happen, she drifted into the darkness.

Eliza had almost forgotten to mark the new tunnel, but she assumed it was a better late than not at all type of situation. Unfortunately for her, this tunnel had its drawbacks. While the other tunnel had at least four feet of room, this tunnel had close to half that. The air was thick and humid and much harder to breathe. She knew she could breathe, but it was an uncomfortable feeling knowing that the oxygen might get too thin at any moment.

The ground flowed like an ocean in a storm beneath her feet. It was the most uneven surface she had ever trekked and she wondered what could have caused such a rough surface to form. As she continued on, the tunnel started to twist into a sharp curve. Sucking in her stomach and turning to the side was the only way she could continue through. A part of the side rock still managed to slice through her shirt at her navel, leaving an inch-long wound. She couldn't help but wince at the dagger-like edge when it pierced through her. There was nothing on her that could clean the wound, but she could, for the time being, pretend it wasn't there.

Thankfully, the tunnel opened about a foot more and she hoped that the air wouldn't feel so heavy on her lungs now. The tunnel led her to a wider area where Audrey and Ben could have comfortably walked side by side with her. Her head looked to both sides as though she could see the ghost versions of her friends walking silently with her.

Soft drops of blood pierced through her shirt and continued to drip like a faucet that hadn't been done up tight enough.

Eliza's body flung forward like a penguin sliding on ice, but not nearly as graceful, and not as fun or painless, as she tripped over a piece of stalagmite. Her face stopped right before a puddle of iridescent purple goo—strug.

She fumbled around to find where her phone had flung to. It happened to be only about three inches away from her and she reached out, still flat on the ground, to grab it. As she shone her light in front of her, the purple sparkled. A very pretty, yet oh so deadly sight.

Laughing at her fall, she sprung up and looked around the area. To the right of her, she could see a large body of water. She was sure that she would find the dead in it. Despite her certainty, she continued to the pool and gazed inside.

There were bodies all in the water, or what used to be water. It was now filled with strug and loose body parts, just waiting to turn to nothing. There was no way to tell how much blood filled the pool, but she could see the strug bubbling. Her eyes squinted at the poor lifeless pieces, but she continued to gaze at what floated, hoping that it was no one she knew.

Peering over it, she could only see two faces that remained partially intact. Both looked to be males, based on their facial structures. One had an oval face with a pronounced chin and no eyes left. The other had one brown eye left and a chubby face. Neither of them looked familiar.

Just as she turned away, a loud, guttural growl echoed behind her. As she jumped in surprise, she guessed that it was far from her, but it still sent chills down her spine. She turned her light down the other tunnels leading further into the cave and saw nothing. There were two of them, and without making a fuss, she decided to go down the closest one to her.

As she was about to disappear into the tunnel, she froze. Out of the corner of her eye, she saw movement. What that movement was, she wasn't sure, but she felt like it was a threat. Her heart picked up its pace as she turned around. What she saw caused her disbelief.

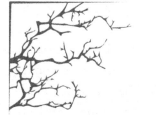

24

Spiders. Ben had never been that fond of them, but he also wasn't necessarily scared of them. In this situation, however, he found everything to be causing his heart to beat faster than it should, but it wasn't enough to keep him from trying to find his friend. He wondered if the girls were also battling spiderwebs and eight-legged masterminds. He had no idea what type of spiders were hiding in the crevices, but he was grateful that he was at least given the gift of a wide tunnel.

The webs had taken over so much that when his light cast on the sides of the tunnel, large shadows of giant webs were projected on the ground in front of him. He assumed, for his sanity, that the spiders were not dangerous ones. In this scenario, even if they were, they would not be the most dangerous things in this cave.

His mind kept drifting to memories prior to the last couple of days. He welcomed the thoughts like he would a blanket on a cold night. The memories jumbled around. First, he thought about trips with Harper and wondered for the first time why he had never called him "Dad." He knew it didn't have to do with when he'd came into his life, since he had been so young, but it almost made him upset at himself for not doing so. Harper had never acted like it hurt him, but now he wondered if he had hidden the pain of raising a child that didn't give him the title of Father.

Ben guessed that deep down inside of him, he had felt the word was somehow tainted. And all that blame would go to his biological "father." Harper had been more of a father to him than anyone, and a better father than most. He hoped that he'd known that and would ask his mother about it if he were to make it out alive.

As his thoughts drifted back to more happy memories, he realized that the cave was almost too straight. He'd assumed there would be a lot of twists and turns, but he had to have been walking in an almost perfectly straight line. The twists and turns never came, and he became suspicious of the path. There was no good reason for him to analyze the cave structure, but there he was analyzing anyway.

Being alone makes your mind go to some weird places—places that normally would stay hidden underneath all the saner ideas—and Ben was only another victim of it.

Just ahead, he spotted a shadowy figure, much larger than a spider. He hoped that his eyes weren't playing tricks on him and that it was Theodore waiting to be rescued.

He continued on, cautiously though, and held his knife tightly at his side in case it was an Eltrist lurking in front of him. A person was in front of him, a mere few feet away, crouched down on the icy ground. Ben ran up to them, but they didn't move. He shined his light on the body, fearing that he was too late. When his light hit the person's face, they jumped up in fear and shouted, "Who's there?"

"Oh... no way. Gerald, is that you?" he asked, surprised.

The man stumbled back and was shaking. Ben cautiously stepped closer to him. "I'm here to help."

His arm raised to block the light, before saying, "Could you lower your light?"

"Sorry, yeah. It's Ben. We met the other day. I can't believe I found you."

Gerlad stepped closer to Ben. His face brightened. "Ben, yes... yes, I remember. The one Eliza was so fond of."

Ben chuckled a bit and said, "Yes, the same one. Are you okay? Audrey and Eliza are also searching for survivors to get them out of here."

"Oh, Ben, you shouldn't have come. So many are dead. I managed to escape from the main area, but I'm pretty sure someone we thought was a friend is partially behind all this," he said in a grave voice.

"Who?"

"Wyatt. He just sat and watched as the window burst and each of us was snatched up by these... these huge dragon things." Gerald raised his hands up as wide as he could get them, while his arms shook. "We were all so confused. We thought he had been possessed or something." His voice quivered.

"The monsters came?"

"Yes, about six of them." He stopped to peer to the side of him, as though he was peering through a window. He continued with, "Wyatt wanted them to take us. I remember seeing a grin the size of a watermelon spreading across his face as I rose off the ground in horror."

All Ben could think to say was, "But why?"

"There must be some benefit for him. Or he's not really Wyatt?"

"When we left, we found some books, and after reading them and what you've just said, it's possible that he's summoning them here for immortality."

Gerald face paled, and Ben immediately regretted oversharing with him. He couldn't imagine what he was going through at this moment and hoped he would never find out.

Ben finished with, "Well, I can explain more later after I get you to safety."

"I can't leave the others!" he said just above a whisper.

"You've seen more?" he asked, his eyes wide and full of hope.

"Yes, at least ten."

"Have you seen Theo?" Ben felt almost ashamed to ask about him instead of just wanting to get everyone out.

"No, I haven't seen him. Sorry."

Gerald placed a hand on Ben's shoulder, but Ben couldn't believe that he was gone just yet. For now, he needed to stay focused on who was currently alive that they knew of.

"Can you take me to them?"

Gerald nodded his head and they journeyed through the hole.

It was a vast space. His flashlight couldn't even reach where the walls were. Then he saw them. A group of people huddled, weeping together. More were standing alone, just waiting to die or waiting to wake up from this nightmare that couldn't possibly be a reality. All of them had the same marks on their backs and blood stains from where the El-trist's had grabbed them to take them here.

As Ben looked around, he felt much less like a hero; in-stead, he felt so afraid that he wanted to turn back and run. Seeing all the people taken made him realize what a night-mare this was. He wondered how he could be a savior in all this. He knew that he would never forget the torment on their faces. It would stay branded in his brain forever.

"Everyone let's get out of her. I know the way out," Ben said, his voice sounding hoarse.

A voice cried out in sheer happiness, and then the group of people came towards him. There were a few hesitant ones that stayed away. "Please we have to go now." Ben called to them. A few more got up and followed the others out of the tunnel. Gerald was able to convince the last few people to come with him. Ben didn't pay too much attention to the faces he saw walk past him because he knew that not one of them would be Theo, and all they did was remind him that he was more than likely now just a puddle of strug.

As Ben watched the last few people go into the tunnel, Gerald held off for a moment. Ben was about to tell him how to get out and to go on ahead and that he would follow behind, when a familiar voice greeted him. Only, he wasn't a friend by any definition of the word. Gerald stopped and looked back towards Ben.

"Follow the glowing markings. You'll reach a big area that will lead you to a tunnel directly below this one. Take that and you'll end up outside. Look for footsteps and follow them to a large rock that's right next to an actual path. That path will lead you to the parking lot."

Gerald nodded his head, and then asked, "Where are we?"

"Harthsburg National Forest."

Gerald hesitated.

"Go. Save yourself and the others," Ben urged.

With one last look at Ben, Gerald pushed the group forward. Ben watched them leave, knowing that Gerald would get them to safety, but not knowing if he would be so lucky himself. He knew Gerald would be able to be the leader they needed.

"Oh, Ben. Is that you?" the voice cackled.

"Who's asking?" Ben glared into the darkness, knowing full well that no one could see his menacing look.

"Come to the sound of my voice," the voice cooed.

"Can't you come to me? You can see my light, can't you?" Ben said, irritated with his game, but also not ready to face him.

"If that's what you really want?"

Before Ben could respond, Wyatt stepped directly in front of him, or at least he thought it was him. Wyatt no longer had bags under his eyes or thin skin that looked more gray than light brown. He looked as though twenty years had just been reversed, or they had time traveled back to when he was a young adult, which Ben seriously doubted. Even his hair flowed like he had just been to a salon, and when he smiled at Ben, his teeth gleamed a white sheen instead of the coffee-stained yellow he'd previously had.

"So, the stories are true then?"

"Oh, have you been reading?" He smirked.

"Glad you've found humor in me. What is your problem anyway? Is killing people really worth it?"

"Oh, my dear, yes. Every last drop. I get to have an almost untouched body and just a few measly people have to die for it. And the beasties get to feed too. This is a treat for them really."

"How old are you?" Ben said, clutching his hands into fists.

"Let's see, I called the Eltrists to me when I was a mere twenty-six and I lost count after a hundred years. I always return to my twenties when they get to feed again, and, you know, I think that Eliza and Audrey would be smitten with me. Especially Eliza." He snickered.

"Why would they give a shit about a murderer?" Ben replied.

Wyatt stroked Ben's cheek with his index finger and said, "Oh, you really don't know, do you? I assumed that she might have let you in on her little secret by now."

Ben stumbled back from him, too confused to reply.

He laughed. One of those laughs that makes you want to punch the living shit out of someone. Ben slipped his knife out, and without much thought, shoved it directly into Wyatt's belly. Wyatt's eyes were like fire when he pulled the knife out and chucked it into the darkness. He put his hand over his wound, bleeding through his fingers.

"You're fucking lucky that my rejuvenation has already begun. I will heal from this. In the meantime though..." Wyatt placed his fingers in his mouth to whistle. "While I get some rest, I hope my winged beasts will keep you comfortable."

And just like that, Wyatt was gone. Loud thuds vibrated the tiny rocks beneath Ben's shoes. The sound of ragged breathing filled the room and Ben quickly looked to where Wyatt had thrown his knife. Thankfully, he spotted it, grabbed it and ran down the tunnel he'd came through. He left his mind blank, except for the word "RUN" flashing in his head like a red neon sign.

25

Audrey cursed the whole way and repeated in her mind how stupid they were to split up. She already had guilt for a hypothetical situation in which Eliza was to die. She knew that she would forever blame herself for that death, and Audrey wasn't sure if she could live with herself if that were to ensue.

As she crept down the tunnel, sounds would echo off the rocks randomly, but they didn't sound threatening, so she ignored them. She assumed it was water dripping down the cavern ceilings, or perhaps some animals who lived in the cave. Either way, she wasn't scared of the noises.

It was clear that the tunnel wouldn't be that difficult of one, until about five minutes in where it changed. In a moment, she would have to suck in her stomach and anything else she could squeeze in to continue. The jagged walls had left little room for error, and so far, she had managed to get by unscathed.

Her light flashed ahead, and her feet stopped suddenly just before she walked into a serrated piece of rock that poked out far enough to impale her, above a large stone that laid in the path. Before she continued, she made sure that she could maneuver her body properly to avoid injury.

As she pulled herself up on top of the rock, she twisted her body to the side. The rock was only a couple feet wide, and to hop down would be hard with avoiding the jagged sides. She shimmied to the side and turned to face forward as much as possible before jumping down. Audrey looked at her stomach, hoping that it wouldn't have a gash in it. She ruffled through her shirt, and still no cuts were to be seen. Audrey turned to the sharp rock and put her hands up to it like she had won in a fight.

Once Audrey felt like the rock had been put in its place, she continued. The tunnel began to open back up and began to decline more. Her lungs thanked the little bit of extra air they were receiving. The faint echoes she was hearing from time to time now sounded like they were only a few yards away. Her hand shook as she moved her light toward the noise, but it was still in the distance, and she saw nothing but dark walls all around her.

Quietly, she cursed and forced her body to keep moving. She repeated under her breath, "Theodore will be up ahead." As her mind relaxed back to her previous mental state, her right shoe stuck to the ground. Audrey looked at her foot like she was disappointed with it. The substance was strong, and the more she pulled, the less successful she was. She half suspected her body would get dragged away at that very moment, like she had seen in countless movies.

Since she had no way of freeing herself, she decided to go on without her shoe. It wasn't something she had considered happening, but it definitely wasn't the worst thing that could have happened either. She hoped this wasn't a sign for what was to come. The chilly ground clung to her foot like an icicle. She hadn't realized how cold it was in the cave, but her foot now knew. Cautiously, she continued, hearing the noises grow louder. Now she was sure that they were the sounds of dripping, but what was dripping she was unsure of.

A mere few minutes later, she was at the end of her tunnel and strug reflected off her light. As her light bled into a new part of the cave, she crouched down, hoping to seem less of a threat to anyone if they were in there.

As her light moved around the cavern, she immediately placed her light into her pocket and her hands rose to her mouth like a magnet to hold in the amount of screams her body wanted to produce. Eltrists were slumbering around the room. As they hummed in their sleep, their mouths hung slightly open and their spiked tails curled around their fluffy bodies like tendrils. Audrey could just about see how sharp their teeth were. She imagined that they could tear through a car quite easily.

Brave is what Audrey chose to be. A surprise even to herself as she took out her light and peeked around the room. She hoped that she could save someone in the room, but she found only Eltrists and another tunnel opposite her. As she thought about the tunnel, she assumed that that was where all the prisoners would be. Why else would the Eltrists all be there, except to guard their food?

Of course, this would be no easy feat for her, and an Eltrist was just in front of it. She thought that if she went back, this would all have been for nothing. No, she knew she couldn't turn back empty-handed. Her socked foot stepped into the Eltrists' lair first, and it was clear that she wouldn't need her flashlight the closer she got to them because they glowed. Her hand stayed fixed to her mouth when she took her next step, and the next and the next.

The first Eltrist was so close to her that she could compare their sizes. Its face was larger than her whole body, and Audrey was not short in stature. In fact, she had had many men who were too scared to date her because of her height.

Tiny horns protruded out of their foreheads that were maybe as long as her fingers. They didn't look terribly sharp, but nonetheless, she wouldn't want to get rammed by them. Each one had their own markings and colors on their fur. The one closest to the tunnel's entrance had a mostly white coat with patches of dirty yellow and dark purple ovals. The one next to him had all brown fur and seemed to be enjoying its dream by the smile it had plastered on its furry face. It was probably dreaming about all the people it would eat once it woke up from dreamland. Ghastly creatures, but they were an enchanting sight to see, regardless of their appetites. Their whole torsos glowed in a magnificent lavender.

As she got closer to the tunnel, she realized she would have to step over the white one's tail that was at least two feet wide at the largest part. Audrey moved down to the tip of its tail and decided that was where she would cross. Its tail had bumpy charcoal protrusions that swelled all over it in a spiral pattern. Carefully, she analyzed the best way to hop over and took her first step in sheer panic.

Panic that was luckily locked away in her insides. When her foot made it over successfully, she balanced to get the other one over. With a small leap, she cleared it. If she hadn't been worried about getting eaten at any moment, she might have done a victory dance, but this wasn't the right time.

Maybe later when she wasn't in danger of becoming some-one's lunch.

She started towards the tunnel and was just in the clear when it happened. Her shoe kicked a rock that bounced down the tunnel, causing an echo the whole way. Audrey froze with her eyes closed, before opening one eye and peer-ing over her shoulder. This time, she yelled, and not under her breath, "FUCK!"

Run.

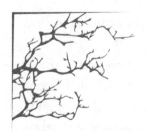

26

A slender man, about six feet tall, with tattered, and what once was a professional champagne colored button-up that was now stained with dirt and blood, stood staring at Eliza. He was the exact person that she wanted to see. Hope filled her very bones.

"Theodore? Is that really you?" she called, straining her eyes to see. The ghostly version of the man walked in the opposite direction from her. Again, she called his name, but it was like he was in a trance. She ran over to him and grabbed his shoulder, which she immediately regretted. His body whipped around and looked at her with wide eyes and his jaw hanging open like a pelican about to feed.

"Brother, are... are you okay? It's Eliza... your sister," she said, stumbling over her words.

As if in a drunken stupor, he replied, "Eliza. Yes, yes." His long arms reached out to grab her, but he only caught the air. His legs stayed planted in place, unwilling to move in the direction in which his torso hoped it would.

"What happened to you?" she asked. She had her theory, and she was sure that it was similar to what had taken over Ben.

"I'm honestly not sure. Eliza, please help me!" Again, his arm reached out, but this time, Eliza grabbed his hand—something she hadn't done since they were children. She let him lead, so she wouldn't harm him.

"Of course, I will fix this," Eliza said as his body moved quickly down the tunnel in which she'd came. "At least this is the way I came in. This goes towards the exit. I bet I could drag you out of the tunnel, even if your body wants to move another way, once we get to the main area."

"Why did you come?" His voice quivered a bit.

For a second, she saw a glimmer in his eye, but he blinked and it faded away. Pools of tears stayed in her eyelids, while she tried her hardest to keep them from flowing down.

"Ben came looking for you; Audrey is also here. You knew I would come for you. When we get out of this, I am taking us home."

"Ben and Audrey are here?" Theodore shouted. He eyed his sister with disappointment. "How could you let them come? You know what the Eltrists are capable of. I mean, I'm happy Audrey would want to come and save me, but I don't want her dead! You know what she means to me." His glare could have burned through her soul if it was capable.

Eliza bowed her head. "I'm sorry, Brother. The only way I could have kept them from coming was if I'd told them everything. I couldn't do it. I thought maybe we could save other people and you and that would make up for what I've done."

Grabbing Eliza's chin, he looked her dead in the eyes like a parent concerned for their child. "Little Sister, I under-stand the unfortunate situation that we have been given, but we must make decisions that are best for those we care about. Perhaps we have stayed here too long." As his body continued to pull him like he had an imaginary rope around him, Theodore contemplated what they could do now.

Eliza glared off into the distance, before saying, "Theodore, listen... Wyatt is responsible for all of this. He has turned against us."

"I suspected that he wasn't here to make amends. You know what this means, right?" Theodore whispered.

"You're not suggesting that he wants to start a war?" Eliza muttered, like she was trying to piece together a puzzle.

"That's exactly what I am suggesting. You saw how mad he was when his contract was up and Dad wouldn't renew it. He wants to do more than be an ambassador between us and the Eltrists. He wants power, and I can guarantee you that if the Eltrists want to use him as a sign of war, they will."

"I was hoping this was just some temper tantrum, like one last time he could make his potion for immortality. I think you are right, Brother. Why else would he have them take you, if not for war?"

Theodore nodded, his eyes hardened with wrath. "We have to get word to our parents. They might not know that Wyatt has struck a deal with the Eltrists. If I can't make it to Folengower, please go without me. Tell them that the Eltrists have declared war and taken me as prisoner, and that Wyatt is helping them. If Wyatt wasn't here to summon them, we could have stayed hidden."

A frown grew on Eliza's face as she contemplated her brother's words. Her long fingers caressed her cheek, before her eyes twinkled with surprise like she had just cracked the mystery. "Maybe Mom and Dad knew that a war was coming? It would make more sense than telling us that we had death threats from someone. I mean, it's been years, and they supposedly still haven't found out who was making them? No, they probably knew there was an Eltrist uprising and wanted to protect us."

"That does sound like something our dear old dad would do," Theodore sneered.

Just as his eyes rolled, his body changed course. Eliza focused on following him closely, and they both stopped their conversation. Eliza remembered that Ben had also been under some sort of trance, but he had been able to be broken free from it.

"Theodore, do you think you could concentrate at all? I think I have a plan to stop this enchantment on you."

He sighed. "I'm not sure. I am pretty weak right now. I can try though."

Eliza slid around to the front of him and placed one of her hands on his chest. His body was trying to twist and turn to get around her hand.

"Okay, tell your body that you aren't following where it wants you to go. Repeat over and over in your head. I'll try to hold you back to help."

Theodore took a deep breath and closed his eyes. She could see his mouth shake as he recited to himself what she assumed was something close to what she had told him to. Heat from his body radiated into her palm. She kept her feet solid on the ground, but it didn't help her from sliding backward.

"Clear your mind."

"I'm trying!" he shouted.

Moving her hand off his chest, she said, "Sorry. I am just trying to help."

Instead of replying to Eliza, Theodore's eyelids blanketed over his eyes. Eliza stared at him and realized how much he had already changed. Dark bags hung underneath his eyes with what many would have assumed were freckles, but Eliza knew that he didn't have any. It was more likely that the dots were dirt or blood.

Eliza again placed her hand in front of him, almost testing what he would allow. His eyes opened, and he didn't swat her hand away. Instead, he allowed his body to move forward as it had previously, and Eliza walked backwards in front of him. He gained pace, while her feet stumbled over rocks. Not enough to make her fall, but she was one rock away from that happening.

Just as she was about to fall, he stopped. Her whole body almost toppled to the ground, but she balanced herself just in time. Eliza gazed up at Theodore, hopeful. When his body didn't continue, she shouted, "It worked!"

But just as the words floated out from between her lips, she noticed that something was very wrong. Her smile melted. Theodore didn't look like Theodore anymore. A grin appeared on his face, but it was not one that she had seen her brother make before. Again, her heartbeat rose. Her hands fell from him, her head turned away and her mind started to orchestrate hopelessness.

Even his eyes gleamed in a way that she had never seen from him before, which caused chills to go down her spine and bumps to rise on her skin. Silence filled the cavern, while Theodore stayed grinning at her, moving forward. His body was fully upright this time, and he glided past Eliza like a calm stream. As though he was trying to be seductive, he gently brushed her shoulder with his, turned his eyes to her and smirked. Eliza glared at his new demeanor, and hoped that her brother was still very much alive in there somewhere.

Eliza had an inkling of what was happening to him, but she wasn't sure how to fix it. Eliza stared at the ground in defeat—something that she hadn't done since she was a child. The mess that they were in was beginning to feel so out of her reach to solve, and she knew she needed the real Theodore back to mend the pieces.

When she didn't follow him, he wasn't impressed. Quietly, his feet stopped moving and glided back towards her. Holding his hand out, he spoke barely above a whisper, "My dear Eliza, please join me." His voice wasn't scared anymore and the way he spoke to her was not something she'd expected. He wasn't usually sly like this. Eliza knew that the warm slur of her name that flowed out as sweet as sap seeping from an elder tree was no sweeter than she was calm.

Despite every nerve in her body telling her to refrain from following him, she knew that if she declined, she was allowing him to perish, and allowing him—really not him, but who was controlling him—to be cruel to her. Forcing her body to accept, she reached her hand out and pursed her lips together. Once he grabbed her hand, he led her down the corridor like they were about to ballroom dance.

Eliza thought it was best that they were going back towards the entrance, but she wondered for what ill reason. Briefly, she focused on how cold his hand was, and dirty, no doubt. As though tiny fragments of rock were scraping against her palm, she tried to wipe her hand, but Theodore's grip was so tight she didn't want to try any harder and make him angry.

27

A glimmering yellow eye gazed into the tunnel at Audrey. As it breathed heavily in her direction, her palms started to sweat, and she began subconsciously scratching at her fingertips. She dared not look at it, but she knew she could only avert her eyes away for a short time before her curiosity would get the better of her. Its entire head was larger than the whole of the tunnel, which was a relief to Audrey in a way, but not enough to keep her mind from thinking of all the ways it could probably still kill her. Somewhat surprisingly, she thought that dying by strug would be the worst way to go.When Audrey gave in and stared at the Eltrist, her eyes instantly transfixed to the yellow like she was in a trance. They were the dusk right before the sun came fully up.

Audrey raised her flashlight with her sweaty hand to try and break her trance. Its eyes twinkled and blinked twice as it scrunched its face in annoyance. When it blinked, Audrey did too, allowing her to refocus and look away. Instead, she focused on its white fur that glowed with the faintest hues of purple. The glow rippled through strands like she was watching the aurora borealis.

Despite the sheer size of the Eltrist that glared back at her, the idiosyncrasy of the creature was mesmerizing. Audrey gave the tiniest grin when she began to imagine what their babies would look like. She imagined a fluffy, glowing ball, with tiny wings and big eyes that would make anyone melt when they stared into them—much like puppy dog eyes. Her imagination stopped instantly when the monster let out a horrid growl from its wide, dripping strug mouth, causing her to quiver. It was a fierce growl and she wondered if it would echo past her for ages until it reached the very darkest parts of the cave.

All it took was one roar for all the other sleeping Eltrists to rise and stomp over to her not so great hiding place. As the ground vibrated beneath her feet, small pebbles danced around them. Audrey's body had done exactly the opposite of what she needed, as it stayed in shock, her feet cemented on the cold ground. Just when her courage was about to allow her to run far away down the tunnel, her body was swept up by the Eltrist's tail. It twisted around her like a boa constrictor, with its odd bumps digging underneath her ribs. She was thankful that they were smooth and not sharp, but it was still painful. Audrey squirmed in its grasp, but she couldn't grab her knife with both her arms squeezed to her sides.

Audrey contemplated biting the creature, but she relented when she saw the hues of purple swirling around inside its fur. There was no way of knowing if she would get strug in her mouth. She had no plans on being poisoned, so she ignored the urge. Instead, her arms flailed around like a fish out of water. Not the most graceful spectacle, but she had no other real options. When her body grew tired, she was quite sure that this would be the last moments of her life.

No, Audrey wasn't someone who would just give up. Anger bubbled deep down, her breathing quickened and her eyes closed. Audrey stopped moving. Her head lolled to the side and rested atop its soft fur. Despite how she looked, she was far from dead and hoping that her plan of playing dead would work. She had heard of it working on animals, and if it could work on them, she assumed monsters could be tricked too.

The giant tail led her to the center of the cave and dropped her without a care. Despite her heart pounding, she dared not move, not breathe, not think of doing anything stupid. Audrey let her mind drift to a faraway place.

She imagined herself relaxing on the beach with a cold beer in her hand, listening to the sounds of waves crashing. When she looked up, Theodore, Eliza and Ben had all joined her. While they laughed playfully, Audrey went to speak, but nothing came out. No matter how hard she tried, not a whisper left her lips, and her friends acted as though she didn't even exist. Audrey let the daydream fade away and clenched her teeth—even they couldn't put her mind at ease.

As her eyelids lifted a smidge, she realized that the situation was worse than she'd thought. She had hoped that they would forget her, but to her horror, a circle of Eltrists surrounded her. Their faces snarled at the body laid before them.

Audrey shut her eyes to try and stop her body from shaking with fear. After listening to hushed noises, she opened her right eye just enough to see their mouths gaping open. When she looked to the next Eltrist, she realized that they were communicating to each other. It was a curious sight, and she couldn't help but watch their exchange. It was almost like they were playing the Telephone game. The one where you tell one person something and then they tell the person next to them. You should end up with what the first person whispered, but instead, the game always gets muddled to something different. She wondered if they also would mutter inconsistencies. Although their mumbling noises were incomprehensible, she still tried to listen.

Strug slowly dripped down their teeth and onto the ground like toddlers during a teething frenzy. It was now obvious that none of them were paying any attention to Audrey. When she realized this, she decided to take the chance to sneak out, hopefully undetected.

Her leg moved an inch, then her torso, and finally her head. With her heart beating at what felt like a humming-bird's wings speed, she stopped and checked to see if any of them had noticed her movements yet. For a second, she froze, thinking that one of them had, but he was just raising his paw to wipe some strug off his chest that had gotten stuck in his thick, gray fur.

She continued inching away, stopping periodically to make sure they hadn't noticed how much she'd moved. It was when she made it next to one of their paws that she couldn't help but gulp. The exit was in sight. All she had to do was squeeze between the Eltrist's legs and haul ass to the tunnel that had brought her into their den. As quietly as she could, she army crawled underneath and made it to the other side.

Holding her breath, she looked back. Her hands were trembling and her body pumping more adrenaline than she had ever felt in her whole life. None of them swayed at her exiting the circle. She took that as a sign to continue quietly to the tunnel for fear of them hearing her footsteps as she ran. They could swipe her up with little to no effort. Her heart started to echo in her mind and she feared that they would be able to hear the beats growing louder. She had about two feet left to the tunnel.

Audrey quietly cursed when a sharp rock tore into her shoeless foot. Blood wetted her sock and her eyes went as wide as a full moon when she noticed their hushed noises had stopped. Bravely, she looked back, only to find a sea of yellow eyes angrily watching her.

Just as one came trudging towards her to swipe her up, she reached for the umbrella and clicked it open. It was a good thing that Audrey wasn't superstitious, or perhaps she didn't count caves as indoor. If anything, her action allowed her to get to her feet, while they looked at her confused.

Confusion wasn't a bad thing, she thought, as she ran toward the tunnel. The one with black fur reached out to her, but Audrey pushed the point of her umbrella into its paw. The penetration caused a thick and dark tar-like substance to seep out. The creature whimpered and held its wound close to its chest with its other paw cradling it. From the creature's reaction, she started to wonder if it had never felt pain before, or if it was just shocked that a human could cause them harm.

Its eyes squinted down at her with rage glowing brightly in them and its jaw opened hungrily. She moved just in time to escape a drop of strug that was falling fast. The strug had some steam coming off it and it fizzled as it hit the ground. The Eltrist put its paw out again to grab her, but, again, she opened the umbrella and used it as a shield and stabbed it.

As more black tar flowed out, it whimpered again. The others looked on, surprised.

She stepped back and then ran forward a few steps in a hi-yah stance and opened the umbrella again like she was trying to scare off a raccoon or other small creature. They backed up in confusion. Everyone in the room, including Audrey, was at a standstill and a little bewildered from the whole situation. It was almost comical to Audrey, but she refrained from laughing at this moment when she was very close to becoming a gourmet fried human.

An Eltrist with brown fur started toward her. She saw their movement out the corner of her eye and decided not to turn toward it. She wanted it to think that she didn't see it. Slowly, it went around the black Eltrist that stood before her, and she jumped up and turned to the right. Her umbrella opened gloriously wide again. As though she were a knight, she stretched out her arm like she had a sword instead of an umbrella.

Quickly, it moved back, but not fast enough. Its stomach now had a small cut in it. Some of its fur stuck to the point. The winged beast's eyes looked like they were giant gumballs about to pop out of its head. Unlike the other Eltrist, this one was instantly angry and swiped again at her. Her free hand reached down and took her knife out.

The knife tore through the beast's paw like it was nothing more than warm berry pie. The black tar stained its fur and piled together in blotches. Its cold eyes darted up and Audrey turned on her heel, looking up at the brown Eltrist. Audrey followed his eyes to the ceiling, and her mouth gaped open. As though she was peering down a well, a large hole was carved into the ceiling. A glowing body started to descend down it. Its furry body landed several feet away from her. Out of the corner of her eye she saw movement from the Eltrist she was fighting. Its stocky tail swung towards her, and she jumped over it like she was back in elementary school playing jump rope.

Her arms swung at it, and she was able to pierce its tail with both the umbrella shield and her knife. Two small puncture wounds were marked on its tail. Her little attempt at saving her life was about to be cut short when another Eltrist, who was standing in the back, became bored of her displays of bravery. Audrey made a run for the tunnel and slid under the legs of one of them like a guitarist at a show shredding. As her legs folded back, she picked herself up, and a smile ran across her face as she dove into the tunnel.

That was until she felt it. The warm sensation trickled down her back. Her head turned to look, and she dropped her now slightly mangled umbrella and knife to the ground. Her fingertips reached her shoulder blade and felt the warm liquid of her own blood running down them. Her body delayed the pain, but she knew it had torn through her skin like a surgeon's knife. Quick and clean.

While she stared at her hand in shock, she heard chatter. Her head turned and looked back at the Eltrist grinning at her with one claw held up. It dripped with bright red blood, like it was taunting her.

Her eyes grew wide with fury, her nostrils flared and she picked up her knife and shook it at them. She wanted to go back in there and end each one of them, but she knew that it would only be a death sentence for her. Instead, she turned and walked away into the darkness, hoping that she wouldn't bleed out.

28

Eliza held Theodore's hand reluctantly for the most part. The smaller part of her was happy to be reunited with her brother again. As they walked, her hand quivered as he periodically smirked and rambled on about things that Eliza only ignored. Each syllable made the hairs on Eliza's head stand up.

They were now close to where they had all split up, and Eliza hoped that at least one of them would be waiting for her there.

Audrey limped to the tunnel's exit in hopes of finding the others. She had thought about retrieving her shoe as she'd passed it, but that would have taken more energy than she had left, so instead, she flipped it off. The tunnel felt like it went on for miles. When in fact, it was not that long of a journey back. But being injured and alone could definitely add minutes, even hours, onto the mind.

Finally, the exit was in sight for Audrey. Chatter could be heard, and lots of it. She hoped that one of her friends had been victorious in their mission. At last, light cascaded through the tunnel. A few more steps and the tunnel would end.

At the same moment, Ben was running tirelessly for another day of life. He wasn't in any immediate danger, but that could change at any moment. Sweat beaded down his brow. With a knife in hand, several new spiderwebs were cut down—more than he'd thought existed when he'd first went through. He was now not far behind the people he hoped he'd saved.

Ben could see a light bouncing off the walls and heard a faint voice call down to him. The voice shouted at him to hurry. It repeated again and again. Ben ran like an Eltrist was close behind. It took a few more seconds for a hand to reach his. A smile fluttered at who stood before him. Many faces were gathered in the wide room. Several were vacating the cave and waving goodbye. They ran quickly out. Ben hoped that they would make it far, far away from here. Then the greatest thing that could have happened, happened. They all were staring at each other once again in the very spot they'd departed from.

Ben spoke first. "Eliza? Theodore..." he said, perplexed. He turned his head as Audrey joined them with bloodied hands. "Audrey! What happened?"

With a hoarse voice, she replied, "Well, the short version is that my tunnel went to a bunch of sleeping Eltrists. Although, my dumb ass woke them up, and right before I escaped, one got me." Audrey turned around to show her bleeding back. Her breathing was rough and she was trying to relax her body.

Gerald, who'd surprisingly never made it out of the cave, examined her wound. Gerald cut part of his shirt with Ben's knife. "Audrey, I'm going to wrap this around your shoulder to help stop the bleeding," he said calmly.

Audrey turned her back to him and winced when he placed the warm fabric over her shoulder and underneath her armpit. He tied the piece together as tightly as he could. The gray shirt turned a crimson hue. It was clear that the shirt would only help the blood from flooding. How much time they had was another story.

When her eyes reached Theodore's, for the first time in a long time, her eyes welled up and tears gently dripped down. She even let out a laugh like they had really done it. They had saved him. But when she hurried to him and put her arms around him, he didn't reciprocate. In fact, he continued holding Eliza's hand and wouldn't let go. He curled his lip, and Audrey knew that something was wrong. He smirked at Audrey and stayed silent.

"Theodore, it's me—Audrey! What's going on?" Her eyes shifted to Eliza for an explanation. Eliza held her shoulders up and shook her head in confusion. Ben's fears were confirmed. He had noticed the hand holding when he'd first came in and wasn't sure what to think, but now he wanted to grab Eliza away from him. He began to march up to her, but she caught on to his body language and motioned with her other hand to stay back. Ben looked hurt, but his emotions were too strong to handle the situation with sanity.

"Now that we are all present, you should all follow me to the gathering ceremony." Theodore spoke excitedly in a voice that wasn't his. His eye sparkled, and he reached down and lifted Eliza's hand to kiss it. Eliza's initial reaction was to pull away, but then she felt that the consequence of her doing so could put everyone in danger.

Ben and Gerald exchanged looks and it was clear that they wanted to formulate a diversion, since Theodore was obviously not himself. "Actually, we were all about to leave. Can you come with us, Theodore?" Ben said as nonchalant as possible.

Theodore's eyes darted to his old friend with cold and vengeful eyes that he had never seen from him before. His friend was long gone. He saw no piece of him left, except for the outer flesh that stood before them. Gerald, who had worked with him for many years, looked at him with distaste for the first time. Audrey was lost in confusion and sadness. There was no way of knowing what had happened to him.

Eliza, on the other hand, had an idea of what was happening, but she had no idea how to get that message across with her fake brother watching and listening to them.

"Ben, while I appreciate what you wanted to do, there has been a change in your plans. I will be leading us to the ceremony. Honestly, you would regret not seeing it," he snickered.

Unsurprisingly, Ben's eyes danced with flames. His anger was flaring up over losing his friend, possibly for forever; Eliza potentially being hurt; and poor Audrey losing a close friend, if not more.

"Alright, you've had your fun. I'll be taking Eliza, Audrey and Gerald with me. Now, if Theodore is actually around, I would love to take him with us as well," he snarled.

"Honestly, this was what you wanted, wasn't it? To find your friend? You went through all this trouble and only saved a couple of handfuls of people. Well, this is what you get. I'm Theodore." He turned his head as though an audience were to the side of him, while he grinned. "At least, the new and improved version." He stopped to itch his head, and when he raised his left arm, he revealed an interesting mark on his forearm. Only Gerald saw it. It piqued his curiosity because he knew that Theodore didn't have a tattoo there. He highly doubted that he had randomly gotten one the day before he was taken.

Theodore scratched his head more and blood stained his fingertips. Audrey wrinkled her nose and scrunched her eyebrows at the display. Audrey eyed Ben with her distaste and then stared directly into Eliza's eyes. Eliza was relieved that they had seen what he was doing.

As he stared at his friend, Ben wondered sadly if he had strug in his head like he'd had. He felt a tug of control when it was inside him, and he hoped that this wasn't what the end result would have been if it had never vacated. Theodore was now just a puppet in this ever-growing, complicated and confusing situation. Audrey ran over to him to tackle him, but Theodore threw her off him with superhuman strength. It was like he'd flicked an ant off his shirt. Eliza tried to pull away from him, but he held her hand tighter.

"You listen to me. I will release you when it's time. For now, you will stay in my sight and at my side at all times. Do you understand?" he said to Eliza.

"Why? Why are you doing all this? You are NOT Theodore!" Audrey shouted in defiance. Theodore raised his right eyebrow at her deliciously, with a smile that consumed everything in sight.

Ben grabbed Audrey from the ground, and as he was about to lift her up, Gerald came over and whispered, "Left forearm. Look." Gerald and Ben helped Audrey up by letting her use both of their shoulders to stand. Her wound spewed with blood, rendering the makeshift tourniquet useless. Ben took his shirt off and cut it in half. He wrapped it over Audrey's wound. She thanked him, and Theodore almost looked jealous.

Ben walked over to where Gerald had stood. He waited until Theodore decided to move his arm again to get a look, but he didn't. Instead, Theodore said, "Eliza, you really need to come with me, and the rest of you will find out soon enough what is going on. Come on, it will be fun. I will be expecting you all to merrily follow Eliza and I down the tunnel now." He turned his back and Eliza followed him.

They walked into Audrey's tunnel, and Ben mouthed to Gerald, "Run." Gerald shook his head. He wasn't going to leave them to go into battle without assistance. Ben wasn't going to fight him on the issue, grabbed Audrey and let her put some of her weight on him. "Where's your shoe?" he asked her quietly.

"Well, it looks like I'll be able to see it again. It got stuck to the ground by something." She shrugged. Ben almost laughed, but given the situation, nothing was feeling funny anymore.

Theodore walked alone in front, confidently. He didn't need to look behind him to make sure that they were all following close behind. When the tunnel became narrow, Eliza held his hand while he walked in front of her. The tunnel looked like it was exhausted from all the bodies that were gathered in it at once, and the tunnel knew, as well as Audrey, that shortly, the jagged edges would be hard for some of them to go forward unscathed.

Eliza moved to the side and pointed to his forearm. The mark was showing, and Gerald stopped to move, so Ben and Audrey could see it with their flashlights. It was the same mark that Audrey had drawn on herself. The same one that was drawn inside this cave. It couldn't have been a coincidence. The problem was, they had no idea what it meant or what it was doing to Theodore. With Audrey, it made her mad and forgetful of what she had done. Was it some sort of controlling curse, or something else? They had no way of looking it up now, but they could potentially get it off his arm. It looked like it was just drawn on with charcoal.

Eliza was brave and touched the mark to see if she could quickly brush it off. Theodore turned around wildly and grabbed her hand. He squeezed it so hard she felt her bones crack. As Eliza screamed, Ben moved Audrey to Gerald's side, ran up to Theodore and punched him square in the face. Theodore instantly stumbled back and released Eliza's hand. He put his hands over his nose and winced. Ben grabbed Eliza by her waist and moved her behind him. Blood trickled down Theodore's mouth and chin. It was clear that he hadn't been expecting Ben to retaliate.

"Ben, what the fuck?" Theodore retorted. The real Theodore.

"If you hurt Eliza again, I'll fucking kill you!" Ben shouted, before he noticed the change in his voice.

"Dude, what are you talking about?" he replied, raising his head to try and stop the bleeding.

"Theodore?" Ben stared at him like he was looking for something. Anything to prove to him that this wasn't just another trap.

"Yeah, of course it's me. I wouldn't hurt Eliza." His eyes welled up with tears.

"If you are faking this, I swear you will regret it later."

"Ben, it's ME!" he yelled.

"Let me see your forearm," Ben commanded. Theodore moved his arms to him unknowing of which forearm he was referring to. Ben looked at the mark closer. "Why, is this on you?"

Theodore looked down and inspected his arm like a child inspecting a new object for the first time. "I have no idea. I didn't have it before I got taken," he said sincerely.

Ben looked back at the others to see what they thought. Eliza held her wounded hand, and just as Ben looked back, he looked straight into Theodore's fist. Ben crashed against the side of the wall, causing a small gash in his torso. Small specks of blood trickled down. Theodore had punched him in his left eye, which swelled immediately. Ben didn't care. He lifted his fists and popped Theodore on the side of his cheek in two swift punches, sending Theodore's face swinging wildly to the side. Theodore held up his hand in surrender and laughed as he spat out a bloody tooth.

"Gerald, help me," Ben called. Gerald knew exactly what he wanted. Gerald held Theodore down while Ben rubbed at the marking. It was thick and wouldn't come off easily. The most he could do was smudge it so it just looked like a black streak. Theodore closed his eyes and his body shook. Gerald held him down tighter, but then he realized that something else was happening.

He wasn't fighting back; he was having a seizure.

Ben held his head so he wouldn't crack his skull open. Audrey turned away from the scene and faced her head into Eliza's shoulder. Eliza had never witnessed Audrey emotional like this, which made everything even harder. Eliza needed her brother back, but seeing him in this way gave her little hope.

Theodore stopped shaking. He started to breathe rhythmically again.

Gerald waited to lift his body up and Ben waited for his command. Theodore slowly opened his eyes, but they immediately closed again. His eyelids were too heavy to lift now that he had no energy pulsing through his veins. His mouth twitched silently.

Audrey ran over and placed her hands on either side of his cheeks. Her forehead rested softly on his and her eyelids closed in deep sadness. Their breathing became rhythmic to each other's. Theodore's eyes, even though they struggled to do so, opened. Unfortunately, his eyes fought to blink, closed and repeated. Audrey moved her hand to where Ben had his behind his head. Ben moved back and Gerald followed to give her space. Theodore opened his mouth and a purple cloud of smoke puffed out. His eyes shot open, startled.

"What the hell was that? Is he dead?" Gerald blurted after seeing the smoke glide down the tunnel.

Theodore replied, "If you are referring to me, then no, I'm not dead. Although, I feel like I almost am." He stared at

Audrey and brushed her hair behind her ear. "I didn't think that I would see you again."

Audrey gave out a sigh of relief. "I didn't think I would see you again either," she replied, happy tears running wildly down her face.

"Audrey, be careful. We can't be sure he isn't faking again," Ben replied.

"I believe it's him," Audrey said.

Ben looked to Eliza and Gerald and they both shrugged. Gerald seemed less convinced than Eliza.

"That symbol must be some sort of controlling spell. I wrote that same symbol on my arm to remember it, not knowing what it was. It made me try to hurt Ben and Eliza. I'm still not sure what it is, but maybe that's what made you act the way you have been. Whoever drew it on you could have attached a different spell to it to control you," Audrey said to Theodore.

"It could be true. This whole situation seems to be dipped in magic, but how do we know for sure that the spell is gone?" Gerald said.

"Did you see the smoke that left his body?" Audrey replied.

"Yes, but again, unless one of you is a witch or something else magical, I don't think we have any clue what we are dealing with," Gerald stated.

"Gerald's right. We don't know. Theodore, I think it would be safer if we kept a close eye on you. Do you remember where or why you were leading us this way?" Eliza asked.

Theodore, now damaged in many ways, wanted nothing but to leave. He looked at Audrey and knew that he wanted to see her beautiful face for more than just today. "Let's get the fuck out of here then," Theodore said, giving his best impression of a smile.

Ben reached his arm down to help him up. He hugged him once he was on his two feet again. Theodore hugged back like bark hugs the phloem on a tree. Ben had succeeded in finding his friend. It was clear that he felt bad for punching him and causing the loss of his tooth, but in all fairness, he was attacking who had invaded his body.

Audrey stepped away to where Eliza was and looked over her hand. Eliza was pretty sure that at least her middle finger had a broken bone. Gerald was the only one who felt out of place. He knew everyone, but not on the same level.

The five of them started to exit the tunnel the way Ben, Audrey and Eliza had come in, and all seemed like it would be alright now. Audrey walked next to Theodore and held his hand—something she had only done a couple times previously. It felt so natural and seamless. She wondered why she'd thought that she couldn't have a relationship with him while moving up in the company. Fear was the only conclusion she could come to.

As they walked, Ben kissed Eliza's injured hand. Her eyelids closed and she softly smiled. Gerald watched the two pairs in their hopeful bliss, but he had been to war before—he saw this as no different, except perhaps worse, since none of them were prepared for what creatures they needed to escape from. He didn't mention to them that he thought this was far from over. Instead, he allowed them to have a moment with each other. A moment that was sure to not last for long.

They had hardly taken more than five steps back down the tunnel when Gerald knew that he was right to assume more danger was to come. Before them stood a tall shadow. Any moment now, they would see who the shadow belonged to.

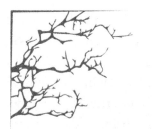

29

The shadow was accompanied by the sound of boots that moved through the tunnel with confidence. Whomever the shadow belonged wasn't worried about who they would find, as they walked and breathed without caution. Without a thought, Ben, Eliza and Audrey drew their knives while they watched the shadow grow far above their heads.

Audrey's hand shook, while she tried to hold onto her knife and flashlight. She blurted out, "Who's there?"

All eyes were now on Audrey instead of the shadow. Ben placed his index finger up to his mouth, his eyes wide. Audrey ignored Ben and pointed her hand in the direction of the shadow. At the same moment, the sound of wild laughter traveled down the tunnel and a silhouette appeared.

Before they noticed her, they noticed her crimson boots. An introduction that only Gerald and Theodore would need catching up on. Audrey was the first to shift her focus upwards. Taylor slouched her weight onto her right hip and gave Audrey a wicked grin.

Audrey shined her flashlight in Taylor's eyes like she was about to interrogate her, which in all honesty was exactly what she wanted to do. "Taylor, what the flying monsters fuck are you doing here?"

When Audrey shouted her name, Ben and Eliza stared up at Taylor, bewildered. Eliza glared at Taylor and shook her head. Theodore understood what Eliza was thinking and proceeded to glare as well. Ben stood frozen in place, unsure of what he should do. He had wanted to trust Taylor, especially since she'd saved his life, but her being in the cave sent off all the alarm bells he had that she was in fact danger itself.

Gerald instantly didn't trust her. The main reason was because she just happened to be in the same cave that a lot of people had died or would die in, and she still had a smile on her face like she was entertaining guests at a party. The second reason was she looked like she had just stepped out of a magazine—one that he would personally never read.

"Aren't you all heroic?" Taylor smirked. "Would you mind lowering your light, Audrey?"

Audrey complied only once Ben replied.

"What are you doing here, Taylor?" Ben asked.

"I don't even get a hello or anything?" She paused and no one answered. "Alright, well, if you must know, I came to help. It's what Harper would have wanted."

"Then why are you so giddy right now?" Audrey glared.

"Calm down, girl. I'm just shocked that you are all still alive. You are dealing with some serious monsters, remember? I'm relieved; honestly." She batted her eyelashes.

Ben stepped forward to moved past her, while he said sternly, "Well, glad you came, but we are all just leaving."

Taylor grabbed Ben's shoulder before he could pass, and asked tauntingly, "Did you kill the monsters?"

Ben moved Taylor's hand off him.

"No, which is exactly why we are getting out of here," Gerald snapped.

Taylor eyed Gerald with a disgusted look, like a rich snob looking at a servant. "And who are you, old man?"

Fire danced in their eyes. Taylor felt the heat from their gazes, but she merely rolled her eyes and tapped her boot like she was in a hurry.

Gerald put his arm in front of Audrey, who was remarkably close to losing her temper, and said, "I would watch what you say. If I cared to explain to you some manners, I would. Seeing the situation, I'm going to ignore your comment."

As though they had all just went for a stroll, Taylor took out a piece of gum from her pocket and put it in her mouth. A pastel pink bubble the size of a lime grew between her lips. It made a loud pop when it smacked back over her lips. She sucked the gum back into her mouth. "I will follow you all, but we aren't leaving."

"Taylor, you can stay if you want, but the rest of us are getting the fuck out of here," Audrey shouted, her fists growing tighter by the second.

Taylor raised her right eyebrow at her and grinned. "You got a mouth on you, girl. You three owe me a little trust, don't ya think? Ben here wouldn't even be kicking anymore if it weren't for me." She was right and that made Audrey want to curse at her even more, but she knew that it wouldn't help them.

"You're right, but why would you want us to stay?" Ben asked curiously.

"Don't you want to finish the job?"

"I've heard enough of this. I'm not inclined to play games. We are leaving!" Gerald snapped.

The five of them were about to march out of there, but Taylor held her hand up in the hope to get one more minute to persuade them. However, none of them cared to listen. More than one of them potentially needed medical attention, and they weren't willing to gamble with their lives after coming so close to becoming survivors. As Audrey walked past Taylor, she brushed shoulders with her. Theodore looked over his shoulder at Taylor as they passed by and gave her a once over. When their eyes locked, his brain felt like something was wiggling around in it. He ignored the movement and continued past her with his arm over Audrey's shoulder. It was unclear if Taylor took the insult to heart because she stared on and didn't even flinch.

Gerald followed behind them, then Eliza and Ben. Taylor waved her hand in front of Ben and Eliza. They both froze. A moment in time was lost for them, and the only knowing party was Taylor. Gerald realized that he couldn't hear their footsteps anymore, so he turned his head back. Taylor's lips were moving, but nothing she was saying was audible to him. Eliza and Ben both stood like statues, their eyes glazed over, looking straight ahead at nothing. It was like they were peering into space in a trance-like manner.

Gerald was about to grab them and pull them along, but then Ben said robotically, "We are going to stay behind." Ben's amber eyes were now stoic.

"Really, Ben?" Taylor perked up and smiled with a grin the size of a boat.

Again, Ben spoke without any sense of self, and answered her with a formal, "Yes."

Taylor grabbed Eliza and Ben and squeezed them like a mother would her two children. Except neither Ben nor Eliza had a smile on their face. Really, they had nothing but dead expressions. Their jaws started to sag as the moments passed.

Audrey and Theodore backtracked their steps when they didn't hear footsteps behind them. They turned and saw that Gerald was motionless. Audrey raised her face up in a quick motion to alert Theodore to look over at Gerald. Gerald wasn't sure how to proceed, but he wasn't a dummy and knew that Taylor had done something to them. It was in his blood to protect people, and he wasn't about to forget about that.

"I'll be taking them with me." Gerald moved toward Eliza and Ben calmly. He touched Eliza's wrist and tapped on her forearm. She was unresponsive. Her body stayed straight as a knife. Taylor squeezed them tighter and smiled like a demented goblin. Gerald strode over to Ben and tried again. The same happened. Absolutely no movement. At that moment, Theodore and Audrey came running back towards them.

They weren't sure what had happened, and even though Gerald had witnessed the change, he still had no more knowledge of what was playing out than them. Audrey gazed at both Eliza and Ben, knowing full well that she wouldn't be pleased with what she would see. Her body started to shake and her hands gripped tightly together in small but deadly fists. Her fear of Taylor was being shocked through her whole body like a lightning bolt.

"What the fuck is going on over here?" Audrey shouted.

"I don't know what you are talking about. It seems that Ben and Eliza have come to their senses and are ready to exterminate the beasts."

Taylor made some more pink bubbles between her thick lips. Her nonchalant attitude was not something that the rest of them took lightly.

Audrey stalked over to Eliza.

"Look, I don't know what Taylor said to you, but we can't defeat them. Believe me, I was in a room with several of them, and I still am not sure if they can die from anything in this world."

Eliza stared off into space, completely mute. Taylor nudged her arm a bit, and then Eliza spoke one word clear and direct, "Fight."

Theodore, a surprise to everyone, reached his hands up to grab Taylor. Before he could, Audrey and Gerald stepped in front of him.

"Look at me, we don't know what she has done to them," Audrey whispered, while she stared intently into his eyes and lowered his hands back down to his sides.

Theodore nodded at Audrey and twitched his neck. Audrey's eyes darted back and forth between Ben and Eliza. Her fears for the worst started to bubble up in her throat. Her once rosy complexion had become pallid like she had seen a ghost. Audrey grabbed Gerald and walked a few feet away from Taylor.

"Gerald, what is going on?" Audrey whispered.

Gerald lowered his voice and said, "Taylor did something. I'm not sure what, but she has to have done something to them." He rubbed his forehead and shook his head in disbelief.

Audrey knew exactly what he meant. Exactly what she was afraid of. And she began to answer questions in her head about the shack near Taylor's house. While she tried to understand why Taylor would have been the one tracking down spells to relive what she had such a long time ago, Audrey motioned to Theodore and Gerald to follow her lead.

"Okay, do you want us all to come and help you defeat the Eltrists?" Audrey asked.

"Only if you want to, dear, of course. If you want to volunteer, I would be happy to have the backup," she said.

"Tell me one thing." Audrey placed her hands on her hips and glared.

"Ask away, but remember the clock is ticking. Especially for Theodore."

Audrey looked over at her love, who was itching away at his head the same way Ben had been. Audrey clenched her fists. She was angry at Taylor, angry at the Eltrist that had sliced her, angry at the whole lot of them for taking the majority of their community, angry at the world. "Why would you want to kill the Eltrists if you know that in a few days or so they will be gone anyway? Why not just let them leave? Unless, of course, you have something to kill them because we collectively do not."

"That is a juicy question. I, in fact, do have the exact thing that could kill them. However, I need a distraction to do so." She pointed at them.

"So, we are just the bait?" Theodore snarled.

"Well, I wouldn't use that harsh of a word, but I guess if you want to look at it that way, then yes. Yes, Mr. Negativity, you and your friends would be bait." She blew another sphere out of her mouth and let it pop. As she sucked it back in, she stalked toward them. Eliza and Ben moved slowly with Taylor. It was like they were floating on a cloud with just the wind to guide their steps. "So, what will it be, folks? You coming or not?"

Audrey shook her head, but then asked, "How long does he have?" She didn't need to say his name for them to know who she was talking about.

Taylor put her hand on Theodore's head and closed her eyes. "I would suggest we hurry," she said spiritedly. Audrey looked at Theodore sadly and held back tears.

The tunnel back was not somewhere that any of them wanted to continue down, but to save their friends they would do it. Audrey didn't want Taylor to put some sort of spell on them too. That would make it increasingly hard to get away from her later. Taylor proceeded to a small crevice in the rock. She extracted a black velvet bag. It reminded Audrey of the time she went to a rave and there were all these people with drawstring backpacks. She'd always made fun of people like that, but then again, she'd made fun of raves, and she had ended up at one, nonetheless.

Taylor carefully placed it on her back and then whispered in Eliza's ear. Eliza perked up and started walking. Then she did the same to Ben with the same result. "Shall we?" she said to the remainder of them. Taylor pushed Ben and Eliza to the front and Gerald, Theodore and Audrey followed.

Theodore walked right behind Audrey and held her hand. She squeezed his palm tightly. Theodore knew that shortly his brain could very well turn to mush and wanted to feel her soft hand against his for as long as he could. Audrey felt the same, but her mind drifted away from his failing health. Instead, she thought about how she would get them out of this whole mess. She also needed to know why Taylor couldn't just let this all go. If she needed revenge, it was certainly not something Audrey or the rest of them wanted to be a part of, but there they were walking down a murky tunnel, waiting for the darkness to swallow them.

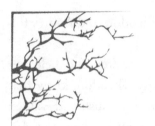

30

Every breath they took sounded like tiny echoes from long ago bouncing around them. Gerald thought of the faint echoes as something else entirely. He suspected they were the cries of the others that were left behind to melt into a puddle. He hoped that his mind was making up something quite elaborate, but in all seriousness, he had seen that exact thing happen just hours ago. Needless to say, he was mentally prepared for anything to happen. He put on his war paint and proceeded with caution.

The tunnel was narrowing and it felt even smaller with all the bodies that now resided in it. The tunnel felt like its insides were about to explode at any minute. Luckily for the tunnel, they were not capable of destroying it at that capacity. The jagged edges of the tunnel seemed to scrape against at least one part of each and every body that followed it. It would have felt comforting to the tunnel walls, but given that only one person was meant to walk at once, and in this case there was an excess of five, the tunnel felt suffocated.

A rock stood in the way; the same rock that Audrey had had to jump over not once but twice. Taylor let Eliza hop over it first, but since Eliza was not herself, she didn't account for the icicle-like rock that protruded from the right side. It pierced her side the second she stood on top of the rock. Eliza fell to the other side. Ben did nothing; instead, he stayed quiet while waiting for his turn.

Taylor looked over the rock at her and flicked her wrist. Eliza sat up like she felt no pain, but her body made it clear that she had been torn through like a bag of flour. Tears streamed down her emotionless face, and her breaths sounded hoarse. Gerald was the only one not in a trance that saw the whole thing. He pushed Taylor out of the way and slowly stepped over the rock to Eliza. Sucking in his gut as much as humanly possible, he was able to get over the rock with only a little poke. A loud breath came out of him as he released air. He wrapped Eliza up in his arms and placed his hand on her wound. Her shirt now had a growing circle of blood.

"Help her!" he shouted to Taylor.

"Me? What could I do?" she scoffed. "She will be fine. The point didn't go through an organ or anything."

Taylor took her backpack off and tossed a small glass bottle to him. Gerald caught it effortlessly. He examined the bottle and from what he could tell there was blue liquid inside. What the liquid was, was perplexing to him. "Pour a drop onto her cut," she stated in annoyance.

At that point, Audrey was able to see what had happened and pulled Theodore over to her enough for him to see what had happened too. "Eliza, are you okay?" she tearfully shouted. Eliza didn't say anything. It took everything for Audrey to not grab her knife and slit Taylor's throat right then and there. Theodore shuffled in front of Audrey and stood in front of Taylor's face. He was so close to her that he could smell her fruity bubblegum seeping out of her mouth with every breath she took.

"What the hell is wrong with her and Ben? I'm fucking done with this game you are playing." Theodore's body shook with frustration.

Taylor blew a big pink bubble that grazed his nose. Theodore saw red and was about to attack when Audrey stepped in front of him.

"Looks like your girl has some sense left," Taylor mocked.

"I may have some sense, but I'm not above protecting my friends, and if that means taking you out of the picture, I will do so. You shouldn't test me, bitch."

Taylor giggled the most annoying and evil giggle. It was enough to make anyone want to choke her. Audrey refrained. Taylor pointed to the bottle that she threw to Gerald and said, "Why is everyone so upset? She isn't going to die. That bottle will stop the bleeding."

"See, the problem is that our friends are not themselves and we know it is because of you. If I had to guess, you aren't exactly human, and whatever you are, I would say you aren't one of the good ones," Gerald stated.

Quietly, Taylor said, "It's true. Maybe I'm not entirely human anymore, but the things I do are for a greater cause."

"Well, then why are Ben and Eliza in a trance?"

"I needed to convince at least one of you to go, and it was clear that you would all stay behind if one did, so here we are."

"Give them back their minds and we will continue and convince them to follow. If you don't, you will have a mutiny on your hands. And we are all armed," Audrey said.

"You know I could do the same to you as I did to them, right?" Taylor was unconvinced of the little group's ability to actually harm her, but she also knew that she wasn't allowed to do certain things. It would go against her mentor's orders. She wasn't about to state any of this to the others though.

"Yeah, that's true, but if you are good like you state, why would you?" Theodore asked.

"Well played." She whispered into Ben's ear and his body collapsed. His knees bent in and his arms fell to the floor, but he caught himself just in time from falling completely to the cold, hard ground.

Then Taylor crossed over the rock to Eliza and did the same. Gerald was already holding her steady. He knew her legs would go limp and wanted to be prepared.

Eliza's eyelids closed and then flung back open with surprise. Her body bent to the left and she placed a hand over her wound. "Ahh, what the hell happened? I... I don't remember anything. Did I get a concussion or something?" she shouted.

Gerald patted her back and was about to speak when Taylor said, "We have no idea what happened. You were walking and you must not have seen that sharp piece of rock."

"That wouldn't make me forget everything about how we got here, would it?" Her words sounded more confused by the second.

"Yeah, and what about me? I don't remember why we are in this part of the cave either," Ben balked.

Audrey, Theodore and Gerald let ideas rattle through their brains on how to address what had happened. The reality wouldn't suffice because that would put them on opposite ends of Taylor, which wasn't good for any of them. They would explain later. In this situation, it was definitely better to not tell them until they were far away from her. At one point, Audrey wanted to say, "We'll tell you when you're older," but obviously besides it causing a few confused laughs, it wouldn't stop them from asking.

"You two succumbed to a strange odor that the Eltrists give out. It can cause you to forget. That must be what happened. If you so much as get too close to some strug and breathe it in in just the right amount, it has some nasty effects," Taylor said in the most motherly voice that any of them had ever heard.

"How do you know all of this?" Audrey said.

Taylor rolled her eyes, "Well from reading of course."

Ben and Eliza looked to their friends for confirmation. Gerald, Theodore and Audrey all shrugged and nodded their heads in agreement with her.

"That explains why we can't remember, but why are we deeper in the cave?" Ben looked to Taylor.

"You don't remember?" Taylor said surprised. They both shook their heads. "Well, we talked a bit more and we all agreed it would be better to kill them, so they couldn't hurt anyone else. Ben, you were quite heroic about it all and started spouting off that that's what Harper would have done, and you needed to finish the cycle for him."

Ben once again looked to each of his friends, who all nodded reassuringly even though they all hated themselves for it.

"Well, that does sound like you, Ben," Eliza said.

"Yeah, I guess it does. Do we have a plan?"

"The Eltrists are just a little further through this tunnel, and when the time comes, we can rally them up. I have some very effective tools that will get rid of them for good."

"What about Wyatt?" Ben asked.

"None of us have seen him, right?" Audrey scanned the other faces. Theodore looked utterly confused, but Taylor looked smitten. Audrey wasn't sure what to think of Taylor's expression, especially since she couldn't have known who he was. But maybe she was just excited that they were looking for another person.

"Wyatt from work?" Theodore said in all seriousness.

"Yeah, we found out that he is not really who he pretended to be. He's actually a witch or something like that, and from what I can tell, a pretty powerful one. He's the reason why the Eltrists are here. I saw him when I found Gerald and the others."

Theodore stumbled back a bit from Audrey and his eyes darted to Eliza. "That guy?" Theodore shook his head in disbelief.

"I know it seems unreal, but that's the truth. He uses the Eltrists' strug to stay immortal, but it's something that needs to be replenished, it seems. Strug is the purple goop that was melting people." Audrey had her hand on his arm as she tried to quickly bring him up to speed.

As she blew another bubble out of her mouth, Taylor said, "While I would love us to stand around and just catch up with each other, we really should be going. The Eltrists aren't going to wait around forever."

"Fine, let's keep going," Audrey said.

Taylor hopped over the rock with no help from Gerald, who moved away just as she outstretched her hand like a lady would getting down from a carriage. Taylor glowered in his direction, but he didn't so much as give her the acknowledgment of seeing her scowl. Then Audrey stepped over, followed by Theodore, who was quite careful to not get stabbed as well. Noises echoed off the walls, much like an orchestra. It was nowhere near as eloquent sounding as that though; more like what you would assume a bear would sound like if it could talk.

While they were all frightened as to what lay ahead, Audrey calmly looked at her wound, while on the inside her thoughts were full of panic. Ben was in the lead now and tried to grab Audrey's shoe as he passed it. He found out on the first pull that he would need some help to get it unstuck. When Theodore made it to the shoe, he tried as well and Audrey let out the faintest laugh. Theodore heard and looked up at her, while his back was still crouched over as he carried on trying to pull her shoe up. Not surprising to her, the shoe did not release. He let it go and accepted the defeat. Audrey grabbed his hand and gave him a pity kiss on the cheek. His grin could have stretched over entire realms.

Light glowed through the opening up ahead that could have been mistaken for hundreds of fireflies. Only, fireflies didn't give off a purple glow. The glow was mesmerizing and Taylor looked at it in wonderment. Ben speculated if she had seen this display of light before when she had been taken. If anything, he assumed that seeing it again would be more like having an episode of PTSD come back. In all honesty, he feared that all his old camping spots would give him that reaction from now on. Taylor seemed more pleased than anything else, but perhaps she was putting on a brave face. Though he doubted it.

The entrance to the larger cave was merely a few feet away. Everyone stopped when they saw what was lurking inside. The glowing light was caused by several Eltrists who were standing in the room. They stood next to each other on all fours in a relaxed manner. Their mouths were moving slowly and the strange noises that were heard in the tunnel were now amplified. There was no doubt that they had their own language, which Audrey had already known.

"Now what?" Ben asked.

"Let's see, you five will walk into the center and create a distraction so that I can have time to use my spell," Taylor stated.

"So, how long will you need?" Gerald growled.

Taylor rolled her eyes and gritted her teeth, before saying, "About five minutes. Maybe less."

Eliza's eyes connected with Audrey's and they had a moment of best friend telepathy. She knew something was off, but nothing could be done at the moment. Eliza squeezed Ben's hand and hoped that he would get the message. She then spoke to Taylor. "Tell us when."

"The Eltrists all seem to be out of the center, so NOW!" she shouted as she pushed Gerald out first.

The four others were angrily closing in on Taylor when they saw the Eltrists start to surround Gerald. Audrey leapt in, taking her faithful umbrella out once more that still had their tar-like blood on the tip. Theodore followed her. Ben and Eliza were the last to run out, but immediately drew their knives from their back pockets, ready for a fight.

Taylor, ignoring the fighting sounds around her, casually sat down next to the tunnel. She grabbed her velvet bag and took out a ripped piece of paper that had writing on it, and another one that wasn't ripped. Along with the papers, she took out a small bowl and a dagger. With one clear swipe, she cut the side of her hand and let the blood drip into the bowl. As though she had done this a hundred times, she did not show even the slightest bit of discomfort when the knife cut into her.

She rose to stare at the others, who were now surrounded by Eltrists. A brown Eltrist was near her, so she sauntered over to it with her knife and the bowl of blood. Her arm stretched out and grabbed it by its tail. Before the Eltrist could turn back, she cut off the tip of its tail. The Eltrist flailed rapidly and reached its paw out to grab her by the throat, but somehow, she was already back in the safety of the tunnel.

A desperate screeching noise came from the hurt beast, alerting the others. They stopped surrounding the group and went towards the hurt Eltrist. The five of them took that as the perfect time to escape. Audrey yelled to them to follow her down to the other tunnel that she'd never got more than about a foot in prior. Audrey's foot touched the cold ground. A small tear had formed from her walking on the rough surface. Swiftly, she turned around and gazed over to see what Taylor was doing.

Taylor's mouth was moving and her hands were in the air—one with the dagger dripping with fresh blood and the other with the Eltrist's tail dripping black and purple ooze into the bowl beneath it. Gerald tugged on Audrey's arm to keep going down the cave, but Audrey's feet stayed frozen in place. Her eyes were fixed on Taylor, and it was a good thing too because she saw him appear when the others didn't. Wyatt stood in the middle of the cave with his back to Audrey and the rest of them. He walked over to Taylor.

There was no way of knowing what words they exchanged, but given their body language, it would seem that it was at least cordial. Then Wyatt snapped his fingers and the world around the five companions changed as quickly as lack of air would smother a flame.

31

The room was glowing. No more artificial lights danced on the cave's surface—only the glowing orbs lighted the room, creating more of a sort of dim light that you would associate with romantic dinners. Sadly, there was nothing romantic about being held captive in a cave. The purple lights were like fluttering insects that moved all around them like they were floating or underwater. It would have been a magical moment, if those glowing lights didn't equal a hot, melting death. But as they all knew by now, that was exactly what it meant.

Gerald, Eliza, Ben, Audrey and Theodore all stood in the center of the cave. Slowly, their eyes opened. Eliza reached out to her left and could feel a hand. It was rough and about twice the size of hers. She could tell that it had to be Gerald's. She hoped that it was Gerald's. The hand grabbed hers back and it rubbed hers with its thumb.

Her left hand stayed clasped to the person's as she reached out her right and found another as well. It was definitely Audrey's hand. They had held hands on many occasions, as girlfriends tend to do. Audrey held hers back with a tightness that only someone does when they are in extreme pain or, like in her situation, feeling intense fear.

At that same moment, Ben was holding Audrey's and Theodore's hand. Theodore was holding Gerald's with his other hand. They were sat in a circle with their backs to each other. The entire room felt alive. Quick breaths, the sound of pitter-patter against the cold floor, and the quiet, rumbling voices of the Eltrists. Eliza's eyes were finally the last to fully adjust to the darkness, and her mind drifted to another time, another her. This was the first time that they truly understood why people referred to them as Twilight Breathers. The array of light that danced around the room was like seeing the twilight after staying up late.

As Audrey's brain jolted like a firefly gleams when it becomes night, her body shook frantically. Theodore's words flooded her brain: "Gathering ceremony." Theodore, or whoever was speaking for him, had wanted them to follow him to it. Now she was kicking herself for not asking more questions about it. There was a good chance that he would have been vague, but the small chance that he would have boasted about the ceremony is what filled her mind with regret.

A voice whispered into their ears. It was a familiar one; one that they cared to never hear again. "If you are ready, we can begin," Wyatt spoke softly to someone.

They didn't hear a reply, but assumed who he was talking to was Taylor. Only one of them was brave enough to ask anything. Audrey's voice shook as she asked, "What is going to happen?" Gerald's hand gave her a reassuring squeeze.

A hand brushed against Eliza's dampened face. Wyatt wiped away her tears and grabbed both of her arms to stand her up. Gerald and Audrey held her tightly, but Wyatt waved his hand once casually and broke the bond. Gerald and Audrey went to stand up, but an invisible force kept them in place. Even their voices were silenced. Audrey and Gerald were the only ones who knew that she was taken.

Wyatt walked over to the other side of the circle, and Ben immediately screamed, causing his throat to feel raw. The screams were all for nothing, and Wyatt only grinned in response. He brought Eliza to the middle of the broken circle, where he welcomed Taylor to the center.

She brought over a book, a large black candle, some wooden bowls and small vials. As she entered the circle, she took out some red powder and blew it into the faces of the four still sitting. The powder went up their nostrils, and a second later they were standing, facing inside the circle. Their hands weren't connected anymore. Ben went to reach out his hand to Eliza, but he wasn't close enough and his feet were sealed in place.

Ben's heart was beating so fast, he thought that he might be having a heart attack. Of course, this wasn't the case. The stress his heart was now under was seemingly too much for him to handle. The fear of the unknown was crippling him. Much like the other four, he had no idea what Wyatt was going to do to Eliza and felt like he had failed her. Eliza wasn't a helpless person, but she felt like the size of a pebble. Tears slid down her soft cheeks, but no sound came from her mouth. It wouldn't have been much use either way.

Taylor gazed at Eliza like she was trying to get with her man. "What is she doing out of the circle?" Taylor gripped her supplies tightly and squinted her eyes to glare at Eliza.

Wyatt's face turned sour from her tone and he brushed more tears from Eliza's face, while he stared at Taylor. Taylor's face began to turn red with rage, but she held her tongue. "She will help us perform the ceremony."

"HER? Why? We don't need another person to perform it."

"Tay, listen to me, you don't know what you are talking about. I may have kept a secret or two from you. This is, after all, your first ceremony. Don't forget, we need the other bodies for our magic to move through."

Wyatt brushed Eliza's dark hair behind her ear, like someone who was caring would do, but she didn't feel like this was to make her feel comforted. He saw the others piqued with curiosity as to what their bodies were needed for.

"I can tell that while you four hold your tongues, you want some clarification," Wyatt announced boastfully. "A gathering ceremony is quite special and the Eltrists will be happy to take you as a small sacrifice. The Eltrists will gain a thin slice of each of your souls. It provides them with many benefits. Normally, they are fine with the souls they have already consumed, but in this situation, I need to offer more."

"Will I be sacrificed too?" Eliza asked warily.

Taylor smiled and moved her lips to say, "Yes," but Wyatt moved his hand up to her to shut her up. "Eliza, you know that I couldn't possibly sacrifice you, but I guess what I have planned will be like a sacrifice on one life at least." Eliza's eyes blinked as though dust had settled in them. Taylor glowered, and she did not so much as breathe in their direction.

Eliza thought about saying a lot of things, but none of it would matter. It was unlikely that she could do much about the situation.

"Bitch," Taylor said under her breath, but loud enough for all of them to hear her.

Just as quickly as the word left her lips, Wyatt backhanded her across the face. Her head swung to the side in surprise. Eliza even flinched. Taylor raised her hands and Wyatt flung backward in a spiral. Taylor stood in attack mode with one leg in front of the other and her arms outstretched in Wyatt's direction. She held her gaze on him, but he leapt up, and within seconds, Taylor was on the ground. Her body laid motionless and silent.

Wyatt walked over to her and kicked her side. Her lips parted in distress, while Wyatt beckoned to her to stand up. When she didn't follow the orders, he made her. His hand motioned her body to rise, and slowly but surely, her eyes opened. Wyatt held her jaw up and whispered, "You may not like how I do things, but you will follow my lead. The girl is of no concern to you, my little Tay. I will grant you eternal life, but it will be given to you on my own will. If you choose to be unworthy, that will be taken away. All I have to do is leave you out of the ceremony."

He took a breath and gazed into her saddened eyes. "Now, what will it be, Tay?"

One tear scurried down her cheek and she nodded her head. "And, remember, Tay, I can take away all the extra nourishment you need to keep the immortality flowing through your veins later. Don't even think about getting any future ideas."

Taylor brushed her tears away and her arrogance stomped back across her face with vengeance.

"Good, now can we start?"

Taylor's head nodded again. Wyatt smiled and grabbed her hand, before placing his lips fiercely upon hers. She kissed him back with longing and desperation. Eliza rolled her eyes at the exchange.

Wyatt led Taylor back to the middle where Eliza stood. It was clear she still didn't want Eliza to be anywhere near Wyatt, but she had no choice in the matter, so she remained calm for the time being. "Now, Eliza, give me your hands and we shall begin."

Eliza pulled away and said defiantly, "No."

"You saw what happened to Tay. Would you like the same fate?"

"Go ahead. I'd rather die than have you curse me."

"I knew you were strong-willed, but I didn't know to what extent. How about this then—every time you choose to not do as I say, one of your friends dies."

"I thought you said you needed them?"

"It's true I need bodies for this, but I can easily send out an Eltrist to bring me more. How many lives would you like to sacrifice for your stubbornness?"

Ben tried to move to Eliza, but he was still stuck and mute. Audrey's eyes welled up and Theodore reached out for her hand, while he tried to be strong. Gerald looked like he was formulating a plan, but in the situation at hand, none of them would work.

"Fine, I'll do what you ask, but you have to do something for me first."

"Living is not enough?" He genuinely looked disappointed.

"You need to allow my friends to live unharmed and give them back their free will."

Wyatt licked his lips and then took a deep breath, before he said, "Really?" Eliza's eyes gazed into his, and he couldn't stop staring back for a few minutes, before he finally looked away and said, "Very well, I can do that for the most part. But if they disobey, I cannot be accountable for my actions."

"What do you mean, "for the most part"?" Eliza frowned at him.

"Well, for the ceremony to work, I need to provide a tiny bit of their souls, as I told you before. There could be some side effects from it. As you know, nothing to probably worry about, but normally I allow the Eltrists to have a meal of the volunteers after the ceremony. In this case, they won't eat them."

Wyatt sighed and placed his hands on her shoulders. "The spell requires something in exchange for my immortality. Things have changed, as you know, and my soul has been picked away at so much that it will not be enough anymore. They don't need to know everything just yet, but you do need to decide now if you will take my offer. If not, consider your friends dead." Wyatt stood in awe of her and his heart was skipping a beat while he waited for her surrender.

Eliza looked into each one of her friends' eyes and made them nod in agreement to the plan. Ben didn't want to agree, but he obliged as Eliza's face grew increasingly hollow.

"Very well." Wyatt snapped his fingers and all was right with their free will again, or at least, the facade of it.

Ben said, "Eliza, I promise I will fix this."

Wyatt began clapping. "Good one, lover boy. Keep it up, and maybe she will stay madly in love with you. Go ahead, Eliza, give him one last kiss goodbye."

Eliza hesitantly walked over to Ben and hugged him. He squeezed her tight and whispered in her ear, "Don't give up hope just yet." Eliza pressed her cold lips against his. For a moment, it felt like they were the only ones in the room. A magical room with dancing fireflies. Alas, there were no fireflies and no happy tales to speak of, just a grim future that lay ahead.

Wyatt held his hand out in anticipation. Eliza whispered in Ben's ear, "I'm so sorry," before she turned away from her friends and gave one last sorrowful look in each of their eyes. Her hand hovered over Wyatt's like it had a mind of its own. Finally, it relaxed into his, and he held it gently with a smug look of success on his face. Eliza couldn't help but glare as one tear ran down her cheek.

"Let's get this over with," she replied.

"Tay, will you join us?" Taylor, who had felt heat rising deep in her very bones from jealousy, plastered on a fake smile and reached her hand out to Wyatt. Wyatt's hand fell into hers effortlessly. Her hand had held him more times than she could count, and out of all those times, it had never stung until tonight. Her hand felt foreign in a once safe haven, but being the person she was, there was nothing that would stop her from getting her prize. A prize that was decades in the making. And tonight, she would finally be granted that prize.

"Hold hands and do as I say. If you do so, you will be allowed to leave with no scars. That is, no visible scars." He gave a loud, guttural laugh. His voice echoed and the only other person who seemed inclined to snicker quietly was Taylor.

Ben, Audrey, Theodore and Gerald once again held each other's hands around Eliza, Wyatt and Taylor. Two circles formed. Two very different circles. The forgotten, and then the ones who would thrive well past their intended time on Earth. Nonetheless, they held hands tightly and hoped for the best possible outcome, which in Ben's mind was killing both Wyatt and Taylor and saving Eliza. While Ben muddied his mind with unrealistic ideas, Wyatt began to speak.

"Creatures of twilight, I call you to thee. Grant me your substance, so I too can stay immortal. I bring you four brave souls that will honor our bargain greatly."

The Eltrists moved around the larger circle and batted their wings gently around them; so gently that they could barely hear the movements. They looked like they were barely floating above the floor. The whole display reminded Eliza of watching a children's show where the characters bounced from cloud to cloud. The beasties gently fluttered up and down. One let out a scream that itched into their very eardrums. Theodore's body flung forward and he started convulsing on the floor. His eyes rolled back in his head, while his tongue lolled out. Wyatt held up his hand, and again everyone had frozen in place except for Theodore, whose muscles continued to spasm.

Eliza's eyes almost bulged out of their sockets as she tried to leap towards him. Audrey lost sight of the fact that she couldn't move more than a wiggle. Her hand started clawing at Gerald's, and she realized when it was too late that her nails had dug down deep into his tough flesh. Blood trickled over his palm, but he didn't so much as wince at the pain. Instead, he kept his eye on Wyatt and allowed Audrey to go with her instinct. Her fingers stopped scratching for release and the coldest, most animalistic face grew on her. Even Taylor had to look away from her scowl.

Ben looked at the Eltrist who had caused the chain reaction. He couldn't pinpoint if this was just part of the ceremony or if it was a deal gone badly wrong that could get much worse.

"Kinsington, I hear what you are saying, but I have more than enough souls provided and next time I will gather more if necessary." Wyatt stayed calm and collected for the most part, but it was quite clear that he hadn't expected what had happened.

The largest of the Eltrists, Kinsington, held his gaze with Wyatt and floated over to Theodore. He reached down to a very damaged Theodore, whose body was still going against his own will. Kinsington's eyes changed from a storm cloud to a bloodbath of rage. His paw scraped up Theodore's broken body and he squeezed him. Theodore gave out a desperate plea, but Kinsington kept squeezing.

Theodore looked so small in his paw. Tiny bits of strug started to seep out of Theodore's nose, ears and mouth. It bubbled out in spurts and Kinsington licked up each drop as it came. One last squeeze and Theodore's mouth dripped out the last sliver of strug. Theodore stopped moving. His eyes stayed open and no words so much as touched the air in front of him. His arms released and draped over the sides of the paw.

The Eltrist larger than the rest and as black as the darkest day of the year, licked up the last bit of strug that lingered to Theodore's chin. Then he very carelessly let him roll out of his paw and onto the cold ground right in front of Audrey's feet. Even though her body was contained, her emotions were not, and her tears fell just as clouds release on an unforgiving, rainy day.

Surprise and anger seeped out of every pore that Eliza had. Ben felt much the same. Gerald may have blocked out the whole situation because all he did was grasp Audrey's hand tighter and had the appearance of someone lost in a daze. Wyatt didn't take his eyes off Kinsington, who now had the whole family of Eltrists at his sides. Taylor rubbed her thumb against his to signal her discomfort. Whispering softly in his ear, she asked, "What is he upset about?"

Wyatt spoke out loud to her without the hushed tone that she'd spoken with. "Kinsington says that you cut off part of a tail, and that we are not offering enough for what they have at stake now."

Frightened, Taylor backed away to reply, "Yes, I did, but it was only to experiment with later. Something to use for other spells. I thought you would be pleased."

As Wyatt pulled his glaring gaze away from Theodore's lifeless body, he turned it to Taylor. "Oh, so you think you can do what you want with them? Let me tell you again, since it must have escaped your mind, the Eltrists are not your playthings. We have an agreement with them. Now, put his tail back or I will feed you to them."

Taylor gulped before pulling the tip of the tail out of her bag. Her eyes closed and she opened her hand. It floated back to the Eltrist, sealing in place as though it had never left.

"Thank you," Wyatt said annoyed.

"This breaks our agreement, Wyatt. You promised no one would be harmed or killed," Eliza spoke between gritted teeth.

Wyatt instantly reached his hand to Eliza's throat. He raised her up slightly so that she was now eye level to him. As oxygen was failing to make it to her body, her brain screamed to her hands to pull his off her throat.

"I'm only going to say this once, my dearest Eliza. You are part of something much bigger, and I will have you again. If I need to bind you, I will. Make no mistake that I granted your wish out of kindness, not out of necessity." He released his grip and let her fall to her knees. Her body shook with terror and she coughed. "Why did you have to change?"

Eliza gave no reply, eventually standing back up. Ben mouthed to her, "What does that mean?" Eliza shook her head softly in response that it was too much to explain. Wyatt was oblivious to it all, since he had much bigger problems both figuratively and literally speaking. Kinsington gave a new plea in a language that no one seemed to understand except Wyatt and the other Eltrists. It was a calm but predatory conversation. One in which Wyatt stood quietly, intent on listening to his concerns.

Kinsington stopped moving his mouth and strug dripped sparingly down to his stomach. Wyatt paused before responding right away to his demands.

"What does he want?" Taylor asked nervously.

"Leverage... against the upcoming war in Folengower," Wyatt said as he paced back and forth.

"In what form?" Taylor asked.

"What war?" Eliza screamed.

Wyatt raised his hand up in the air and said, "Shhh, let me think." He walked around the circle. "How long would you need him?"

Kinsington replied, but only to Wyatt.

"Yes, I realize that the ceremony must be completed within the hour. I need time to think," he shouted. Wyatt waved his hands, and just like that, Audrey, Ben and Gerald were all released from his grip. "Don't you so much as think of leaving," he said sternly to the three of them.

Their bodies relaxed and Audrey fell to the floor, wrapping Theodore in her arms. She brushed his thick hair out of his face and kissed his cheek, while tears streamed down hers. Ben walked over to Theodore and placed a hand on his chest. He quickly removed it and then placed it back. He grabbed Audrey's hand and put it where his had been. Audrey felt his heart beat, not once but twice, within thirty seconds. Ben put a finger to his mouth. Audrey nodded.

As Wyatt paced, Audrey continued holding Theodore. Wyatt stopped, and as though a real light bulb had just turned on above his head, his eyes lit up with joy.

"Kinsington, I will accept, as your ally. I will also not call you again to feed out of your normal cycle until the war is over." He took a deep breath. "However, you must grant Taylor immortality, and me another dosage of mine. We will also need some extra strug in case we need more for upkeep." Wyatt spoke with as much confidence as he could muster.

Kinsington turned away from Wyatt and huddled around the other Eltrists. They glowed brightly as their fur shimmered in the light they produced. Kinsington turned around a few moments later and stated his response to Wyatt. Wyatt grinned. "So be it! We have reached an accord, ladies," he boasted to them, but only Taylor seemed pleased.

Eliza glared at Kinsington and let her hands ball into fists. She stayed quiet and watched as the Eltrists went back to fluttering around them, while dripping purple orbs. Wyatt called to the group to join hands once again and do as he instructed.

The next minutes that followed were both terrifying and beautiful. While they held Eliza's hands, Wyatt and Taylor chanted in unison in quiet voices at first. The Eltrists flew to the side of the them, circled around a large pile of strug about the size of a boulder that no one seemed to have noticed before. However, Ben wondered if it had been invisible to them before or if they had been so caught up with Wyatt that they had neglected to look around at their surroundings.

How they hadn't smelt the stench coming from it was another perplexing matter. The ghastly smell filled the air around them—it was like rotting flesh with a hint of mildew and bile. Pieces of limbs and eyeballs jiggled around in the blob of strug. It was clear that all the strug was now being reclaimed and brought back in one giant pile that expanded several feet high and wide. It was mildly discolored to a faint pink in some places. Apparently, the blood from its victims was still in the process of melting into nothing.

Wyatt yelled, "Now raise your hands and chant, "Creatures of the other world, we ask that you feast upon our brothers and sisters!'" Even though they all were undoubtedly disgusted, they repeated the words. Then Wyatt added, "So that we can give a proper offer to you in exchange for a most blessed gift." They repeated again, but they spoke with tensed mouths and fists. Taylor and Wyatt started chanting in ecstasy. As Taylor's chanting grew louder, she twirled here and there.

Kinsington and the rest of the Eltrists grouped around the strug and opened their mouths in unison. Their teeth were as sharp as spikes, but in reality, they didn't need their teeth to suck down every last bit of strug. They used their tongues to toss the pieces of gelatin-like slop into their gaping holes. The strug slushed around their mouths and made a slurping sound.

Once the last of the strug was gone, Wyatt held up a hand to signal to stop chanting and the room fell silent a moment later. The Eltrists began to glow more brightly now that their bellies had grown by another stomach in size and were starting to look like furry lanterns.

"Now for the final part of the ceremony. Please, Kinsington, take your pick of the souls." Kinsington nodded and walked up to Audrey. He placed his paw on her like she knew he would. He was the one who'd torn into her flesh, and it only seemed right that he would choose to take more from her, given the fight that had ensued between them earlier. He still had her blood on his paw, but now it was dry and flaky.

Audrey showed no fear, but wrath was pouring out of every pore. Kinsington stared deep into her fiery eyes. This made her even angrier. Kinsington placed his blood-encrusted paw over Audrey's mouth, which caused a bodily spasm where Audrey's head jerked back, giving her whiplash. He gently placed his other paw behind her head. She started clawing at him for air, but instead of giving it to her, he pushed one claw down her throat, scratching it. Holding his paw about an inch from her mouth, he waited.

Something wiggled inside her very core. It felt small and huge all at the same time. It swam up to her throat and pried open a hole a mere centimeter more and leapt out right into Kinsington's paw. It was about the size of a dragonfly and shimmered with a silver and green color. If you saw it at a glance, you would think that it had a face and body, but given a closer look, it would seem that it was just a ribbon of shining light.

Kinsington closed his paw and shoved the object in his mouth. He wasted no time in swallowing it, and once finished, his eyes closed. It was like he was savoring his favorite food.

Audrey wished she could smack the happiness out of his very core, but that would be a suicidal move, and she wasn't going to die after all this. To her relief, the hole in her throat seemed to magically close on its own a few seconds later. Wyatt observed as the next Eltrist came up and picked Gerald. After seeing what had happened to Audrey, he merely let it happen to him without any struggle.

Ben was next, and then Wyatt allowed one to take Taylor. Taylor screamed and yelled at Wyatt. Wyatt merely said, "For your immortality, there has to be some sort of trade, my dear." Taylor was irritated at that comment, but she eventually held still and allowed a part of her soul to fade.

The last Eltrist fluttered over to Theodore's damaged body and was about to do the same to him, until Taylor shrieked. Eliza had taken her knife out, pushed Wyatt with all her might against the wall and was slicing the blade into his throat. His eyes were wide and his mouth hung open speechless, blood bubbling out of it. Taylor went to grab Eliza, but Eliza pointed the knife directly at her. If she would have moved another inch, the blade would have pierced her cheek. Instead, the tip was merely getting friendly with the feel of her skin. Eliza turned back to Wyatt as Taylor backed away.

Wyatt grabbed his throat, using every ounce of energy to try to call for help, but only Eliza answered. With one rage filled movement, the blade tore through his hand that held his wound. Eliza pushed it deeper, until she could feel muscle. For a moment, Eliza looked away from her knife to gaze upon Wyatt's now remorseful eyes. Sweat beaded on her brow and her eyes stayed watchful of his as she pushed the blade as deep as she could force it and then turned it with not even an ounce of regret in her heart. Wyatt slouched to the floor and Taylor gasped, before running back to the tunnel.

Theodore, cold and on the verge of death, was lifted wildly by Kinsington. His fur glowed like he had swallowed a billion lavender fireflies. Strug slid out of his mouth and he used his right paw to swat it away, while his left carried Theodore. As his head and legs dangled over the sides of Kinsington's paw, Audrey couldn't help but think how small he looked in his grasp. Kinsington and the other Eltrists disappeared a moment later, taking Theodore with them.

"Brother!" As Eliza called out to him on her knees, she screamed, "Traitors!" Her knife clunked to the cold ground and her eyes closed tightly. Ben started towards her, but she put her hand up to stop him.

"Eliza, what is going on?" Ben asked, confused.

"I'm not who you think I am," she replied as she wept.

Audrey and Gerald walked to Ben and waited for Eliza to say something. Anything that would make sense. But instead, Eliza got up and disappeared through a different tunnel. Perplexed, the three that were left called out to her, but she didn't come back. Ben went to follow her, but Audrey and Gerald held him back. A part of Ben felt that he had to let her go, despite the gnawing need to know more.

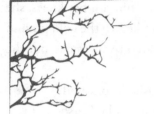

32

It had been two weeks, too many stitches and too many sleepless nights since leaving the cave on that nightmare of a day. Alert as always, Ben stood up straight at his table and sipped on some hot tea to calm his nerves. Audrey came downstairs the same as she had done every day since the cave—with disheveled hair and biting her right index finger like she was sure it would eventually make the madness stop. Her eyes were angry with pain.

Theodore was gone, and possibly now only a corpse. Audrey sat at the table again with a new set of books that she had come across on her last trip to a library about two towns over. The books busied her mind and gave her an escape. An escape that would hopefully lead to Theodore. Gwen had also stopped by and brought more for her. However, nothing mentioned Folengower.

The air felt different in Harthsburg, and Ben knew that the world he was going to have to live in was one he would fight tooth and nail to change. Eliza had vanished and had yet to make a reappearance in their lives.

Ben waited a day before he ransacked what was Wyatt's house, only to find a facade. After that, him and Audrey had driven straight to Elderberry Lane. When they'd turned the knob to Taylor's house, it had opened with ease. They had done so quietly, but Taylor hadn't been there to hear their hushed and cautious footsteps. When they realized she wasn't home, they stole all her books and anything else that could prove significant later from her main house and the shack.

Gerald had stopped by a couple of times, but he was busy with the survivors from the cave, and ones that had hid in different parts of the town. He helped with their mental states and made sure they had food, since most of their jobs were now non-existent.

The town was quiet, but Gerald was adamant on not letting the creatures ruin the town that he'd grown up in and loved. Maggie helped by baking donuts again and handing them out for free. She was lucky that her sons had hid her away after they saw a neighbor disappear into the sky. Either way, they were all trying to do their best.

Audrey was scanning a page in a book that had no cover; at least not anymore. It was riddled with moth holes and soot. "Ben, look at this!" She shot out of her chair and brought the book over to Ben. "Look. Read right here."

He scanned the page and read, "Folengower is a legend to most, but many druids have the ability to venture into the vast lands. Fear this place if you enter alone."

Ben's mouth opened wide. "Finally, we've found something. But how would we find a druid?"

"I guess we'll have to find out," she said, a little deflated.

"Have you found anything on where Eliza might be?" The hunger in his eyes was almost too much to bear.

"No, Ben, I'm sorry." Audrey placed her hand on his shoulder.

A knock at the door made both of them jump. Audrey walked over to answer it, expecting it to be Gerald again. However, what was on the other side of the door was clearly not Gerald, and not a man for that matter. It was Taylor.

"BEN, get the fuck over here!" Audrey yelled.

Ben's face went pale. "What are you doing here? Has something happened to her?"

"To Eliza? Oh, nothing, unfortunately. We have a problem though. If you want to see Eliza again, come with me."

That was all it took for Ben to leave his home with no other questions. Audrey came with and sat in the back of Taylor's car, ready for anything. Ben sat silently and waited to see where they go, but he already knew they were going back to Elderberry Lane.

The steps ached with every stride they took up them. The house felt deranged; like it had a strange energy. It moved through them like the wind glides through leaves. They would have been lying if they'd said that the surge of energy that moved through them was not cause for concern. Taylor smiled at the mortals' change of expression from feeling the power that was just behind the walls.

Taylor opened the door with not even a whisper to them and moved her hand to command them inside. The house looked the same, but what ached in their bones was another story. It was louder than they remembered it. An old record player blared classical music loudly in the living room where Ben had been cut open. Ben's body quaked as he saw a small drop of his blood that had failed to be cleaned up.

"Are you going to give us a heads up about what we should expect?" Ben peeled his eyes away from the single stain and looked at Taylor.

"Well, that wouldn't be any fun now, would it? Besides, I'm not allowed to say anything," Taylor said in irritation, rolling her eyes.

Ben decided to not ask any more questions, and while Audrey was normally an in your face type of girl when it came to things that seemed fishy, even she was quiet. It was a surprise to even Ben, who waited for Audrey to say something, but she only kept following Taylor. When they'd visited a couple weeks ago, they'd never walked this far into her house. It was darker and smelled of earth.

The hallway ended at a door that mirrored all the others. If you happened to glance at it, there wouldn't be a second thought, but Ben and Audrey knew this was no ordinary room. Taylor turned the knob and pushed the door open.

A coldness swirled around them and a single silhouette sat at a wooden table, facing away. Before Ben stepped in the room, he knew it was Eliza. His heart fluttered, but his mind wouldn't let him step any further. As though he knew Eliza would not be the same person he knew just a few weeks ago, he stood frozen in time and listened to his heart pound loudly with grief.

Maps of Folengower were hung slightly askew on the wall with x marks and red circles that took over the mossy and periwinkle striped wallpaper that ached to be a focal point again. The area seemed to be divided into two parts, but before Ben could make out what it all meant, Audrey moved away from him.

She began to rush over to the table, but Eliza stood before Audrey could get close. Audrey's feet stopped still and silent, afraid to make the wrong move. The silhouette's body moved slowly and turned without so much as a word.

It was, in fact, Eliza, but she looked to be closer to the age of eighteen now. Her forehead was now adorned with an intricate tattoo of small lavender circles that got smaller as they met in the middle. The middle had a black upside-down triangle with smooth edges. With a solemn face, she looked directly into Ben's eyes. Ben couldn't look away.

"Is there anything else you need from me, Ancient One?" Taylor said quietly, her voice shaky with fear.

Eliza calmly shook her head. "Close the door on your way out and do not bother us," she said with as much bitterness as she could muster.

Taylor bowed her head slightly and quickly exited. Ben and Audrey couldn't even glance at each other. They were so stunned by who, or what, was in front of them. Eliza realized their reluctance to speak, so she spoke first.

"I have missed you two so much." Eliza hoped that they would want to give her a hug and say they felt the same, but all she got was two people staring at her like she was an anomaly. "Let me start again. Would you two like some water and to sit?"

Ben finally spoke a quiet, "Yes, please."

Eliza closed her eyes and within minutes Taylor opened the door with a tray of glass cups with water and ice. They had just sat down on the red tufted couch and with water in hand, when Ben and Audrey both spoke at the same time.

Along the lines of, "What the hell is going on?" As Taylor fled the room, Eliza cautioned them to stop talking.

"I have lied to you both, and I had hoped that secret would never reveal itself. I have a whole life that I've left behind in Folengower. A life that I'd had no choice but to leave behind for the good of our people."

"Who the fuck are you?" Audrey shouted. Ben placed his arm in front of Audrey to calm her. She pushed his arm away and stood up with her face uncomfortably close to Eliza's. Eliza could smell the wildness radiating off her lips.

Despite the enraged eyes that stared back into Audrey's, she still proceeded to scream, "I trusted you!" She turned back to Ben and waved her hand to him. "Ben trusted you!" Tears built up by anger dripped out.

Eliza kept her composure, despite the chaos that filled her eyes. "I understand that you both have so many questions, but know that my feelings towards both of you are real and genuine."

Audrey scoffed and sat back down next to Ben.

"Are you the one from the *Eltrist* book? Taylor called you "Ancient One,"" Ben uttered.

The power that flowed through Eliza's veins silenced Ben and Audrey. The fog had cleared right before their eyes, yet the light was not behind it. The darkness would awaken a new life. A new beginning as familiar to Eliza as the trees expected rebirth in springtime.

Calmly, Eliza turned away from their wide-eyed faces and said, "I'm not the one they refer to as Ancient One; that's always been Theodore."

Made in the USA
Monee, IL
24 January 2024

51790123R00173